MW01134220

HONOR HOUSE

a novel by

Mark H. Massé

HONOR HOUSE
Copyright © 2020
LCCN: TXu 1-976-817 (8/5/15)
United States Copyright Office
Washington, D.C.

All rights reserved. No part of this publication may be reproduced, stored in a retrieval system, or transmitted in any form or by any means, electronic, mechanical, recording or otherwise, without the prior written permission of the author.

ISBN-13: 9781090977427

Printed in the United States of America

Although this book includes reference to actual people, places, organizations and incidents, it must be read as a work of fiction. This novel is a creation of the author's imagination. All dialogue is invented, and characters and events have been altered or reimagined. Except in specific instances where noted, any similarity to real individuals, living or dead, is coincidental and unintended by the author.

Credit: Cover photograph is in the public domain (Author: Nyttend, https://commons.wikimedia.org). It represents a fictional building and university location.

Credit: Author photograph by Jenny Lesselbaum

Credit: "The 30-Year Secret: A crime, a cover-up and the way it shaped Oregon" by Nigel Jaquiss, *Willamette Week*. Published May 11, 2004. Updated January 24, 2017. Retrieved September 1, 2020. https://www.wweek.com/portland/article-3198-the-30-year-secret.html

DEDICATION

For my wife, Mykie, and all who heal others

For our dear friend Sue, may she rest in peace

For Lee K. Abbott and Frank Bentayou, steadfast mentors gone too soon

HONOR HOUSE

"Every man has some reminiscences which he would not tell to everyone, but only to his friends. He has others which he would not reveal even to his friends, but only to himself, and that in secret. But finally there are still others which a man is even afraid to tell himself, and every decent man has a considerable number of such things stored away."
(Fyodor Dostoyevsky, <u>Notes from Underground</u>)

<u>Voices of Honor House</u>

"We let them get away with it." (Alex Merten)

"Should have nailed the bastard long ago." (Nick Delamore)

"Nick warned me not to go with him." (Allyson Chambers)

"Stay away from those pretty college boys."
(Clarice Johnson's boyfriend)

"Burn every last one of those damn frat houses to the ground."
(Megan Bradley)

"Cut loose the wagons, boys!" (Bruce "Bru" Van Pelt)

"We are bound by our creed to live with honor, loyalty and truth." (Omega Epsilon Tau)

Prologue

Almost midnight in McAllen, Texas, and a weary priest holds the remote in a trembling hand. He winces as *CNN*'s Wolf Blitzer drones on. Former congressman Bruce Van Pelt has won the Ohio Republican gubernatorial primary, defeating state attorney general Richard Reasoner. He will face Democrat Kwame Imani in the fall election. When live coverage shifts to Van Pelt's enthusiastic supporters, Father Alex Merten closes his eyes in prayer.

The beaming victor waves to the crowd in the Cincinnati Convention Center. He kisses his stylish wife and three doting daughters. Two towheaded grandchildren cling to the imposing man's trousers. He strides to the podium draped in adulation.

Merten knows Van Pelt will use his good looks and soft Southern accent to charm and seduce. The tone is soothing, the message polarizing: "It is time to reclaim what is right in this Christian land of ours. I am unwavering in my defense of traditional American values. And I am committed to leading the great state of Ohio and contributing to the national discourse about our cherished way of life."

Merten watches the newscast on an old Zenith TV a thousand miles from hometown Cincinnati. Here in McAllen, most folks would find it strange their pastor is so interested in Ohio politics. He has lived in this Texas border town for some 30 years. *Yo soy Padre Alejandro. Mi iglesia es San Filippo. (I am Father Alex. My church is St. Philip.)*

He turns off the television and shuffles across the rectory apartment, floor boards creaking under the threadbare brown carpet.

His gait slowed by bulging discs and arthritis, he eases down on the straight-back wooden chair. The modest kitchen table is where he composes his Sunday homilies and tries to balance the parish's accounts, robbing Peter to pay Paul as his mom would say when bill collectors clamored for payment.

There are no urgent financial matters on this warm Tuesday night, May 1, 2012. A joyful Cinco de Mayo draws near. But Merten is mired in sadness, seeing that poor woman slumped in a shower stall. His heart races and static grows louder. *Clear my mind, Lord. Grant me peace.*

In Carlson, Indiana, about 100 miles from the site of Van Pelt's raucous tribute, another sixtyish man watches Ohio primary results. Nick Delamore, a journalist with the local *Times-Union* newspaper, is more animated than Merten.

"Un-fucking believable," he says, spittle spraying the screen as he downs his third tumbler of Dewar's.

In Lakewood, Ohio, a western Cleveland suburb, Megan Bradley is also tuned to *CNN* when she takes a call from A Safe Place, the women's shelter and crisis center in University Circle. A hotline worker timidly asks, "Megan?"

Bradley pauses. *You know who this is. Why do you have to ask?* But she doesn't chide the employee. She understands how difficult it can be talking to the shelter director this late at home.

"What's going on, Karen?"

"Sorry, Megan. But everyone is either with clients or out sick tonight. Didn't know who else to call. I'm sorry."

"You don't have to apologize. What do you need?"

A sexual assault nurse examiner at the UH Medical Center has called for a victim's advocate. In the emergency room, Bradley will explain the rape kit process and support the woman during her forensic exam, debrief with her dormmates and argue with a rookie Cleveland cop, who had been questioning the Case Western student. Attacked at a campus party, she collapsed on the steps of St. Rocco's Church, having wandered disoriented and disheveled through the Little Italy neighborhood of Murray Hill. When Megan Bradley gets home five hours later, she has nearly forgotten how mad she was when Bruce Van Pelt won his primary.

FOX-News and conservative media applaud him, but liberal pundits say his candidacy has been a well-orchestrated sham, citing the Ohio Republican's minor achievements in multiple congressional terms. Yet even critics note his impressive network. The brain trust includes his brother, Jerome, the Wall Street hedge fund founder and campaign treasurer.

Merten and Delamore knew the Van Pelts from their frat days at Merriman University. Bruce (Bru) was two years older than his nebbish sibling. Bru was the alpha male, boisterous and charismatic. Jerome (Jerry) was known as "Casper the Friendly Ghost."

Merten's college moniker was derived from his black hair and moustache. His Omega Epsilon Tau brethren called him "Garcia," referring to the character from a popular childhood TV show: *Zorro*. The hero was a rakish outlaw in California during Spanish rule. Sergeant Garcia was a hapless chubby soldier who pursued Zorro.

Father Alex's faithful would be shocked to learn their gentle white-haired priest had been in a fraternity a year before entering the seminary. He is a celibate man of God not a drunkard or fornicator. How could he live that type of sinful life? As much as he loved his congregation, he could no more tell them than he could his own mother.

With His divine grace, there will be a reckoning. Merten must persuade or provoke Delamore. Years since their last contact, he wonders if Nick has any loyalty to Van Pelt, his ex-teammate and "big brother." They were kindred spirits: pranksters, brawlers and heartbreakers.

He summons the words, but his thoughts are muddled. His clever wit mocks him. Crumpled pages burn in an empty Maxwell House coffee can in his stained kitchen sink. Days pass until inspiration returns amid tearful reflections. His letter concludes, "May Christ strengthen and protect you."

After Friday evening Mass, he hurries to the mailbox by a Tex-Mex restaurant. Owners Ramon and Elena Alvarez are at their silver Escalade and eagerly wave.

"Hola, Padre Alejandro!"

He greets them with an upraised hand.

"Come join us, Father," a strapping gent with shoulder-length hair shouts from down the block. His friends cheer with bottles and cans. A symphony of car horns resonates at the impromptu fiesta before the historic Mexican holiday.

"Gracias," he says when the noise subsides. "But it's past my bedtime."

"Adios y buenas noches, Padre." The affable fellow bids him farewell, echoed by a chorus.

"Buenas noches, mis amigos," he replies with a smile burdened from a distant celebration.

On the eve of the annual Hawaiian luau party in Sussex, Ohio, Alex Merten is with a band of men drinking Mogen David ("Mad Dog") 20/20 from wineskins. They watch Mitchell Crouse and Bru Van Pelt rotate the carcass of a whole pig, the fire spiking and crackling with greasy drippings. The ceremonial roasting continues as frat president Van Pelt boasts, "Wait till my little Pi Phi is sizzling on my spit."

Merten hates his lewd remarks. *Shut the hell up!* But he laughs along nonetheless. *Just go with the flow.* His reticence is a prelude to that fateful first weekend of May 1973.

Father Alex again leaves the rectory this Friday night, wearing his black pants, short-sleeve black shirt and white clerical collar. Balmy air envelops him as he moves toward the banks of the Rio Grande, where a vibrant sunset has settled. A full moon cascades light on the masculine river.

The heat lingers, rising from gritty streets. Revved up muscle cars and far off voices are comforting. These are his people, and how grateful he has been for their embrace. If only he felt worthy.

He studies the current. The sound of the rushing water is calming. He recites the rosary, faded black beads in his calloused, tremorous hand. He ends with an Act of Contrition, groaning as he rises from his knees.

He is alone on the tranquil riverbank as legions of stars shine above. Soon the festivities will begin in this humble neighborhood. There will be fireworks and gunshots in the air. Many will invite beloved Padre Alejandro to their homes. But their calls will go unanswered.

He removes his worn thick-soled black shoes and places them on a large flat rock at the river's edge. In one shoe his wristwatch and wallet, in the other his rosary and clerical collar. He shakes his head to quell the static and banish the image of that lifeless woman. The weary priest prays for his family, his parishioners, for Nick Delamore and those on the path to perdition. *May almighty God bless and forgive all of us who seek eternal rest.*

—

4

Chapter 1

Nick was surprised by the envelope from St. Philip's Church. He initially thought it was a request for donations. But this letter was escorted by problems that couldn't be alleviated with a check.

"Van Pelt's latest victory has brought back painful memories. You once told me to forget the past and move on. Yet my penance continues. I am writing now because the time has come to expose our fraternity's crimes. But I lack the courage to act alone."

He could anticipate what was coming. Alex would ask Nick to help him "take arms against a sea of troubles and by opposing end them." How many times had he quoted from *Hamlet*? And how often had he begged Nick to let him go to the police?

"Don't be stupid," he had warned his guilt-ridden pal in the days following Clarice Johnson's death. "We moved the body. That makes us complicit."

As Nick read the letter, he saw them struggling to carry the woman out of the frat house cloaked in sheets and blankets. Alex described events from that desperate night in meticulous detail as in a deposition. The letter was written less like a clergyman and more as a law student, which he had aspired to be.

He appreciated Nick for trying to protect him. But they should have done much more. Alex asked him to examine his conscience and course of his life. "Are your personal and professional failures from the regret you have carried as I have?"

More of Merten's psychobabble. What did he want? To see Van Pelt charged with rape and manslaughter after 40 years?

Delamore used to relish taking on the "bad guys." At the height of his career with the Cleveland *Plain Dealer* newspaper, he followed in the footsteps of colleagues like James (Jim) Neff, award-winning journalist who wrote the 1989 book *Mobbed Up* about the Teamsters union and its powerful president Jackie Presser's links with organized crime and the FBI. After Neff left the *PD*, Delamore continued investigating the Cleveland Mafia's role in local construction trades, waste management and Great Lakes iron ore transport, which fueled the Midwest steel industry through the 20th century. But unlike Neff's successful trajectory in the media, book publishing and academia, Nick's heady days were short-lived.

He became a casualty of ego and reckless behavior. He couldn't be trusted with prime assignments, and his outbursts alienated editors and colleagues. He was on a downward spiral but didn't see it that way. He kept saying, "I'll be back on top of my game in no time."

His nadir was unceremoniously reached in fall 2011 when he landed at a 25,000-circulation Gannett-owned paper in central Indiana. He was a grumbling reporter going through the motions, writing on deteriorating infrastructure (i.e., potholes) and local celebrity sightings (e.g., Santa visiting the mall via a garbage truck). Nick was barely surviving in an age when thousands of journalism jobs were being eliminated nationwide. Younger staff at the *Times-Union* viewed him with curiosity or disdain. They knew little of his distinguished past before the term multimedia was ever uttered. He was a "lost cause," and his obstinance was hastening his irrelevance.

The one-time football player listed when he walked like a fishing trawler on stormy seas. His chronic bad back the result of injuries and 10,000 days and nights hunched at typewriters and keyboards. He was overweight and battled kidney stones, a nagging prostate and colitis. He popped tiny green Imodium A-D pills like Tic Tacs.

He was proud of his full head of hair flecked with gray, though his dense brown curls had become brittle. He dated comely pre-menopausal women, but the twice-divorced Delamore wanted no long-term commitments or companionship beyond the bedroom. Most nights he would nod off in his worn leather recliner before the 11 o'clock news, a Dewar's on the rocks by his side.

Lethargic and surly, he was unsuited for anything redemptive much less valiant these days, which was fine by him. Those who still loved the man could counsel: Lower your expectations. Prepare to be disappointed.

Rereading Merten's letter, he poured a scotch and popped a Lean Cuisine dinner of chicken, rice and green beans in the microwave. "Another fabulous meal for me, myself and I." But he didn't finish eating as his cell phone rang twice that May night. The first call was from Jim, Alex's older brother.

Nick asked how he had tracked him down in Indiana. He wasn't on Facebook, LinkedIn, Instagram or Twitter. They were a waste of time and self-indulgent. He had no need for such preening or a smartphone for that matter. A cheap flip model was fine and dandy for this Luddite.

"Talked to Megan," Jim said. "Nice you two have stayed in contact since … ."

"Since we split up," Nick said abruptly.

He apologized for his rudeness and offered his condolences when Jim informed him of Alex's "apparent suicide." Nick didn't mention the letter, but he now understood its intention.

"The funeral is Saturday in Cincinnati. Hope you can be there."

"Absolutely. You got it," Nick said. "And I'm sorry for your loss."

"And for yours," Jim said. "Alex considered you a brother."

"Thanks, appreciate that. Almost forgot, where's the funeral?"

"We wanted it to be in the cathedral downtown, where he was ordained. But, due to the manner of his death, the diocese won't allow a Catholic service. It will be noon at Armbruster's Funeral Home on Colerain Avenue by the Gateway Mall."

When the call ended, he sipped his watery scotch and thought of Alex. How he would go on in his Cincinnati "twang" about his hometown honey, Donna Carvel. Nick either pretended to listen to his excited ramblings or ignored him. Merten said Delamore was "a jaded man who didn't know the meaning of love."

But he was there when Alex's romance came crashing down. Donna got pregnant the first time they had sex, and he borrowed money from Van Pelt to pay for the "sad, awful" December trip to New York City. They broke up just before Valentine's Day.

Nick would find him moping in their small second-floor room, listening to the same Cat Stevens albums. Donna wouldn't respond to his letters or phone calls. Those were dark days, but the worst were to come.

Merten spiraled into depression, dropping out of Merriman the summer before his senior year. Back in Cincinnati, he withdrew from the outside world, reading the Bible and sleeping in his twin bed. He would complete his undergraduate studies in the seminary.

Nick had teased that Alex chose to be a "man of the cloth" so he could wear colorful Sunday garments, give rousing sermons and drink gallons of free church wine. But he gave him props when Merten protested for social justice and "walked the walk." He thought Alex had been content in his poor south Texas locale. In the wake of his death, he questioned why it wasn't enough to sustain him.

"We did the best we could." Nick spouted hollow words in the kitchen of his sparsely furnished unit. As if in a spell, he was reopening the squeaky wooden door of that second-floor frat house bathroom, stunned by the rush of steam from the showers and stench of booze, vomit and excrement. He gulped his scotch before answering the next phone call.

"What a bummer about Alex. I can't believe it."

Megan Bradley had a rapid-fire Dorchester dialect, although she had spent much of her life in the Midwest. She talked and walked faster than most. In their early days, her energy and antics attracted Nick. Over time these same traits aggravated him.

"You gave Jim Merten my number?"

"You didn't want to know that Alex died?"

"To be accurate, committed suicide."

"That's what Jim said. So sad."

"Happens to the best of us, even a priest."

"I hadn't seen him in years. But he was such a great guy."

"Amen to that, sister."

"I figured you'd make a joke."

"Amazing how you can read me like a freakin' book," he said gruffly. Nick had also lived in the Midwest most of his adult years, but he was a metro New York native.

"Didn't call to fight with you. Wanted to say I was sorry for Alex and that I'll be at the funeral. I assume you're going."

"Wouldn't miss it for the world."

"Geez, you're on a roll. Hitting the scotch pretty hard tonight?"

"Megan shoots and scores! ... I gotta go. *Deer Hunter*'s on."

"Don't you ever get tired of those Vietnam War movies?"

"Not when it's Robert De Niro."

—

"I'll leave you to your bromance. But we need to talk after the funeral."

"About what?"

"For starters, what we can do to beat Van Pelt."

"What we can do? Who's we?" Nick asked sourly. "You mean you and Kwame?"

"Cut the crap."

"You forget I'm a journalist? A little thing called conflict of interest."

"Like when George Will wrote speeches for Reagan."

"Think it was the first Bush."

"Whatever," Megan said. "You don't have to do anything official. Strictly behind the scenes."

"Cool, I could be Deep Throat," he said. "No thanks."

"Don't you care that he could be governor? You know him as well as anybody, Nick."

"Knew him years ago. Maybe he's changed."

"Men like him don't change. He was and will always be fucking evil."

"Not everything is so black and white."

"What? Are you making excuses for him like he was some frat boy Romeo? Is that what you're saying?"

"Not talking about him specifically. What I'm saying, if you'd let me finish, is that there are false accusations. Like what happened with the Duke rugby team."

Megan sighed. "It was the lacrosse team in 2006, and that case failed due to a lack of evidence not false accusations."

"I stand corrected."

"The vast majority of sexual assault victims are being honest," she said. "You of all people should know that."

"Things are so different today. Sexting, online dating, the hookup culture. It's crazy out there."

"Rape is rape."

"But I'm hearing more stories of women lying about consensual relations. And if the guy's convicted, he's labeled a sex offender or worse. This falsely accused angle challenges conventional wisdom in crime reporting."

"Where are you hearing these so-called stories? And conventional wisdom from whose point of view? There's nothing new about people in power saying they're being falsely accused."

"But what about those instances where a man *is* the victim?"

"What about it? The percentage of women who false report is very low," Megan said. "Most suffer in silence."

"And that's my point," Nick said. "The fact it's rare makes it valid as a story idea."

"So go ahead and challenge your version of conventional wisdom. What do I care?"

"How did we get off on this tangent?"

"I was asking for your help, and then you began ranting."

"Hey, if Van Pelt wins, he wins. Nothing I can do about it."

"You sure have flamed out, Delamore. We're done here. Give my best to Robert."

"Robert? Robert who?"

"De Niro," she said before clicking off.

They had last talked months earlier when he congratulated her for being invited to the White House by Michelle Obama, who had organized a national panel on domestic violence. Megan Bradley was chosen for her exemplary work directing Ohio's oldest women's shelter. She had started in social services as a grad student in the Campus Counseling Center at Merriman University.

Nick and Megan's relationship had been passionate and problematic, befitting strong-willed East Coasters. After they divorced in 1995, Bradley's career flourished as Delamore's declined. Some said she had propped him up, and when she left he lost his bearings.

He turned on *The Deer Hunter* and couldn't believe his timing. A late-night commercial was airing for the charity Gather My Sheep. Bruce Van Pelt and his wife, Susie, were in a godforsaken African village surrounded by happy children. He had two in his arms and was laughing with them. It was a well-produced spot that made him seem downright saintly.

At the end of the ad, the Van Pelts asked viewers to donate with "loving hearts and minds." Had Bru changed? Was there an epiphany on his road to Damascus? *Who the hell knows?*

Chapter 2

Alex Merten's service was attended by an overflow gathering in a suburban Cincinnati funeral home. Rows of folding chairs filled the main parlor and extended into the hallway, where portable bulletin boards displayed photographs of young Alex, collegiate Merten and Padre Alejandro. Nick studied the pictures as an archeologist might view artifacts. The dynamic duo in fraternity days, arms entwined. More photos at weddings and reunions before their lives had diverged.

Nick hugged Jim, Alex's polar bear of a brother, and expressed condolences to his frail widowed mother and grieving relatives. He was searching for an open seat when Megan pointed to an adjacent empty chair. Her bobbed hair was an appealing shade of auburn. She had a trim figure, striking blue eyes and a cute upturned nose.

"Still look like a leprechaun," he whispered.

"And you've put on a few pounds."

"Can't argue with that, but I carry it well. Don't you think?" he asked as she concealed her amusement. "So where's Roger?"

"Cleveland State's graduation today. He was just named dean of the law school."

"Good for him," Nick said, staring at the framed photograph atop the closed casket of a youthful priest in his vestments among adoring faces. There would be no more chatting about Bradley's love life. And she knew better than to ask if he was seeing anyone.

"Who's the Clint Eastwood look-alike up front, and what's the deal with the red running shoes?"

"Father Gary Scott, a friend of Alex's from seminary. Jim said they always wore red when they ran marathons."

"Alex did marathons?"

"I can't believe they wouldn't allow the funeral in the cathedral."

"That's a tough union, and they don't like suicide. Bad PR."

"Well I think it sucks."

Scott, the off-duty Jesuit in dark suit, open-necked white shirt and red Adidas, said they had come together to honor a man not solve life's mysteries. *Fair enough. But how had Alex endured the priesthood? Celibacy must have been grueling ... and all that bureaucracy.*

In college he had quietly rebelled against institutional hierarchies that crushed individuality. Then he became a cog in the machine of the billion-plus Holy Roman Catholic Church. The tradeoff was his joy in serving the poor, where he found his true calling.

"I wish each of you could have met some of those beautiful souls in that close-knit McAllen community," Scott said. "They loved Padre Alejandro. Their Father Alex. And how he loved them."

Alex had been reinvented. What Nick couldn't grasp was why after all the years and all his good works, he would take his life. *Surely God had forgiven this tenderhearted man for any transgressions.*

There were bittersweet anecdotes from Jim Merten and Gerri, one of Alex's sisters. Megan cried with many others while Nick was stoic remembering his old chum. Father Scott closed the ceremony by thanking all for coming, and Delamore hurried to the restroom. When he was at the sink, a compact man with thinning hair entered. No immediate recognition but intuition.

"Gunner, that you?"

The man grinned before shaking hands.

"Long time, Dago."

"Damn straight. How you been?"

Glen "Gunner" Gunderson was in the same pledge class as Nick and Alex. Liberal-minded friends, they were the only Omegas to vote for McGovern versus Nixon in 1972.

"You still live in Cinci?" Nick asked, buoyed by this chance meeting.

"Came back to care for my mother. How about you?"

"Carlson, Indiana. Can you believe it? I'm living in the boonies."

"Had a cousin who went to Hempstead. Not a bad college town," Gunner said, gazing in the mirror at the faint scar above his left eyebrow.

"Says you."

Jim Merten opened the bathroom door. "Nick, we need you as a pallbearer."

"Be right there."

He and Gunner exchanged business cards and assurances to keep in touch. Walking into the parlor, Nick wisecracked, "You voting for our favorite Nazi, Van Pelt?" Gunner replied with watery eyes. Then he disappeared into the group exiting the funeral home.

Alex was buried on a hometown hillside that May afternoon. Nick joined mourners at Jim Merten's Tudor-design house. Megan cornered him by the staircase as he was eating a ham sandwich and German potato salad off a paper plate.

"Who were you talking to at the funeral home?"

"Why? You trailing me?"

"Did he go to Merriman?"

"Gunner, I mean Glen Gunderson. One of the real nice guys in the frat."

"Good of him to come. Alex impacted many lives."

"He sure did."

"You should know I also got a letter from him."

How far had Alex gone? Had he broken their vow of silence?

"Who said I got a letter?"

"He told me he had written you. So drop the act, OK?"

Nick put his plate of food down as Megan described how Van Pelt had called Alex. Said he was contacting the old Omegas. Tried to bribe him with a big donation. But when Alex said he would never support him, the camaraderie ended.

"He threatened to tell his bishop about him being in the fraternity, borrowing money to pay for an abortion and more 'shameful actions.' 'We're brothers 'til death do us part,' he said."

"Alex told you all this but not me? Doesn't make any sense. Why would Van Pelt think he could hurt his election chances?"

"Maybe he wanted to make sure *you* didn't do anything to screw things up."

"Enough with the conspiracy theories," Nick said. His "bad" left knee throbbed as he leaned on the black metal railing. "Van Pelt could have easily called me."

"He must have had concerns."

"Concerns? What can I do? I'm at a podunk paper in Indiana."

"You have plenty of Ohio media contacts."

"Like I said before, I can't ... ."

Color rose in her cheeks as she glowered at him.

"You're involved whether you admit it or not, no matter how you try to erase your past and people like Alex Merten and Allyson Chambers—remember her? Alex hoped you could help us stop Van Pelt. But you're not going to. What I could never figure out is the fucking control he has over you."

"Not so loud," he said. Megan could curse with the best of 'em. Raised in a hardscrabble Boston neighborhood, she was no shrinking violet. He drew close enough to kiss but chose to rebuke. "Try showing some respect for Alex."

"How dare you!" she said, pushing him into the railing. "Don't talk to me about respect. His death wasn't enough for you to know what he wanted? Are you kidding me?"

She left him fumbling for answers among uneasy and unintended onlookers.

The trip back to his crummy one-bedroom apartment and dead-end job in Indiana was slowed by orange barrel lane closures on I-275 West. If he had stayed on I-75 South, he could have revisited Lexington. Stuck in traffic, he detoured via remembrance to verdant Kentucky: June 1972.

With his estranged wife, Linda, and son, Joey, back in New York, 19-year-old Nick Delamore wanted to let loose, and Bru Van Pelt provided a great escape. He told him to pack his swim trunks, golf clubs and something decent to wear. Nick's "formal" attire consisted of a beige corduroy sport coat. That was until Bru bought him a new outfit at a classy men's store. "Here to lend a hand, little bro, head to toe."

Van Pelt and high school teammate Jonah "Moby Dick" Moore shot hoops with Nick on the full-length backyard court. Moore was a black inner-city kid who earned a scholarship to attend Bru's prep academy. They had ruled their basketball league. This summer Saturday the three men played ball and lounged at the pool, drinking cold Coors beer that Bru's father,

Brian, had flown in from Denver as he did each month on his company's private jet.

After Sunday brunch at the Lexington Country Club, the Van Pelts hosted a niece's 12th birthday party at their house. Bru gave a gaggle of children golf cart rides. Boys and girls were squealing, clinging to him as he raced "like Bobby Unser at the Indy 500." Nick had seen a photo of JFK driving a cart full of Kennedy kids at Hyannis Port that was very similar to the scene he observed in the Bluegrass State that enjoyable weekend.

Based on what Megan had said, he was supposed to forget such days ever existed. He should treat Van Pelt as the enemy. Alex must have also decided Bru had no redeeming values. What about the $500 he loaned him for his trip to New York with Donna, never asking for repayment? Or that St. Patrick's Day party when he rescued Merten from a savage beating?

The ghosts of Merriman had returned courtesy of Bradley's guilt trips, admonitions and assertions. She said Nick was defending a "despicable predator." But his fraternity bonds had long been broken.

Media ethics aside, how could she ever believe he would assist Kwame Imani, who had been his rival since college? For all he knew, they had resumed their entanglement. If that were true, he wanted no part of any campaign, regardless of how he felt toward his Republican foe. Anyway, Imani had little chance of winning. Van Pelt was backed by the Tea Party, affluent patrons such as the Koch brothers, prominent advisors and strategists, including business and civic leaders throughout Ohio and the Midwest, many of whom were Omega frat brothers.

And if the odds weren't stacked high enough, the Democratic candidate had an Islamic name. With the bigotry and anti-Muslim sentiment in post-9/11 America, could Imani sway a meaningful number of Ohio's white electorate? Possibly with a small "p," following President Barack Hussein Obama's trailblazing efforts in 2008. But before his victory, Obama had to counteract the doubters and haters, assuring voters he was a practicing Christian. Imani also had to "prove" he was reinstated by his "first" religion. He had excellent verification, notably his 1986 wedding to the devout niece of Rev. Otis Moss Jr., civil rights pioneer and pastor of Olivet Institutional Baptist, one of Cleveland's historic black churches.

Nick drove to Carlson for two hours in heavy thunderstorms. As was his custom in bad weather, he checked on his aging neighbor across the way.

"Gloria, it's Nick," he said outside her door. "You OK?"

Would she wobble out to meet him? Maybe she had turned in for the night. He had his keys in hand when her door opened.

She was a solidly built woman with bad knees and no family in town. Each week Nick picked up her grocery list, stocked her shelves and filled her refrigerator. She gave him cash, which he left unspent when he delivered her food and prescriptions.

"I'm fine. Bless your heart," Gloria said, leaning on a metal tripod cane, her eyes blurred by cataracts.

"How's the trash situation? Let me take it down for you."

"Oh, don't want to bother you. It's late."

"No problem," Nick said, stepping past her and into the narrow kitchen, where a small plastic grocery bag was tied to a knob on the sink cabinet.

"Thank you for looking out for me," she said, giving his arm a little squeeze. "You're in my prayers every day."

"I need all I can get. You're saving me, Gloria."

"They were discussing the way to salvation this morning on *The 700 Club*," she said as he left with a wave.

ESPN's *SportsCenter* was muted while Nick downed a tall glass of Dewar's, awaiting the day's inevitable flashbacks: Mrs. Merten sobbing into her handkerchief. Megan confronting him on the stairs. Gunner walking off teary-eyed.

He pulled a business card from his overstuffed wallet, reflecting on how he had nicknamed Gunderson for his long-range basketball shooting prowess. Shy and soft-spoken, he was regularly on the receiving end of pranks by Van Pelt. Was that why he got emotional when Nick asked if he was voting for him? He decided to call though it was almost 10 p.m.

"Gunner, it's me, Dago."

"Who?"

"Nick. Nick Delamore."

"Oh, Nick. Hey, it's kinda late. Got an early meeting tomorrow."

"Was just wondering why you transferred to Cincinnati before senior year?"

Gunner's fatigued response was more of a plea.

"Come on, Nick, it's late. UC was closer to home."

"But you liked Merriman."

"Don't want to go into it, OK?"

"Can I ask you one more thing?"

"Can't we do this some other time?"

"Why did you react like that today when I joked about voting for Van Pelt?"

"When it comes to him, don't have much to say."

"I know he liked busting your balls, but he was there the night those townies jumped you."

"There weren't any townies, Nick. It was Bru," Gunner said, resurrecting his junior-year assault, which had to do with him and Jerry Van Pelt.

"Wasn't anything really going on with you two, was there? If you don't mind me asking."

Gunner chuckled nervously. "Don't mind me asking? Why don't you say what you're thinking? Was I gay? Was 'Fairy Jerry'? Is that why Bru beat me up?"

Gunderson had returned from uptown after a night of beer and pinball with his accounting classmates. Most Omegas were sleeping in the first- and second-floor "rack rooms." Others were in the "tube room" watching Johnny Carson. When he flipped the light switch, Bru was sitting on the arm of his black vinyl couch with a bottle of Jack Daniel's. He ordered Gunner to drink, but he refused.

"Be a man, ya fuckin' homo," Van Pelt said, jamming the bottle to his lips. A stream of bourbon, saliva and blood coursed down his chin. He jerked backward and shoved Bru's arm away, the bottle breaking on the floor.

"You faggot sonufabitch," he said, lurching for him as he tried to escape. Van Pelt dove, making a shoestring tackle. Gunner lost his balance and rammed head first into the doorjamb. When he came to, Bru was kneeling on his chest.

"Swear to God you're not screwing around with my brother."

Gunner was woozy and in pain from his mouth lacerations and the gash on his forehead.

"You're crazy," he wheezed. "Get off me."

"If you're lying, I'll kick the ever-living shit out of you."

"I'm not. I swear."

Bru used a towel and so much athletic tape to bandage Gunner's head that he looked as if he wore a candy cane turban. Van Pelt later concocted the tale of how townies jumped him outside an uptown Sussex bar. Bru had found Gunner in his room "bleeding like a stuck pig" and took him to the infirmary.

"Had no idea," Nick said.

"Nobody did. He may have been psycho, but he wasn't dumb."

"Why didn't you tell anybody?"

"My word against his? He was untouchable in that fraternity. And you forget how his millionaire parents endowed the new business school at Merriman? Nick, you were the only one who could stand up to him."

"Sorry, Gunner."

"Not your fault. I've had a good life."

"You married? Kids?"

"Yes, married. My husband and I recently celebrated our 20th anniversary and fifth year as a legal couple."

"Your husband?"

Gunner's response was good-natured.

"Dago, for a wise-guy New Yorker, you're a little slow on the uptake."

"Coulda fooled me. You had great-looking dates, and you played a mean game of b-ball. You could shoot like Jimmy-what's-his-face on *Hoosiers*."

"Chitwood."

"Good call. Hey, we should get together sometime."

"I'd like that. Take care and don't blame yourself for what happened back in college."

Nick had believed the bogus story on Gunner getting mugged. All of it a lie and all because Bru was incensed over an illicit affair in the Omega house, where homosexuality was ridiculed and feared. He had told Nick how he was "severely punished" as a boy for trying to shield his "effeminate" brother from his father.

Brian Van Pelt was a decorated Marine in World War II, who saw horrific combat in the South Pacific. He returned home determined to be successful and respected. Or there would be hell to pay.

Nick learned the source of Bru's explosive temper lay in that Lexington mansion. His father, a heavyweight champ in the service, had a ring built in the basement. That's where Bru was taught to box and where he was disciplined. Brian would throw sharp punches as he lectured and hectored his son.

"Either you're a leader or a follower. A lion or a lamb. Which are you, Bruce?"

If he hesitated, Brian would cuff him on the head or jab his ribs. If he argued, the penalty would be more punches. When he was older, he fought back.

"If I tagged him, that was all she wrote," he said, describing how his dad would deliver a knockout. Left or right temple or an uppercut to the jaw. "Timber!" Brian would say as Bru fell to the canvas, to be awakened with a bucket of ice-cold water.

And where was his mom, Val, when all this was happening? Likely passed out. She had endeavored to be a "good" wife and mother in her children's early years. She would get the boys off to school and either meet in town for cocktails or open a bottle at home. Val would be "napping" when Bruce and Jerome came home, arising in time to make a tolerable supper and chat with her husband and sons. After more wine, she would fall sleep downstairs or alone in her luxurious bedroom.

Brian's relations with his wife had ended months before their second son was born. He preferred bored suburban housewives and high-priced call girls. When Bru was 14 and his pecker deemed man-sized, he lost his virginity "the Van Pelt way" with a prostitute in one of Cincinnati's finest downtown hotels. Brian wanted to ensure Bruce got a taste of quality poontang so he wouldn't fall prey to a homosexual predisposition, as dainty Jerome was destined.

Val knew of her husband's dalliances. They had agreed if affairs were discreet, they would be tolerated. However, one of her trysts occurred literally too close to home. On a day when Bru skipped classes as a high school senior, he saw his mother and her "greaseball lover boy" art instructor au naturel in the backyard pool.

"Nice visual of dear old Mom."

"Skinny dipping?" Nick asked, accustomed to his frat house candor.

"Her big white ass in the shallow end."

"Man, that's rough."

"No big deal," he said. "And that was how his shriveled pecker was—no big deal. Saw him when he toweled off. Mine was twice as big as his."

"Maybe the water was cold," Nick deadpanned.

"Good one, Dago," he said. "Must have been freezing out there."

Gunner said he shouldn't blame himself. But he knew what Van Pelt was capable of, and he hadn't stopped him. Megan said he had acquiesced if not collaborated. And last but not freakin' least, Alex was begging for atonement beyond the grave. With another scotch in hand, Nick lumbered toward his recliner. *Leave me the fuck alone. What's done is done.*

Chapter 3

Sullivan "Sully" Kirby was Bruce Van Pelt's father-in-law, mentor and benefactor. The 78-year-old Kirby had announced he would not seek reelection to the U.S. Senate in 2013. The Republican's legislative career had spanned five decades. He liked telling his Ohio constituents how he was first elected to Congress in 1976, the bi-centennial year. And how he wanted to serve until the tri-centennial, but "the Good Lord has other plans."

Kirby's homespun ways evoked the late Sam Ervin, who chaired the Senate Watergate Committee in the 1970s, resulting in the resignation of then-president Richard M. Nixon. Each was an amiable small-town denizen who had risen to national fame. But Ervin was a god-forsaken Democrat, and he a die-hard member of the Grand Old Party.

Kirby was heavyset with a ruddy face, full white beard and twinkling eyes behind tortoise-shell glasses. Kris Kringle comparisons were obvious and endearing to media watchers. He played the part, effecting a deep-bellied laugh and droll demeanor. *MSNBC* teased his speaking style as being "equal parts Jed Clampett and Gomer Pyle."

His public persona obscured a Machiavellian mindset. He had long been on choice Senate subcommittees. He wasn't opposed to bipartisanship if it could burnish his reputation. But he was no damn progressive.

As Ohio lieutenant governor to Jim Rhodes in May 1970, he recommended National Guard troops be sent to Kent State

University armed with live ammunition. After the killings of four students, Gov. Rhodes condoned the show of force with anti-war protesters at the blood-soaked campus. Kirby confided that he regretted more of "those dirty longhairs" weren't shot.

The senator, a poor farm boy from West Milton, Ohio, became rich and influential, securing his family from scrutiny. The Kirby children shunned the limelight, except middle daughter, Susie. As a college intern in the Treasury Department, she promised her father she would one day run for office. But then she met Bruce Van Pelt. In the Reagan years he was working for his father's international textile firm.

The general public was unaware of how many lines of designer jeans were manufactured in sweatshops in Thailand, India and Mexico. The low labor costs benefitting Brian Van Pelt's clothing empire were typically offset by tariffs on imported goods. But thanks to Senator Sully Kirby, taxes on those foreign-made jeans were reduced significantly by waivers. Kirby's rationale: The jeans were packaged and marketed in the U.S., generating American jobs and revenues "here at home." The product line would expand to private-labeled items such as running shoes, sold in Wal-Mart, K-Mart, Sears and J.C. Penney stores.

Brian was a global success, but he took nothing for granted. He dispatched son Bruce to meet with trade officials, international business reps and retailers. He was a natural corporate emissary—handsome and gracious, attracting allies and desirable women.

Susie Kirby wasn't the prettiest of Bruce's Capitol Hill conquests, but she was the best-connected. Bru told his fraternity alumni, "Not a great lay but the most valuable." The off-color line was classic Van Pelt: crude and brutally frank.

Bruce and Susie became a Washington power couple. They were the darlings of the new Christian right coalition, embracing people like Newt Gingrich and Ralph Reed. The Van Pelts learned how religious affiliation was critical to political success. Each was raised mainstream Protestant. But with Reed's solicitous overtures, they soon joined the evangelical flock.

Susie created a charity for orphans in third-world nations where Van Pelt factories were located. Bruce assisted his wife in promoting Gather My Sheep. The fundraising employed extensive advertising and publicity, which generated important name recognition. The telegenic pair were frequent guests on the Sunday morning talk-show circuit.

Upon Sully's advice, Bruce declared residency near his alma mater. In subsequent congressional campaigns, the Kentucky-native emphasized his wife's Buckeye roots and his college years. He became a well-liked though unproductive legislator, bolstered by right-wing media outlets.

He left the House of Representatives in 2010, ostensibly for philanthropic pursuits. Meanwhile his operatives were forging strategic alliances. Columnist George Will defined Van Pelt's future as "Kennedy-esque," which nostalgic Democrats termed blasphemous.

The Republican candidate's media marketing and advanced analytics were eclipsed by Sully Kirby's influence. He knew Ohio's rural voters and "white bread" suburbanites. He was positive of victory over Cleveland Mayor Kwame Imani.

"We'll whip Kwazi bigtime. He doesn't have a chance statewide."

"Kwame," Van Pelt corrected. "It's Kwame."

"Kwazi, Kwame, I don't care what his jungle bunny name is," Kirby said. "Let's send him and Obama both back to Africa."

Although frustrated, Bruce remained silent. He knew Sully couldn't take criticism. Van Pelt would never be deemed enlightened on social issues. But he didn't harbor prejudice toward blacks as did many of his cronies. He said his friendship with Lexington high school basketball star Jonah Moore was pivotal to his views on racial relations. Van Pelt would keep the peace with his father-in-law. For he could become a candidate for Sully's Senate seat if he somehow lost the gubernatorial race.

The Ohio contest was a microcosm of the 2012 presidential election: a self-made African-American versus an upper-crust scion. Nick Delamore had no links to Romney or Obama, but he had a unique perspective on Van Pelt and Imani.

Kwame Imani had adopted his Muslim identity when black activism was the zeitgeist, even on moderate campuses such as Merriman. The goateed, sunglass-wearing Imani was a dashing presence at a school with an enrollment of some 8,000, including more than 500 minority students. Serious to a fault, he would drop his guard only with trusted friends. In those venues his cackling was contagious as was his mimicry of African-American comics Dick Gregory, Bill Cosby and Richard Pryor.

In college he and Nick competed for the Irish spitfire and feminist Megan Bradley. The three couldn't have predicted how their lives would intersect many years later. If elected in 2012, the

Cleveland mayor would be Ohio's first black governor. Nick might acknowledge such an achievement, but support his quest? Not a chance.

Did Megan think he had forgotten her affair with Kwame when their marriage broke up? She was free to sleep with whomever when they divorced, but did it have to be with her college lover? The guy before and after him?

Nick may have wanted to hide out in Indiana, hoping the past would stay buried. But that was wishful thinking now that Megan was on a mission, unloading on him at Merten's funeral. No, he hadn't erased Alex or Allyson, a very special someone on that lengthy list of people he had failed.

Allyson Chambers was from the small farming town of Garden City, west of Medina, Ohio. Her brother had been an all-state running back, and she liked football. When she went to Merriman in fall 1971, she naively believed that being a college cheerleader would be as fun and carefree as it had been in high school. This teen beauty with the kid-sister smile also hoped she could keep the "bad boys" at bay like she had dodged them back home.

A strict Catholic, she pledged to preserve her chastity until the wedding night. Avoiding temptation, she dated sparingly her freshman year. But in one heated make-out session, a greedy, nimble-fingered lad undid her triple-latch bra. When he kept probing, Allyson wailed like a woman possessed. He bolted from her dorm room as if chased by Satan.

She didn't care if her ("Easy DZ") Delta Zeta sorority sisters called her a prude or a tease. Allyson Chambers wasn't "going all the way" until she had a husband. But it was exhausting fending off a line of suitors, who saw her as a gift to be unwrapped.

Her virginity vow was intact when she met Nick Delamore in the fall of her sophomore year at an Omega-DZ beer blast. He was keg-side, doling out foamy cups. She was at a safe distance, smoothing a cranberry sweater over new bell bottom jeans.

"Aren't you drinking?" she asked, stepping closer in her platform Oxfords.

"I'll catch up."

Allyson catalogued his assets: strong build, butterscotch brown eyes, a mass of dark curls and a sexy moustache above full "oh-so-kissable" lips. She asked if he was going to play football again.

"Tried to rehab it," he said, patting his knee. "But when you tear an ACL, you're out of luck."

"Sorry. You were really good."

Nick's gaze drifted from the beer blast to crushing gridiron hits. He missed the primal rush of dominating other men. When he looked back at her, his eyes had lost their luster.

Allyson hoped he would ask her to dance as Sly and the Family Stone rocked the party, thrilling the crowd of sweaty white faces. Nick was going to steal a kiss but pulled back when Jerry Van Pelt scurried across the basement rec area like a mischievous child.

"Is he an albino?" she asked.

"No, but he's a weird dude. Hard to believe he's his brother," Nick said, pointing to Bru dancing with a buxom DZ.

"They're so different. Was one of them adopted?"

Nick traced the little twerp's steps. He was sneaking to the bar where red Solo plastic cups were arranged. Chip Trellendorf, Mitchell Crouse and "Face Man" Tom McKinney stood by some sorority sisters. Crouse signaled Jerry, who deposited a pill in each beer cup, a demented Willy Wonka dispensing sedatives. He had gotten the "Sopors" (Quaaludes) from "Mighty Max" Klein, whose motto was "prime the pump and get humped."

Nick said to Allyson: "Don't ever set your drink down at one of these beer blasts. Keep it with you."

"OK. Why you telling me this?"

"Take it or leave it."

"I'll take it. Thanks," she said. "Now that we've got that out of the way, are you ever going to ask me to dance?"

But they never did as Bru swooped down on her.

"Forget him, babe, you're with me," Van Pelt said. He had a metal beer stein in his left hand; his other paw was around her waist. "Dago Delamore is off limits. Didn't he tell ya? Married and has a kid! Too bad so sad."

When Bru was sober, he was intimidating. Drunk, he was a threat. Nick could predict when his thuggish side would emerge, and he was the sole Omega who could handle him at his most dangerous.

They had first competed when Van Pelt was a sophomore tight end and Delamore a frosh linebacker. Bru was loud. He swaggered. Nick didn't like him and knew they would come to blows. When they met in the locker room before the initial preseason practice, he called him "buddy boy" and marveled at his flowing curly hair. He tried to mess with it, but Nick stopped him with a forearm shiver.

"Looks like you know how to box, pardner," Bru said, drawing attention. "Boys, this here Nick *Del-a-more* is a badass from New York. You're *Eye-talian*, right? OK if I call you Dago Delamore?"

"Whatever ya say, Hopalong," Nick replied, pulling the name from an old television Western.

"Hopalong Cassidy. Gawd, loved that show as a kid. You Dago, me Hopalong. Yee-haw!"

At the Omega-DZ beer blast, Van Pelt had Allyson firmly in his grasp. He swiveled his hips and guzzled his beer, accepting hoorays from frat brothers and stares from awestruck women. A muscular six-foot-four, he was like a mythological god come to life. Close-cropped bronze hair highlighted his wide brow, aquiline nose and perfect teeth.

His hazel eyes were riveted on her porcelain features. "You are gorgeous," he said, kissing her harshly. He forced his tongue between her resisting lips. When she tried to pull away, he pressed her to his crotch.

She had felt others bulge with desire when they slow danced. Her girlfriends giggled about "boys and their boners." But this erection frightened Allyson, and she used both hands to escape. When he tried to recapture her, Nick blocked him.

"Slow down, Hopalong," he said, locking eyes with him. "You're scaring this nice girl."

"Oh, I get it. You want to tap this pretty young thing. Where's your wife and baby boy? They go back to New Yawk?"

He pushed by Bru and toward a recoiling Allyson. From behind came a stream of beer and then a spike as a metal mug clanked off his head. Music was blaring, but people quieted as the big men squared off. Van Pelt wore a tight white Ban-Lon polo shirt, chinos and Top-Siders. Delamore had on a gray sweatshirt, Wranglers and tan work boots.

"Don't pussy out on me, Dago."

Nick went into a boxer's crouch, fists cocked by his chin. He saw the roundhouses coming because Bru was telegraphing his punches. He ducked and deflected them as his challenger called for him to fight.

When Nick moved in, he was hit with a stiff jab to the face. But Van Pelt reacted too soon, raising his arms triumphantly, expecting Delamore to go down. He surprised him by launching a pure shot to the solar plexus, which felled the giant, his huge frame collapsing in a heap on the linoleum floor. Nick ran the back of his hand over his lips and tongue along the top row of teeth. *All good.*

Van Pelt was helped to his feet, and Delamore went looking for Allyson, who was at the front door.

"Hey, where you going?"

"I don't like fighting. It scares me," she said.

"We were only fooling. Come on, I'll walk you home."

"Are you sure? What if ... ? Oh, I don't know."

"Everything will be fine. Promise."

Outside her dorm, she thanked him with a kiss.

"Is it true what he said about you being married and having a son?"

"Yeah, but things didn't go well, and I haven't been a very good husband or father."

"You seem like a good guy to me."

"Thanks, but we just met."

"Do you want to come in?" she asked. "It's cold out here, and my roommate went home for the weekend."

As with most of her sorority sisters, Allyson lived in the same dorm where the DZ suite was located. There were no sorority houses at Merriman. Campus administrators believed that by limiting Greek women to rooms instead of buildings, they would be less inclined to engage in wanton socializing.

Nick knew the layout: two beds, two desks, a double-dresser and cheap closet doors with full-length mirrors. The first thing that caught his eye was a poster of James Taylor in her tidy room. Plush penguins were everywhere: on the pink and gray bedspread, windowsill and nightstand, encircling a 5x7 family photo and black clock radio.

"So you like penguins and JT," he said as she clung to him.

"Love penguins and JT. 'Fire and Rain' is so romantic."

"Good song," Nick said, his work boots planted on the floor.

"Sit down, silly," she said, sliding the toy animals off the bed.

Allyson nuzzled his neck. Nick took it slow, choosing to talk first. He asked what she was studying and her post-college plans.

"I'm in special ed," she said. "Told you at the beer blast. But you got distracted by that big jerk."

"Van Pelt," he said, reliving his perfect punch. "What grade level?"

"Elementary," she said. "I love kids."

"Good for you," he said, hands in his lap as she fawned over him. "You know you're turning me on."

"Am I?"

"How far do you want to go?"

"Why can't we just kiss?" she asked. "Why isn't that ever enough?"

"Sometimes it is," he said. "With or without clothes?"

Her body stiffened, and she began pacing on her pink shag rug.

"You think I'm a big prude, don't you?"

"I think you're fine," he said. "It's your call."

She was glowing as she pushed him backward and knelt on his sturdy chest.

"Thank you. Thank you. Thank you."

"Should I stay or go? It's getting late."

"You can stay, but it's a small bed."

"OK if I take off my boots and dungarees? Nothing else."

"Dungarees? Don't you mean jeans?" she asked haltingly. "Can I trust you?"

"Can you?"

"Hope so," she said. "I want to put on my pajamas, but I'm keeping my underwear on."

"Put on your bathrobe if it makes you feel better," Nick said, entertained by her funny pout. He shielded his eyes as she got ready for bed.

"Don't make fun," she said, displaying her red flannels.

"Are those?" he asked, inspecting the background pattern.

"Yup, penguins."

"And those are our school colors. Onward, Merriman."

Nick was amazed the night would end this way, cuddling the voluptuous Allyson, who smelled of citrus shampoo and baby powder. Her kisses were driving him crazy. God, how he wanted to make love.

"What's wrong?" she asked in the perfumed darkness.

"You sure we can't?"

"I want to be a virgin when I get married. I'm Catholic."

"Me too."

"Were you a virgin when you got married?"

"Not a virgin, but I had only been with Linda."

Allyson pulled him closer. Despite the industrial-strength pajamas, bra and panties, her rhythmic rocking aroused him. When she started cooing in his ear, he was a goner.

"Did you?"

"Yeah," he said. "What goes up must come down."

"You're funny and so gosh darn cute."

"That's what they all say."

In the morning, Nick sneaked out of the dorm. Allyson was at her window as he jogged through campus, a big curly-haired teddy bear. She knew they were meant to be together forever.

Chapter 4

The night of Alex's funeral, Nick slept fitfully. Too much scotch and too many thunderclaps. As storms crossed central Indiana, Nick was beset by fleeting visions from his Merriman days. In this dreamscape the Omega house was cavernous with a bizarre decor: black vinyl couches, La-Z-Boy recliners and rows of church pews.

He was reading a *Playboy* and ogling the centerfold when a lean and tanned Alex appeared, wearing jeans, high-top red sneakers and a Hawaiian shirt. He snatched the magazine, tearing it to pieces before shoving the shredded pages in his mouth. Merten was gyrating like a holy goof when Delamore grabbed for him, but he slipped away and then vanished.

Nick stumbled down the wide tilting corridors, unable to keep his balance on these funhouse walkways. He heard a woman scream from the first floor, tracking the noise to a darkened room with the door ajar. Were these cries of torment or pleasure?

Ghoulish figures were watching a big bare-assed man humping someone on a floor mattress. He strained to see who was there. But all he could see were writhing bodies in the shadows.

Nick yelled ("Hey, get off her!"), but his words fell silent. The man was grinding away as a woman moaned beneath him. He gasped for air, escaping to the bright hallway.

Naked men in American Indian headdresses ran by him and into a bathroom, where an obese woman was slouched under a steaming shower, her pale skin covered in red blotches. She was rimmed by piles of Budweiser beer cans and empty Jack Daniel's bottles as they pelted her with war cries. Someone pulled him from the doorway, and he scuffled before reentering the dusky bedroom. A woman was crying, face down on the bed. He knelt beside her. *Allyson? ... Megan? ... Megan?*

There was chanting from afar: "All hail! All hail!" Van Pelt sat on a throne among his court of admirers. He beckoned Nick. When he refused to pay homage, sycophants bound his arms and legs. He was carried on their shoulders as Alex splashed him with holy water from a glass vial, the type a priest uses to bless those during last rites.

Nick fought to get free, shouting, "I'll fucking kill all of you!"

Then he heard the chiming of bells as in the Offertory of the Mass. *My Lord and My God. My Jesus, mercy.* He awoke sweating and tangled in his sheet. His cell phone was ringing by the bed.

"Nick?" Megan asked.

"Huh?"

"You sound strange."

"Crazy dreams. ... You calling to apologize?"

"What? No. Listen to me, OK?"

"What's wrong?"

"Something happened to Miranda last night."

Nick's mind was clearing. He found a pen and notepad. "Is she OK?"

"She was almost raped at a frat party. Said she got away before it was too late, but her friend is in bad shape."

"Where are they now?"

"At the ER. I spoke with Inez and Christopher."

"Why did they call you instead of me?"

"Because their daughter was involved in a sexual assault," she said. "I'm almost there."

"Where?"

"Wilson Memorial Hospital in Sidney. About 90 minutes from you. Need you to meet me as soon as you can."

"Will Miranda be OK?"

"I'll know more when I get there. But she's a survivor. That's all that matters."

Miranda Delamore was Nick and Megan's niece and goddaughter. Their divorce two years after her birth didn't alter that fact. Nor had it prevented her from being a devoted part of their lives. She was the closest thing Nick and Megan had to their own daughter in what had been a childless marriage.

Miranda was a top student and star volleyball player at Magnificat High School on Cleveland's Westside. She had an independent spirit and enjoyed talking politics with her uncle, who said she better not become "an ink-stained wretch" like him.

"No worries, Unk," she said when he congratulated her at high school graduation. "I'm going to law school, and someday I'll be on the Supreme Court."

"Have no doubt," he told his dimpled niece with the soulful eyes.

Christopher and Inez Delamore were delighted when their only child, Miranda, selected Oakwood College, a small liberal arts institution north of Dayton. They believed she would be safe and get an excellent education. Miranda had an academic scholarship and a starting spot on the volleyball team.

"But she's a survivor." Nick heard Megan's voice as he dressed. He didn't want to think about what could have happened. *Thank God she got away.*

Miranda's roommate wasn't so fortunate. Maybe she was too out of it. Or maybe she had been overpowered. Just like in his college days, heartless bastards hunted their victims. These women needed the guardian angel Megan Bradley, who would do everything in her power to secure justice.

Nick went to the ER and gave Miranda's name to the admitting nurse, who took her time perusing the log of patients.

"You'll have to wait here."

"But I'm family."

"As I said, you'll have to wait here."

He muttered in protest and called Megan. It went right to voicemail. She sent a terse text: "With Stacy. Rape kit. Miranda coming out."

Nick embraced his willowy niece, who had grown into such a stunning young woman. *Thank God she got away.*

"Hi, Unk. Sorry for making you ... ."

"Hey, knock it off," he said. "I'm just so glad you're safe. How's your friend doing?"

"Not good. She's ... ." Miranda choked up. "She's ... ."

"It's going to be OK," he said, his arm grasping her shoulder.

Nick's stomach was churning. He wanted to get the scumbags who did this. He got a second text from Megan, suggesting they go eat. She would meet up with them later.

"How are you feeling?"

"My neck's sore, and I've got a headache. All they gave me was Tylenol."

"Why not some real drugs?" Nick said, eliciting a grin from Miranda.

Then she said somberly, "I'm the one who took Stacy to the party."

"Easy does it," he said, holding her hand as they walked to his car. "None of this was your fault or hers in any way."

He didn't ask about the marks on his niece's neck, certain Megan would soon provide details.

"Want to eat something?"

"Not super hungry," she said. "See you're still driving your old Honda."

"We're both going strong."

Miranda smiled, but her eyes were dull gemstones in need of polishing. Nick saw a small retail area, bookended by a McDonald's and a Subway.

"Take your pick."

"Doesn't matter. Better coffee at McDonald's."

"Mickey Ds it is," he said, trying to sound upbeat.

He saw a booth at the far end of the restaurant where they wouldn't be bothered.

"Know exactly what to get," he said, kissing the top of her coal-black hair.

"OK," she said wearily. "Go for it, Unk."

Miranda examined the tray as he recited: "Cheeseburger, fries and chocolate shake with extra whipped cream. All your favorites."

"Uh, I'm a vegan, so I don't eat that kind of food anymore. And no processed sugar."

"Since when?"

"At least three years ago," she said. "But that was very sweet of you."

"Easy breezy, kiddo," he said. "More for me. What would you like? A salad? A muffin? Wait, that has sugar in it."

"Just some iced tea, please."

"Unsweetened," he said, heading off. *At least three years ago?*

"Can you sit next to me?" Miranda asked upon his return. "I'm feeling sleepy. OK if I lean on you?"

Moving to her side of the booth, Nick recalled a lyric from a Bill Withers tune: *"We all need somebody to lean on."*

As she dozed, he ate and drank everything on the tray. After the second milkshake, he was bloated and regretted his gluttony. But he wasn't going to budge and disturb Miranda's sleep. He thought of her friend Stacy, whose problems could last years. Some never recover from trauma, Megan often said. *All those broken lives.*

When Nick and Miranda arrived at her dorm, Megan was in the lobby. She had brought Stacy back from the ER.

"They gave her a sedative," she said. "Should sleep all day and probably through the night. But you need to stay with her. One of your friends is up there now."

"Thanks so very, very much, Aunt Meg," Miranda said, dwarfing Megan in a long hug.

"Here to help, sweetie. But I'm running on fumes. If you need me, I'm staying at the Holiday Inn Express up the road. Left messages for your RA, who wasn't here this morning."

"She's usually out on Sundays," Miranda said. "There's a central number to call in case of emergency."

"No, I want to talk to her personally and don't want anyone to bother Stacy today. Tomorrow, we'll also meet with the dean of students. Left a voicemail for her too. Your mom and dad gave me permission to speak on their behalf."

Nick stood with hands shoved in his pockets, seemingly invisible and feeling quite inadequate.

"Sure that's not rushing things?" he asked, unable to maintain his silence.

Megan looked at Nick and then at Miranda.

"Don't mind him," she said. "He means well."

"I know," Miranda said, kissing her godparents goodbye. "Love you both. See you tomorrow."

"He's going back to Indiana."

"I am?"

"You'll only get in the way."

"Miranda, I'll call you tomorrow night," he said. "Take care. I love you."

Megan retrieved her phone as Nick viewed the morning sky.

"Going to be a nice day."

"Maybe for you."

"I mean the weather. Geez, cut me some slack."

"Don't bet on it," she said. "I need some food. Saw a Cracker Barrel near the motel."

They sat in the folksy setting with after-church diners. Megan ate heartily as she discussed the chain of events from the last dozen hours: Miranda was invited to a fraternity beer blast by the captain of the men's volleyball team. Craig Owen had been helpful "like a big brother" to her all season. He encouraged her to bring friends to the party, and at first he seemed more interested in Stacy.

"Miranda said she got a little ... ."

"Tipsy?"

"Except they don't say 'tipsy.' "

"A little buzzed. That better?"

"Whatever. She was making out in Owen's room, and ... ."

"But he wasn't satisfied with just kissing, was he?"

"Are you done?"

Nick nodded and flagged the waitress for a coffee refill as Megan continued.

"She let him touch her breasts. But when he tugged at her jeans, she joked, 'No way, José.' And he said: 'Come on. I know all you Hispanics are hot-blooded.' "

"He said that? Hot-blooded Hispanics? What an asshole. Then what happened?"

"He took off his shorts and straddled her. That's when she felt panicky for the first time. He shoved his erect penis in her face. She twisted her head to one side. But he had such big hands, he easily turned her. 'Don't be a bitch,' he said. 'Just suck it.' "

An elderly twosome at the next table were shell-shocked, hearing such language on the Lord's Day. Megan disregarded their stony faces and kept talking.

"Miranda tried not to freak out. She said he was hurting her shoulders, and she couldn't move. If he wanted a blowjob, he needed to let her up. He said, 'Do it and you can go.' When he shifted, she shoved him off the bed and ran out."

Granny and Grandpop rose in unison and took their business and disgusted expressions to the far side of the dining room. Resuming her account, Megan said Miranda rushed downstairs to where Danny Evans, a freshman on the volleyball team, was alone playing video games. She said she had to find Stacy. Evans told her to stay in the TV room. When he left, Miranda realized her phone was in Owen's room. Then she heard yelling and saw Evans carrying Stacy, wrapped in a sheet like at a toga party. Her face was red, scratched and streaked in tears. Her blonde hair was matted, her bangs glistening. Evans said he would drive them home as vulgarities rained down.

At their dorm, she told him to stay in the car with Stacy while she got some clothes for her. When he balked, she threatened to call the campus police. Miranda had him take them to the hospital, where she called her mom and dad.

"Any of this sound familiar?" Megan asked Nick, between sips of coffee.

"Familiar?"

"Same scenario with Allyson Chambers. Or have you forgotten how she was gang raped in your fraternity?"

"Hasn't been a bad enough day as it is? You have to bring that up?"

"This morning when I was trying to encourage Stacy to complete the exam, it was like being back in that Sussex ER with Allyson."

Nick watched the flow of traffic outside.

"How did it go with the cop?"

"He barged in and started grilling her and Miranda on how much they had to drink and what they were wearing. Did they do anything to give anyone the 'wrong idea'? I had to back him off, and he didn't like that."

"I bet. Good for you."

"Stacy was afraid her parents would find out if she filed a police report. But Miranda was pissed, and I told her she could press charges for assault, confinement and attempted rape. When she agreed, I made sure they took photos of the marks on her neck, arms and shoulders. The cop said he was going to the frat house for 'non-custodial questioning.' We both know, Craig Owen and the others will claim it was all consensual."

Nick was listening to Megan, but his thoughts were elsewhere—the night he tried to warn Allyson Chambers about Bru Van Pelt.

Chapter 5

$\mathbf{M}$onday morning, Megan texted her assistant shelter director that she would be out all day dealing with a "personal matter" at Oakwood College. After a bland breakfast in the motel lobby, she called Miranda.

"Left another message for your dean of students. Do you know this Beverly Ward?"

"She spoke to us at orientation," Miranda said. "Seems nice."

"That's what they're paid to be. How are you doing? How's Stacy?"

"I'm OK. She had a bad nightmare but fell back asleep."

"Heading over now. Stay with Stacy until I get there and talk to your RA," Megan said. "See you soon."

Shannon Anderson was the resident assistant at Blandon Hall on Oakwood's lush campus. She supervised students on three floors of the new dormitory, with its widescreen digital TVs, snack lounge, game areas and turbo-speed Wi-Fi. At first glance, Anderson, a psychology major, seemed too timid to enforce a host of rules. But she was very organized in coping with infractions: alcohol and pot smoking, loud music and curfew shenanigans. She believed she was handling her job well. That was before she met "Bulldog" Megan Bradley, as Nick had dubbed her.

"You've got a traumatized woman on the second floor—Stacy Matlin," she said bluntly.

"Sorry?" the RA replied, ill-prepared for an opening salvo at the start of her day. "Who are you?"

"I'm Miranda Delamore's aunt and head of a women's shelter and crisis center in Cleveland. Miranda's parents have given me permission to serve as her advocate. There were sexual assaults involving Miranda and her roommate, Stacy, this weekend. I was with them in the ER yesterday at Wilson Memorial. It's urgent that you do whatever's necessary to support both women, especially Stacy."

"Yes, I understand," Anderson said, scrolling her phone. "But I'm not seeing any reported incidents."

Megan snapped at her: "Do you really think there would be postings already? You better get up to speed. Stacy was gang raped on Saturday night, and Miranda barely escaped."

"Oh, no. I'm always telling our girls to be careful," Anderson said. "They're my friends, you know. My friends."

"That's good," Megan said. "But that's not enough. Have you had any sexual assault training?"

"All the RAs watched a Title IX video with a presentation afterward."

"That's all the training you've had?" Megan asked, sarcasm renewed. "Listen, you need to put off anything else you had planned for the day and make Stacy your priority."

Anderson was taking notes. "I first need to inform the dean of students."

"I'm meeting her at 2 o'clock," Megan said, reading one of her new texts. "I'll tell her we talked and that you want to speak with her."

"Thank you," Anderson said. "I'm so sorry this happened. They're great girls."

Megan was going to correct her. *Women not girls.* But she could see how shaken Anderson was.

Next up: Dr. Beverly P. Ward, dean of students, Oakwood College. Megan expected a frumpy academic not a fashionably dressed middle-aged woman, accented with a scarlet silk scarf and disarming welcome.

"Pleasure to meet you, Ms. Bradley, in spite of the circumstances. I've heard of your work in Cleveland."

"It's Megan, please. And as I said on the phone, I'm here on behalf of my niece and her roommate."

"Understood," Ward said, smiling at Miranda, who wore a brown and white checkerboard blouse, stretch tan slacks and flip-flops. Megan was in her trademark black jeans, black work boots and midnight blue shirt under a black blazer.

"Let me begin by assuring you, Miranda, and your aunt we will do everything possible to determine what occurred at the Alpha Beta house on Saturday night and take all necessary steps," she said, her ruby-tipped fingers interlocked on the polished mahogany desktop.

Megan took the lead: "As I told the RA this morning, the first thing this college has to do is take care of Stacy Matlin. She's a suicide risk."

Ward called the student health center and asked to have a nurse visit Stacy that afternoon.

"Thank you," Megan said. "But she will also need immediate counseling."

"I agree," Ward said. "I'll make those arrangements. However, this is finals week."

"Shouldn't make any difference to you or anyone else here," Megan said. "The welfare of your students is your primary responsibility."

Ward was tight-lipped as she turned to Miranda.

"I hear you also went through a very trying time on Saturday night. How are you doing now?"

"OK, I guess."

"And you filed a police report, correct?"

"Yes, I filed a report."

"But you weren't technically sexually assaulted," Ward said, writing on a legal pad with a blue and yellow Oakwood College pen.

"She *was* assaulted, damn it."

"Ms. Bradley, you're obviously upset. But I will not tolerate profanity in my office. And I would like to complete my interview without further interruption. It's protocol."

"I have a different word for that," Megan countered.

"Craig Owen tried to rape me," Miranda blurted out.

"I have noted that," Ward said. "But I need more background before we proceed."

Megan glared at the dean, anticipating the usual blame-the-victim routine.

"Was there underage drinking at this party, and, if so, how much did you girls have?"

"They're women not girls," Megan said, nudging Miranda. "And if they were drunk, that doesn't mean they were guilty of anything except maybe poor judgment. It sure as hell doesn't warrant being raped."

"Of course not, and I resent your implication. The well-being of our students is my top priority."

"Then act like it and stop excusing criminal conduct."

"Miranda," Ward said, doing her best to bypass Megan. "According to what you told the police, you went to Craig's room voluntarily and engaged in consensual sexual activity. Wouldn't that have indicated you wanted to go further? Would that be a reasonable assumption?"

"Why are you defending him?" Megan asked, piercing the dean's faux armor.

"Craig Owen is one of our honors student-athletes. But he and anyone else involved will be liable for their behavior. What I'm trying to ascertain is whether there's enough here to present to the Student Ethics and Morality Committee. And, to be honest, I'm having my doubts."

Miranda spoke up: "Do you have doubts Stacy was raped in that frat house? She sure doesn't and neither do I."

Ward clenched and unclenched her manicured fingers on the shiny desktop.

"Until Stacy meets with me or files a police report, there is little I can do as far as remedial action. Sometimes difficult things happen in life, but we must move on."

"Move on? Are you serious? Have you even heard of the Clery Act?" Megan stood leaning on the desk, smudging the gleaming surface as Ward frowned. "You're required under federal law to keep accurate records on forcible sex offenses as violent crimes. From what's being reported on the college's website, I'm having *my* doubts about the integrity of your office and this school in general. All of which could result in a complaint to the U.S. Department of Education's Office of Civil Rights."

Ward slid her chair back so far, it crashed into a wide credenza. She stood, her taut face matching the color of her silk scarf, and said with steely conviction: "Go right ahead, but don't try to threaten or intimidate me. I'll be speaking with Craig Owen and other fraternity members this week. If I need any additional information, I'll contact you, Miranda, and Stacy. Now you must excuse me, but I have more work to do and meetings to attend."

Monday evening, Nick watched LeBron James and the Miami Heat win their NBA playoff game as he awaited Megan's call. He had spoken earlier with Christopher and Inez, who were very distressed. They had wanted Miranda to come home with Megan, but their headstrong daughter persuaded them she was fine to finish the semester and needed to be there for Stacy.

"We thought Oakwood would be perfect for her," Christopher had said, trailing off. Nick heard him weeping.

"Hey, bro, there's no predicting when or where something like this will happen. What's most important is that Miranda is OK. You and Inez have done an outstanding job raising her."

"Thanks so much for helping us out," Christopher said.

"You're welcome. But Megan did the heavy lifting. She's relentless in these situations."

Nick knew his brother and sister-in-law wouldn't relax until their daughter was back in Rocky River, Ohio. He wanted to open a new bottle of Dewar's, but he decided to first talk with Megan.

"Another royal cluster fuck," she said, followed by a loud yawn. "The dean of students is a classic bureaucrat, posing by her big polished desk. When I checked back with the police, they said an officer had visited the frat house. But they all covered their asses, even Evans, the one who drove Miranda and Stacy to the hospital."

Nick asked how Miranda was doing.

"You should have seen how assertive she was in the meeting with the dean. Don't have the heart to tell her that likely nothing will happen. No arrests. No hearings. No expulsions. Maybe the fraternity will be put on probation. Or maybe not. And this dean will probably win administrator of the year. ... You still there?"

"Yeah," he said. "You want me to go and see Miranda later this week?"

"You should check on her before she moves out," she said. "But let's talk more tomorrow. I'm fried."

"Hope you know how much everyone appreciates what you're doing."

"Thanks. Only doing my job."

"You were made for this work. You used to say it was a calling."

"Well my bed is calling, and my feet are killing me."

He heard one of her boots hit the wood floor, prompting a honeymoon memory: coating her toned body and feet with baby oil. *Those tiny tootsies could turn a grouchy podiatrist into a fetishist.*

Nick clicked off his phone and checked the calendar for when he would visit Miranda again. Then he poured a well-deserved tumbler of scotch. The golden elixir transported him to his jinxed junior year at Merriman University.

Chapter 6

On Halloween 1972, Alex Merten was in the library cramming for midterms and missing his mercurial girlfriend, Donna Carvel. They had dated as seniors at Cincinnati's Princeton High. She was his first love. He was an expedient boyfriend.

Alex chose Merriman, an hour from home. Donna attended Ohio University across the state. That was a pragmatic choice as she was a budding actress, and OU had one of the best theater programs in the Midwest.

She told him he had no reason to worry. "You know what they say. Absence will make us grow fonder." Her passionless comments sounded prerecorded.

He called her twice a week and wrote poetic letters. She preferred silly cards with dogs and cats at play. He wished for more outward signs of affection but felt lucky to have a beautiful albeit long-distance sweetheart.

As fluorescent cylinders hissed above, he sat in his cubicle holding his highlighter. What if he had to duke it out with someone over Donna? His fingers were small, delicate. Would they shatter on an adversary?

"Why do you stress about things like that?" brother Jim would ask. Easy for him. With his mighty fists he had won all his fights. Same with Nick Delamore, whose New York street battles were like swashbuckling tales.

Next came the usual fretting over sex. Alex knew the mechanics of lovemaking. Although as an adolescent, he and his immature pals thought their peckers would get stuck if they lost their erections during intercourse. When the time came, could he perform, would he satisfy?

Beyond that ongoing anxiety lay the fear of death facing him and thousands of men with low draft numbers. The Vietnam War was winding down, according to news reports. But troops were still being killed, wounded and captured. If he didn't flunk out, he would keep his student deferment. That's what the gaunt Unitarian minister had said last fall. As a kid, Alex watched black and white World War II movies, daydreaming of being a brave soldier. But now he was filled with doubts.

Drowsy from the stale library air, his head felt like a Howdy Doody puppet. He shook himself awake. *Time to go.* He left behind scores of studious zombies and escaped.

People were enjoying the Indian summer twilight. The weather was a reprieve from the onset of a bleak southern Ohio winter. The evening carried the scent of leaf burnings and sounds of students tossing Frisbees and laughter in the quad.

A shaggy gnome with a cannabis smile strolled by barefoot in a purple tie-dyed tank top and frayed jeans: "Don't change dicks in the middle of a screw. Vote for Nixon in '72."

As night fell, costumed creatures lurked by trees and corners of buildings. A werewolf crept toward a woman in cut-off denim shorts and a red Merriman sweatshirt. She was juggling an armful of texts and fiddling with a bike lock. When she turned and saw bloody lips and fangs, she shrieked, dropped her things and slapped at the jokester, who celebrated his stunt before sprinting away. Alex hurried down the library steps, and the student flinched when he rushed to her.

"Crap, you scared me."

"Sorry. You OK?"

"I'm fine," she said. "Just a little spooked."

"Sure you're OK?" he asked, collecting her books.

"Yeah, thanks."

She rode down the tree-lined slant walk, weaving between students and past the Georgian-design brick structures. She was attractive, but Alex wouldn't have pursued her even if she had shown any interest because he was already in love.

He would leave wham-bam romance to Nick Delamore, who had been married at 18 and was a father. Though the same age, they were light years apart when it came to sexual experience. As a 20-year-old virgin in the frat house, Merten was a candidate for Ripley's *Believe It or Not!*

From his melancholy perch high on the concrete steps, Alex saw couples kissing. *What was Donna doing tonight? Was she at her rehearsal or out partying?* He would try calling later, though it would probably only frustrate him.

"You contemplating life or the hair between your toes?" Nick shouted at his brooding friend. "Come on, sad sack. Time for brewskis and pinball."

"And a bucket of saltpeter."

Nick turned thespian: "Where oh where is my darling Donna? Wherefore art thou?"

"I'm not that bad."

"Not that bad? You're the biggest pussy whip on campus," Delamore said, turning heads.

He cracked up when Alex tried to shove him from the sidewalk. They wrestled briefly in Greco-Roman style, which was fitting considering their Mediterranean appellations, Dago and Garcia.

"Econ midterm tomorrow," Alex said as they reached the bars, eateries and quaint shops in the heart of Sussex.

"Just enjoy the view, Poindexter," Nick said, spying a woman in tight orange shorts. "That tush is like a big juicy peach."

"Correct me if I'm wrong, but aren't you married?"

"Getting the divorce papers any day."

"Hasn't stopped you so far."

"Hey, I've been careful."

"Give me a break," Alex said upon entering Bottom Dog Tavern.

The bar's amber lighting and close confines were pleasing to those downing 3.2 beer in booths or at wobbly wooden tables. The watery brew was the only legal alcohol served within Sussex city limits. Merriman students knew they had to drive over the state line into Indiana to get wine or liquor.

The women were subtle, evaluating prospects as they chatted. The men were more obvious, raising beer mugs in search of fair damsels. Thankful for a name and phone number, they would sell their souls for a chance at love on any given night.

"Can't play this stupid game," Alex said, slapping at the pinball machine, his turn ended by an inept attempt.

"Don't bang the flippers," Nick instructed, assuming his pose: feet shoulder-width, head up, fingers twitching. "It's all in the touch. That's what she said."

He was racking up thousands of points, moving like a light-footed boxer. He caressed the glass and rocked his crotch at the clanging, flashing apparatus. When his sensual dance ended, he bowed, having bettered his own record.

"Didn't know I was with Tommy, the friggin' pinball wizard," Alex grumbled.

"What's bugging you? Donna's coming to Viking, isn't she?"

"Said she was, but that was last week."

"Stop worrying; she loves your ass," Nick said, checking out some new women at the bar.

"What if she's cheating on me?"

"With who, some wacko theater nut? Forget about it."

Alex offered Nick one of his Marlboros.

"I keep thinking that ... ."

"That's your problem," Nick said. "Stop thinking. Let it go, man."

"OK, mellow yellow."

A shapely blonde approached their table. When she leaned over, her peasant-style blouse was revealing.

"Allyson. How you doin'? Hey, Happy Halloween."

"Why haven't you called?" she asked, teetering in place.

"You OK? This is my buddy Alex."

She ignored the introduction.

"Why didn't you ask me to the Viking party?"

"What? You better sit down before you fall."

"Why didn't you?"

"Tried telling you the other night. I don't want to screw up my divorce."

"You are such a liar," she said, jabbing her finger at Nick. "Thought we had something special when you spent the night with me, or was I dreaming?"

Alex's eyebrows rose. *Let's see how you manage this one, Delamore.*

"I do like you," he said. "But I'm not ready for a relationship. That's why I didn't call. I'm sorry."

Alex thought this all very acceptable but not Allyson.

"You're like every other guy," she said. "Want to see how much you can get without any commitment."

She stepped toward her sorority sisters, who were waiting impatiently at the door. Then she looped back to Nick.

"I figured I'd give you one last chance because Bruce Van Pelt called tonight. He asked me to the party, and I said yes. He's even taking me out to dinner first."

Her jaw jutted defiantly before she lost her balance, and Nick steadied her with both hands.

"Don't do that, Allyson. Don't go with him," he said as sincerely as possible on a belly full of beer. "Trust me. You saw how he gets when he's bombed."

She pulled away. "He apologized for how he acted. He said I'm a nice classy girl. That's what he called me. Classy."

"Please don't go with him."

"Why? You jealous?" she yelled in his ear. "Gave you a chance, but you don't want to go with me. ... And tell your friend to stop staring at my boobs."

Alex turned away from the woman as she stormed off.

Nick took a drag of his cigarette and shook his head.

"That's messed up."

"Why would she do that?" Alex asked, spinning his empty mug. "After what Van Pelt did at the beer blast? If you hadn't slugged him, who knows what could have happened. Can't believe she would go anywhere near him."

"Beats me."

"So who you going with?"

"Mary Beth Saunders, that stacked Tri Delt who works at the paper. When I said she could write a column on student life, she almost jumped me in the office."

"Was starting to feel bad for you, but ... ."

"But what? What am I doing that's so wrong?"

"You're one of a kind."

"Got that right." Nick slapped the wooden tabletop. "Let's blow this popsicle stand."

The two men emerged from the bar like bears leaving a cave. They joined the line of students wandering back to the bucolic campus. In these environs, crime was ripping off steaks from the Kroger supermarket, parking illegally, swiping a bike, boozing or getting stoned in a dorm room. Violence was left to nightly newscasts and headlines. To most living here, even the Kent State shootings seemed as far as Saigon. This wasn't the real world. It was never-neverland nestled in the bosom of "Mother Merriman."

"Go the back route," Alex said, gesturing toward the residential neighborhood.

"Faster this way."

Alex put fingers to his lips.

"Why didn't you say so?"

When they were sauntering down the darkened streets, Alex pulled a joint from his flannel shirt pocket.

"Halloween gift from Mighty Max."

"Light that sucker up."

Their dialogue became monosyllabic as they walked along fraternity row, past the Doric columns, wide porches, brick walls and vaulted doorways. Alex had first seen these frat houses at freshman orientation in September 1970. He was in a caravan of neophyte males looking impotently at the upperclassmen in dark blue shirts with gold Greek lettering, luring freshman girls with beer and bravado.

"Hey, doll. Not you, dorkface. Yeah you, cutie. Forget that orientation crapola. Come party with us." A sandy-haired Sigma Nu held overflowing plastic cups. "And bring your good-looking friends."

At the convocation, Dr. Wilbur Ackley, president of Merriman University, spoke of the school's history. How it originated in 1806 when Oliver Merriman, who had surveyed much of southwest Ohio, established a Methodist college in the town he called Sussex, after his birthplace on the south coast of England. Ackley's monotonous speech changed when referencing student unrest the previous spring.

"You are the first incoming class since the fateful events on the nation's campuses this past May," he said. "Those were indeed tragedies, but let me be very clear: Our university will not tolerate lawlessness under any circumstances. You are here to get an education and to build the foundation for your adult lives."

Most in this auditorium were unacquainted with protest. But that September day irreverence was in vogue as students chanted Dr. Ackley's name ("Hello, Wilbur. I'm Mister Ed."), accompanied by horse whinnies.

One fraternity fascinated Alex on his way back to the dorm, reminding him of Arthurian legends he read as a boy. The edifice at the corner of College Avenue and Stanton Street was built of limestone and brick. The word "Omega" was painted in black and gold letters above the arched front door. *What would it be like to live behind those castle gates?*

Since then he had shed any illusions about frat life. A century earlier, Citadel cadets created Omega Epsilon Tau as a brotherhood of honor, loyalty and truth. Another myth perpetuated by tradition.

"Home sweet home," Nick said entering the foyer, where he and Alex heard the usual tube room insults.

"Don't look now, but it's Delamore and Merten," Crouse said. "The biggest wetback queers on campus."

"Garcia, how's it hanging?" Trellendorf sneered from the darkness.

"About two inches," came a phantom reply and a round of guffaws.

The Omegas were marked by eerie light from the console TV, burning as an eternal flame in the fraternity. Their ringleader, Crouse, was a whiny warthog. Each night he would park his lard ass on the red leather sofa and inhale greasy double cheeseburgers or pepperoni pizzas after a full dinner. His mouth was in perpetual motion, whether he was stuffing it with food, swigging booze, or lusting for women, real or imagined.

"Fuck you and the whores you rode in on," Nick said.

He and Alex crossed the living room. The rest of the house could get trashed, but this thickly carpeted, book-lined chamber was sacred. It had a chandelier, mantle, fireplace and an upright piano, donated by a decrepit alum. The room was used on rare occasions, such as fraternity rush, Parents Weekend and Homecoming.

They were met at the top of the back stairwell by a new group of Omegas. Max Klein, Spencer Dodd and their fellow "space cadets" were seeking more lonesome travelers to sample the new hash supply. The two joined the line into Klein and Dodd's room, passing their signature cardboard sign: "Dope will get you through times with no money better than money will get you through times with no dope!"

Nick unwound after his spat with Allyson Chambers, and Alex paused his pining for Donna Carvel. Merten would sleep until noon the next day, missing his econ midterm. Delamore "evacuated the rocketship," roaming the hallways in a daze. He reached the second-floor john where burly men stood guard.

"No can do, Dago," said Crouse with outstretched hands. "We have strict instructions from *El Presidente*."

"Get the fuck out of my way," Nick said, trying to push past the clumsy clowns, who normally wouldn't defy him. But tonight he was just another pothead not the feared linebacker. "Who's in there with him?"

"Some slutbag DZ he met at the beer blast," Trellendorf said, fingering a zit on his cheek. "He's not human. He's a humping machine."

When Nick heard "DZ and beer blast," all he could think of was it must be Allyson with Van Pelt. He regained his strength, tossed aside Tweedle Dee and Tweedle Dumb and rushed in the bathroom. He slipped on the floor and grabbed for one of three white sinks.

Two shimmering figures were in the shower. He heard Bru grunting, a woman groaning and a slapping, slurping noise. He had to see if she was with him.

"Howdy, pardner. Want in on this?"

She was red-haired not blonde. Nick averted his eyes. There was nothing erotic about the drenched woman spread-eagled on the lime-green tiles. Smelling the rank odors and spilled beer in that disgusting stall, he gagged as he shut off the water.

"What the hell's wrong with you?"

Bru answered with a smirk. His face and upper body looked sunburned.

"This ends right now. Get her out of here," Nick commanded.

Crouse and Trellendorf came running, and he stood ready to smash either man.

"Boys, back off. Dago is doing his Wyatt Earp impersonation this evening," Van Pelt said, falling as he tried to lift the inert redhead.

"Motherfucker," he bellowed as his kneecaps crunched the slick shower floor. Genuflecting in pain not prayer or deference, he directed his minions to hoist the woman onto his shoulder. "And get towels for me and Lady Guinevere."

When they left the bathroom, Nick vomited in the toilet. He rinsed out his mouth, splashed water on his face and went to the darkened rack room, where men were snoring and farting on double-decker beds. Alex was asleep on the top bunk as Nick lay on his sagging mattress below, glad his lovesick friend didn't witness any of Van Pelt's sleazy actions this Halloween night.

Chapter 7

With Memorial Day looming, Nick wanted some solitary downtime. He had made two trips to Ohio in less than a week. The previous Saturday, Christopher, Inez and he helped move Miranda out of her Oakwood College dorm.

As Megan predicted, no one in the Alpha Beta frat was even reprimanded. The school permanently banned alcohol at all Greek social events. Violations would result in chapter suspensions. Publicly, the Interfraternity Council at Oakwood said it would comply with the ruling. Privately, most viewed the no-alcohol mandate as ridiculous, with an improbable enforcement of the ban at fraternity and sorority parties during the school year.

The Sidney, Ohio, police had interviewed Owen, Evans and other Alpha Beta members. They all disputed Miranda's assertions about the frat house assaults, and Beverly Ward said "her findings were inconclusive." Not surprisingly, the Shelby County prosecutor took no action. Megan called the editor of the *Dayton Daily News*, asking him to investigate rapes and other violent crimes at Oakwood College. The paper didn't publish any such stories except a short piece on the alcohol ban, noting parties that had "gotten out of hand."

Miranda Delamore and Stacy Matlin withdrew from the prestigious private school. Stacy told her folks that a case of mono late in the semester caused her grades to slip. She also used

Miranda's rationale that she could get as good an education at Cleveland State University (CSU) for much less money. Mr. and Mrs. Matlin wouldn't learn of their daughter's rape even months later, when her decline was exposed and a death wish nearly fulfilled.

Miranda didn't hide her disenchantment with Oakwood and desire for a fresh start. She was shifting her focus from political science (pre-law) to social work and would be a part-time staffer at A Safe Place, the women's shelter and crisis center in University Circle. She had also decided to end her college volleyball career after one year. Miranda's mom and dad wanted her to stay at home when attending CSU. But she said it would be more convenient to live with Stacy near the downtown campus.

"Inez and I are nervous wrecks," Christopher admitted to his brother when packing up Miranda's dorm room.

Nick reiterated how resilient she was. His niece was a throwback to Megan's early activism and his own lost passion.

"You can still speak truth to power, Unk," Miranda had said before leaving for Cleveland.

Could he? Would he? Were the stars aligning for a cosmic change? If the universe had something in store for him, he decided it could wait a while longer. Until then he wanted to minimize his workload and sidestep any hassles.

On a blessedly uneventful morning in the newsroom, he read his emails. He was fine until he saw the "high priority" one from Megan. Had the Oakwood College incidents, the Merriman references and talk of Allyson Chambers conjured her up?

"She wants to meet with us. Please call me ASAP."

Why had Allyson reappeared? She must have known of Van Pelt's public life. Was it because he was likely to be Ohio's next governor? Or his "war on women," his regressive policies and threats to cut funding to Planned Parenthood and related social programs if elected? Megan's email had been short, but he could hear her strident voice: *You owe her, Nick. Whatever she wants, you owe her.*

He was late for a meeting at Hempstead University with the student media advisor, Henry Marx. Nick had unsuccessfully begged off the assignment. "Can't you send one of the newbies?" he asked editor Paula Hoagland, poking his head in her office that morning. The zaftig tanning salon devotee was in disbelief.

"What planet are you living on, Delamore?" she replied in a self-described Appalachian vernacular. (Nick was amused by her pronunciations, such as *Ve-HIC-cull*.) "They're our interns. Can't exactly send them to a meeting on internships now can I?"

He stood in her doorway until Hoagland waved him away. He wasn't thrilled he was sleeping with his boss. But it distracted him from the doldrums, granting perks in a job littered with mundane duties.

Finals week at Hempstead, and scantily clad young women in super-short shorts and skimpy tops surrounded Nick as he trudged from the visitors parking lot. They were more like lingerie models than college teens. *Not an ounce of cellulite.* He was unable to divert his eyes from the derriere of a student emblazoned with the words "Hot Pink."

"Truth in advertising," he said under his breath as she sashayed ahead of him. He ambled for a few more luscious seconds before she slipped into a nondescript classroom.

Henry Marx, diminutive journalism professor, waved as Nick entered the *Hempstead Herald* media center, squeezing past "kids" at their posts, scanning Macs and iPhones. Marx said he was: "More Groucho than Karl. Course my students don't know what the heck I'm talking about."

Nick shook the much shorter man's hand. "Bet they don't. With that stache, you're definitely more Groucho."

Professor Marx stooped and used his ballpoint pen like a cigar as he guided Nick to his glass-walled office.

He thanked him for coming, praising the partnership the school had with the *Times-Union*. "These opportunities provide real-world training for our best and brightest," he said, handing him a sheet of eligible students like an official proclamation.

Fortunately the office air conditioning was working as Nick was perspiring from his campus trek. File folders and paper stacks lined the professor's desk. Nearby was a photograph with his fetching (and much taller) wife and their adorable toddler.

"Henry, have to ask, how do you deal with these coeds? Got whiplash walking here."

"I try not to look."

"You let all that eye candy go to waste? You're a better man than I am, Gunga Din!"

Nick was hoping this would be a short meeting so he could duck into Finley's Ale House for a burger and a beer before returning to the newspaper. Those thoughts diminished when Marx closed his door.

"Thanks for coming," he said. "But the internships weren't the only reason I wanted to see you."

Nick's back tightened as he tried to adjust to the molded plastic chair.

"Familiar with campus pathology?" Marx asked, displaying an article from *The Chronicle of Higher Education*. "Depression, anxiety, bipolar disorder, suicides—all up at schools around the country. And Hempstead is no exception."

Nick skimmed a couple grafs and charts.

"Another serious issue is sexual assault," Marx added. "Surveys show as many as one in five undergraduate women will be raped in college."

Nick was framing his reply. Reporting on this subject could take weeks of work, and he didn't have that kind of time, even if he wanted to tackle the story.

"Need you to keep this off the record, OK?" Marx asked awkwardly.

His twitchy mannerisms and high pitch were similar to the New Jersey-bred actor Joe Pesci. *Maybe Marx hailed from the East Coast.*

"What's this about, Henry?"

"We've been investigating how the university handles violent crimes," he said. "Mishandles would be more appropriate. Know how many rapes were reported last year at Hempstead? Zero. That's with an enrollment of almost 12,000."

"The key word is reported," Nick said. "If students don't file charges, the school can't be faulted for its record keeping."

"Correct, but what if they're discouraged from contacting the police? Our dean of students is known for coddling jocks who get in trouble. He promotes adjudication, but he's more about protecting our brand."

"All this anecdotal?"

"I'm friends with a biology prof who sits on the University Disciplinary Panel, the UDP. She's been in enough hearings to see how the dean operates."

Marx gave Nick a short bio on Dean Dave Worthington. He earned his bachelor's and master's at Hempstead and was hired at his alma mater, moving up the administrative ranks.

"Was athletic director, so you know where his sympathies lie."

"Too speculative. What else you got?"

"This semester one of our football players allegedly raped a freshman student. She didn't want to file a police report, so her RA recommended she see Worthington and request a UDP hearing."

Marx said the woman was made to feel that it was her fault for "leading the young man on, giving him the wrong impression." The dean asked how she was dressed, how much she had to drink, and why she let him in her dorm room. A panel member questioned how she knew she had been sodomized.

"This on the record from the biology prof?"

"The hearings are closed, and it would be career suicide for her to go public. But I trust her."

"That's not enough if you want to publish a credible story. You need a primary source."

Marx recounted another incident where a Hempstead student went to Worthington saying she was drugged with "roofies" and gang raped at an off-campus party. In a 4-to-1 vote, the disciplinary panel concluded there was insufficient evidence to take any corrective action. Even before the hearing, the woman was bullied online and in person. She stopped attending classes and became a prisoner in her dorm room. She couldn't even go to the dining hall because of all the harassment.

"That's terrible, but it sounds like procedures were followed."

Marx continued: "When she learned the men who raped her wouldn't be punished or expelled, she went back to Worthington. Told him she wanted to go to the police and file charges. He said it was too late, and she should 'try to put this all behind her.' "

"How do you know that?"

"She posted texts after meeting with him. Later that week, she almost died by overdosing on sleeping pills. She dropped out last fall. But she recently contacted one of our reporters, whom she knew in high school, and agreed to an interview."

"Henry, I empathize with what you're trying to do. But what do you want from me?"

"Need you back in the game," Marx said.

"Excuse me?"

"You had a helluva career at the *Plain Dealer*. Pulitzer finalist. Going after the Cleveland Mafia. You were the man, kicking ass and taking names."

"Ancient history."

"Hey, the past is prologue. Don't you miss it? I mean you must be going crazy at the *Times-Union*."

"Why can't you run with this?"

"I'm no Woodward or Bernstein, OK?" Marx said. "Can't go rogue. I'm a student media faculty advisor and instructor on a one-year renewable contract. That's why I need your help. We're talking significant FOIA reporting and outreach to the feds."

Nick would learn this muckraker was the son of a Reform rabbi from Milwaukee. Henry Marx reminded him of his younger best self—from the aggressive attitude down to a dapper moustache. But his youth was long gone, and Finley's Ale House was calling.

"Will you think about it?"

"Man, you don't let up, do you?"

"My wife calls me the Energizer Bunny."

"In or out of the bedroom?"

They smiled and shook hands.

"I'll think about it."

"Gotcha," Marx said, extending the handshake. "We need you, Nick, if we're going to blow the lid off this."

"I said I'll think about it."

"OK if I call you Friday?"

"Anybody ever tell you that you're ... ."

"A pushy little ... ? All the time."

Departing Marx's office, he walked by islands of flowers, trimmed hedges and stately oak, maple and hickory trees. All this landscaping was deceiving. As he well knew, a campus was no never-neverland.

Nick had left the meeting enthused. *Adrenaline or an awakened conscience?* The latter was far-fetched given his resigned mindset. He decided it must be adrenaline, which fueled him back when he was a bona fide journalist.

He drove by Finley's Ale House but didn't stop. *Times-Union* employees were surprised to see Delamore back this late. But there he was typing away at his keyboard, fueled by coffee and the urging of a charismatic rabble rouser.

However, the words weren't Henry Marx's. They belonged to high school classmate Jon Kaplan. He was the firebrand who had inspired an apathetic Delamore and others to care about social issues. Frizzy haired a la Abbie Hoffman, with wild eyes and a wilder wit, he published the school's underground newspaper, raising teen consciousness on the Vietnam War, civil rights and student advocacy. He didn't accept the status quo, telling Nick to "use your talents to change the world." *This is all your fault, Kaplan.*

He read a report by the Center for Public Integrity on the systemic and systematic failures of higher education to address campus sexual violence, as institutions overlooked malfeasance while safeguarding their identities and competing for hundreds of millions of dollars in tuition, grants and donations.

Nick was being deluged by Marx's emails and Megan's non-stop messages. She kept asking when they could meet with Allyson Chambers Ryan, who was now living back in Northeast Ohio. And she was still pressuring him to support the Imani campaign: "You can run, but you can't hide."

Hours later, his cell phone rang again.

"Stop stalling."

"Between you and Henry Marx, you're driving me nuts."

"Who's he?"

"Prof at Hempstead who wants me to investigate sexual assault cases."

"Good for him."

"Don't need this aggravation."

"You big wuss," she said. "We're saving your lazy ass."

"Spare me the redemption lingo," he said. "Let's switch gears. How's Miranda doing?"

"Everyone loves her at the shelter. And she's going to register students for Obama. Forty years after I volunteered for McGovern."

"She's your protégé, your mini-me."

When Megan giggled, he hoped he was in the clear.

"Except she's a foot taller."

"That's great to hear about Miranda. Any word on Stacy?"

"From what I can gather, she's not doing well."

"That's too bad," he said. "But I have to wrap this up."

"Me too," she said. "FYI, we're meeting Allyson on Friday, June 15 at noon in Medina. Will text you the location."

"Wait, what?"

"And Lauren Deveraux from the *PD* heard you went to college with Van Pelt and Imani, and she wants to interview you. Bye."

"Wait a minute," Nick said to a dead phone line. *Fuck. Fuck. Fuck.*

Chapter 8

Miranda Delamore's anger rattled within, threatening to erupt. Her father said she was acting like her irascible uncle Nick. Her mother spent more time in tears when they were together. Miranda wasn't trying to be mean or hurtful. She grew up as a happy little girl and an obedient daughter. But today she was a volatile 18-year-old wrestling with raw emotion.

She and Stacy had been so excited to go to college and to be on their own. They were going to have fun and meet all kinds of guys. Then they discovered how some were monsters, who didn't give a damn how much pain they caused.

Since coming home for the summer, the two had been together intermittently. Stacy's texts were abrupt or nonsensical, and she was edgy and impatient on the phone. When they last met, Miranda asked about the coarse red lines on her forearms and ankles. Stacy said they were cheaper than tattoos.

"You seeing anyone?"

"Seeing? That's a good word for it. ... Oh, just kidding."

But she wasn't. Miranda's on-again, off-again beau, Ray Russo, was a square-jawed Cleveland policeman, serving in the tradition of his older brother, father and grandfather. He said he had seen Stacy hanging out on Prospect Avenue.

"Not a good sign. Could be into some bad things."

"You don't know everything, Ray," Miranda said. "Stacy's trying to cope with all she went through."

"Only trying to help," he said, finishing his cheeseburger at Bearden's, one of their hangouts.

"Doesn't sound like it."

"I realize she's hurting, but this won't end well."

"Why do you have to be so negative? She's my friend not yours," Miranda said, abruptly leaving the restaurant.

Nick kept dodging the *Plain Dealer*'s Lauren Deveraux. Before responding he would call an old crony at the *PD*. Larry Rivers was a tough S.O.B. He had been a long-range reconnaissance patroller in Vietnam, an investigative reporter and a government beat writer, respected by Cleveland's pols and powerbrokers. Now in his mid-sixties, he was writing a weekly column ("Life in C-town") and penning detective novels on the side.

Rivers and Delamore raised hell together "back in the day." This call picked up where they had left off. True to form, Rivers was profane and acerbic.

"The fuck you want?" he asked in a raspy voice. "Heard you drank yourself to death. Where you calling from—Cocksucker, Indiana?"

"Carlson," Nick said, pacing a path shaded by oak trees.

"Who cares? It's Indiana." Rivers' chuckling became a hacking cough.

"Who's this Lauren Deveraux? She wants to interview me on the governor's race."

"Why she want to talk to you?" he asked. "You haven't been relevant since ... when?"

"Need some info on her."

"Fast-rising star. Mizzou undergrad, master's at Medill, couple years at the *Dispatch* (Columbus not St. Louis). She got my old beat when I started the column. She's good. No ass to speak of but great legs. Did I say that? Not allowed to go there anymore. They call it harassment."

"And they call you a Neanderthal."

His response was delayed by more jagged spasms.

"Catch your breath," Nick said, explaining how he had attended Merriman University with both candidates. But when that failed to engage Rivers, he mentioned Megan and her crusade against Van Pelt.

"She was too good for you. Sure kicked your butt when you were married. Why is she on the warpath, other than the fact he's an obnoxious demagogue?"

"Alleged sex crimes in college."

"Alleged what?" Rivers asked. Nick heard him typing. "How you know this?"

"Was his frat brother."

"Never figured you for a frat rat."

"Never figured myself for one, but so it goes."

"You knew he was bad news in college?"

"Screwed up. Let him off the hook."

"Hey, man," Rivers said. "Not judging you."

"Thanks."

"But your ex sure is if she put Deveraux on your tail."

"Megan was a rape counselor at Merriman when Van Pelt was there," Nick said. "That's how we met. She worked with some of his ... accusers."

"Accusers? You mean victims. Tell me you're not defending this guy."

"Not defending him. It's complicated."

"This ain't a deposition, man. But you said you let him off the hook. Take it from one fuckup to another: You only have one shot at life. Better get your mind right for your own sake."

Nick watched a mother pushing a stroller as Rivers cleared his throat.

"What can I say, Larry? Blew it. Should have nailed the bastard long ago."

"So what are you going to do?"

"Do?"

"Ever read *The Quiet American* on Vietnam in the 1950s?"

"What does that have to do with anything?"

"There's a quote: 'Sooner or later, one has to take sides. If one is to remain human.' "

"OK and ... ?"

"The main character is an alcoholic British journalist, a real reprobate. He's in a moral dilemma that could get his romantic rival, an American colleague, killed. This Yank, who earlier saved the Brit's life, is CIA—a true believer. Win at all costs no matter if innocent people die. Get the picture?"

"That I'm a degenerate drunk who needs to get off my ass."

"Something like that," Rivers said. "You try sitting this one out, it may end up costing you."

"You my shrink?"

"Drinking buddy."

"Thanks for the advice."

"De nada."

"So what happened to the Brit journalist?"

"Made the hard call and betrayed the American. He had some remorse, but he got the girl."

"There you go. Justice prevails."

"You need to think this through," Rivers advised. "Van Pelt's team won't get distracted by what went down in the seventies. They'll say it's a smear job by Imani."

"That's why I need a favor. You know the drill."

"Damn," he said. "I'm too old for this."

"You're a pro. That's why I called you."

"Ha," he chirped. "Nice try."

"Butch and Sundance ride into the sunset."

"For chrissake," Rivers said, ending the call with another coughing jag.

"Sooner or later, one has to take sides. If one is to remain human." Nick thought he had broken out of a clinch, buying time for his next move. And he was sure Rivers would raise legitimate issues with Van Pelt's candidacy. But his optimism soon faded.

"They anticipated my query about his college years."

"Anticipated?"

"His press secretary brought up *The Confessions of St. Augustine*."

"So?"

"He said Van Pelt was like Augustine when he was young and driven by his passions."

"That's in the book?"

"Written in the fourth century and every bit as timely today, seductions of the flesh and all that."

"Didn't you press him on the sexual assault angle?"

"Don't be a ball-buster, Delamore. This guy knew no charges were ever filed. And I'm not chasing a lawsuit at this point in my career."

Nick sat at his desk clicking his pen and looking at Lauren Deveraux's phone number scribbled on a Post-it Note.

"You interviewing Van Pelt?"

"Probably not."

"Why not?"

"Unlike you, bub, I don't have a stake in all this."

Nick waited to contact Megan until the *Plain Dealer* column ran. It was a clever piece, featuring a quote from St. Augustine in the lead and Rivers' sardonic style. He questioned Van Pelt's sacrosanct image and referred to "former Merriman classmates" critical of his college past. Nick thought it might slow his momentum. But poll results showed the Republican candidate's favorability rating with registered Ohio voters rose after Sunday's publication. Megan was livid over his scheming with Rivers.

"You actually believed he would write something controversial? Everybody knows the paper is endorsing him."

"He included the womanizing."

"The playboy who found God and became a family man," she said. "What a crock."

"Maybe, but it's a start."

"Will you please call Deveraux? You said you would, and it's been two weeks."

"Relax, I'm on it."

"And, remember, we're meeting Allyson next Friday."

"That's enough nagging for one call. What are we ... in a *Hallmark* movie?"

Nick and Megan didn't meet rom-com cute. An initial confrontation foreshadowed their rocky relationship. When college football ended, there was a deep void in his life. Nick was indebted to his salty-tongued English professor and *Daily Journal* advisor, Dr. Jeff Kinsey, for encouraging him to work at the student newspaper, where he was introduced to Megan Bradley from Dorchester, Massachusetts.

She arrived on a damp November day at the paper's cluttered offices on the top floor of Dickinson Hall. Nick sat at his massive wooden desk. His armchair and the rest of the room's Early American furniture had been bequeathed by an old Sussex newspaperman.

Nick acquired this and additional trivia from Professor Kinsey in his spring semester Reporting I class. Delamore's journalistic skills showed such potential, Kinsey had suggested he write for the *Daily Journal* as a freelancer. He was rehabbing his injured knee, hoping to return as a starter. But after spring workouts, Nick knew his playing days were over as was his football scholarship. He learned of new full-time paid positions and applied for the assistant editor slot. With his strong writing samples and backing from Kinsey, he got the job.

He was dedicated to learning newsroom operations with the same drive he had on the gridiron. He meshed well with frenetic editor Josh Zinaman from Greenwich, Connecticut. Despite early misgivings, the erudite editor grew to appreciate Nick's work ethic and wit. Their Northeast roots bound them, and they exchanged jokes on life in rustic Ohio.

That memorable rainy afternoon, Zinaman was in class, and Nick was crafting an editorial challenging the university's parking policies. He wrote his draft on a legal pad before typing it on his portable Royal. Nick wasn't bothered by the chatter of those discussing plans for the upcoming weekend; he worked best in the midst of activity.

He was encamped in the rear of the large room. A shabby yellow couch provided the illusion of privacy. People had to scale it to reach his desk. Nick called it his metaphorical moat: "No man or woman shall pass without the shibboleth." When most drew a blank, he told them to consult a dictionary.

"You Nick Delamore?" asked a petite woman in jeans and a shapeless gray hooded sweatshirt. Her hands rested on slim hips, and she acted dismayed with the room's odd placement of furniture.

"That's me."

"Somewhere we can talk privately?"

"Hey, where you from?"

"What's it to you?"

"I'm from New York, and I know a Boston accent."

"Uh-huh. Somewhere we can talk?"

"Come on over, and I'll grab a chair. Those guys up front are getting ready to go."

She was succinct. Megan Bradley was a grad student working at the Campus Counseling Center. She was there regarding his connection to a campus crime.

"What did you say?" he asked as the room of student-journalists watched the mysterious visitor.

"I'm here on behalf of my client." Her intensity contradicted her pert freckled face.

"Who's your client?"

"It's confidential."

"I don't like you showing up here like I'm guilty of something."

"A woman was raped last weekend at a frat party."

"What's that got to do with me?" Nick was cotton-mouthed. He pulled a stick of Juicy Fruit gum from his jeans and tugged the sleeves of his black turtleneck sweater.

"She said you told her not to go with him. So you must know who he is."

That sonufabitch. Van Pelt had said he took Allyson home early because she was sick. *That sonufabitch.*

"Hold on. How should I know who he is?"

"She said, 'Nick warned me not to go with him.' I asked her, 'Nick who?' But she wouldn't say. I convinced her the only way I could help was if she gave me your full name. I swore you wouldn't get in any trouble."

"Allyson Chambers, right? How's she doing?"

"How's she doing? What sort of dumb-ass question is that?"

He started to apologize when she interrupted, stating that anything about her client was "off the record and not for publication." Megan didn't discuss the series of events leading to Allyson's treatment at Sussex General Hospital: How her roommate alerted the RA, who discovered bloodstained and soiled towels in the dorm bathroom the morning after the frat party. How the RA called Megan, who told Allyson she needed medical care to prevent serious infection. How Megan took her to the emergency room and was her advocate that day and throughout her time at Merriman.

"How's she doing?" the feisty counselor mimicked. "The ER nurse said her vagina was torn and needed stitches, and there was rectal bleeding from blunt force trauma."

Nick exhaled deeply. "Was there a police report?"

"No. Said she didn't want anyone to know. She kept crying and telling me she was a good Catholic. Now her world's been destroyed."

He lowered his head and bit his lip.

"That sucks. She's a nice girl."

"Woman," Megan corrected. "Woman not a *girl*. Yeah, it sucks what happened. And she isn't feeling very *nice* because of what some animals did to her."

She didn't want to believe this guy in the black turtleneck with the sad eyes was sincere. Since working at the counseling center for the last year, Megan mistrusted most men on campus.

"That's good you care," she said. "And if you do, then crucify those scumbags."

He rubbed his moustache. "I'll see what I can do."

She pushed back from the desk and stood scowling: "Cut the crap. I know all about the Omega house and Van Pelt, the rich kid from Kentucky, who acts like he can do whatever the hell he wants."

At the Viking party Saturday night, Allyson and Bru were laughing as they hoisted their wineskins. She was a knockout in her leopard-skin outfit, and his hands were all over her. Whenever Nick looked their way, they seemed to be kissing.

He asked sheepishly, "Have you talked to the dean of students?"

"Yardley Smith? That clown? I had a client who went to him last spring. He told her, 'There are times when you need to forgive and forget.'"

"Any other options?"

"The university ethics committee treats sexual assault like a violation of the school's honor code. A student can be put on academic probation or expelled. And guess what? That's never happened in all the years Smith has been dean. He stops women from pursuing criminal charges, saying it will be too hard to prove a rape occurred. He only cares about Merriman's image. He didn't want our Campus Counseling Center to exist. But after Kent State, the administration decided a program like ours might actually be good for students."

Nick was drawn to this impassioned woman, which was nuts. She would throw him to the wolves if she had to.

"Should I try to see her? Would that be OK?"

"She's very shaky. Seeing you could make it worse. But if she reaches out to you, be a friend."

"Anything else?"

"Yeah, you could do the right thing," she said, scaling the couch.

He heard her work boots scuffing the wooden floor. When he looked up, she was gone.

Nick thought of calling Allyson or stopping by her dorm, but he hesitated. Megan Bradley had said: *"Very shaky. Could make things worse. But if she reaches out to you ... ."* One crisp morning as he was going to his creative writing class, he saw her in a baby blue parka, head down in the throng of students, blonde hair cut quite short. He didn't want to startle her.

"Hey, Allyson. It's me, Nick."

She stopped as if to study the carpet of fallen leaves. The autumn had peaked, and dismal weather awaited. He stepped closer, and she leaned on him, fragile in his arms.

"Should have listened to you."

"That's OK. That's OK."

"It's not OK. It's not," she insisted.

A chilling breeze swept the campus, and Nick shivered.

"It's freezing out here. How about some coffee or hot chocolate?"

He led her to the student union. When they started talking, Nick knew he wasn't attending any classes that day. And he knew there would be a showdown. This time he wouldn't let Bru dupe him as he did the night of the Viking party.

Van Pelt was in the tube room watching prehistoric beasts battle in a *Godzilla* movie. He was bare-chested and barefoot, wearing his fur vest and leather leggings. Nick had on jeans and an Omega T-shirt, having discarded his Norseman garb.

"How's your hot mama?" Bru asked as very fake dinosaurs clawed each other.

"She's crashed."

"Where's Garcia and the bodacious Donna?"

"In the attic loft."

"He got the penthouse? Outstanding. Maybe he'll finally get lucky tonight."

Nick asked how things went with Allyson. He was prepared to hear about Van Pelt's latest sexcapade, but he was surprisingly low-key.

"She felt sick. So I took her home. End of story."

The Viking punch was a potent mix of vodka, tequila and grain alcohol. Allyson told Nick that she drank for hours and then blacked out.

"My fault," she said, clutching her cup of hot chocolate. "When I woke up, I couldn't breathe."

"Like somebody was smothering you?"

"He was so heavy, it scared me."

"What did he do when you said you couldn't breathe?"

"Kept kissing me."

"Saw you making out with him on the dance floor."

"Are you trying to make me feel bad? Thought I could confide in you."

"You can. It's just … . I'm sorry. Go ahead."

"Why are you interrogating me?" she asked, tears wetting her cheeks. "I made an awful mistake. Please don't make it worse."

What Allyson didn't tell Nick were intimate details she shared with Megan. She said Van Pelt held her down while methodically removing her clothing. She struggled, but he was too strong. "Gawd almighty, you have a beautiful body," he said, staring at her naked torso. He grabbed her breasts, twisting the nipples so hard she thought he had torn the skin. She yelped when he inserted his thick fingers and began rotating them. She begged him to stop to no avail.

He was growling as he forced himself inside her. She had dreamed of a magical honeymoon night with a loving husband. But now she was being ripped apart. When it finally ended, she was sobbing and hyperventilating. Exhausted from the ordeal, she fell asleep.

Allyson was awakened by sniggering in the darkness. Lights flickered on and off. *Who's there?* Men whooped and applauded, pawing at her. Now she was on her stomach, held down and face shoved so deep into the pillow she thought she would suffocate.

Her legs were spread, and the agony resumed. *Stop. Stop. Please stop!* They were rooting each other on. There was more yelling and commotion in the room as bodies were tossed about and things broken. Then it became strangely quiet.

Van Pelt appeared and tried to comfort her. "You OK? You OK?" he asked, rubbing her down with a towel. The light hurt her eyes. There was blood on the towel and sheets, and she smelled urine and feces in the bed. He drove her back to the dorm in silence, dressed as a Viking warrior. She wore a tattered leopard-skin outfit and was swathed in a plush Pendleton wool blanket.

As Allyson sat crying in the cafeteria, Nick handed her a paper napkin. When she regained her composure, he asked, "Did you tell him no?"

"Yes, I tried, but he wouldn't stop."

Nick grimaced.

"Shouldn't have told you all this."

"Course you should have. I want to help."

"Thanks, but I'm feeling really tired. Can you walk me home?"

That night, Nick went to Bru's room. Omega president Van Pelt lived alone in the frat house "suite," which included a small bedroom and half-bath. He was skimming a *Sports Illustrated* and drinking a can of Budweiser. The room smelled of sweat-soaked gym clothes, pepperoni pizza and Pierre Cardin cologne, which often masked his body odor in lieu of a shower.

"What's happening, Dago?"

"Allyson told me what you did to her at Viking."

"Did she?" Bru asked as Nick stood over him. "You know there's two sides to every story."

"You fucking raped her."

Bru pulled the lever on the recliner, sounding like a petulant child arguing with his mother and father.

"You weren't there. You don't know. And she didn't say no, bro. She didn't say no."

"That's bullshit, and you know it."

"We talked the whole time, and I didn't force her to do anything."

"So why did her RA take Allyson to the counseling center? One of them came to see me at the paper."

"And they want you to do what? Report me?"

Nick's jaw slackened.

"What? You think this is the first time someone's come after me?"

He gulped his beer and belched. "It's always my word against hers, and I've never lost."

"You're a sick prick," Nick said, daring Bru to make the first move. He watched his shoulders and hands for any sign of a sucker punch.

But he sat calmly. "Hey, buddy boy, since when do you care what I do with my dates? You had a chance with her, but you bailed. Is that what this is over? Me tapping a virgin before you could do her?"

Nick balled his fists.

"I'm kidding, OK? Just listen."

"Why should I?"

"Because we're friends. Brothers. Or are you throwing all that away?"

"Keep talking."

He said he carried Allyson upstairs, and she "came to" in his room. When they were kissing, she let him touch her.

"Kept asking if she was OK."

"What did she say?"

"She was mumbling."

"You screwed her when she was passed out."

"Didn't know she was. Took it slow. Didn't want to hurt her."

"Hey," Nick said. "Don't need to hear every freakin' thing."

"She fell asleep so I covered her up and went back to the party."

"Then what happened?"

"Huh?"

"She had to go to the ER. What did you do to her?"

"Wasn't me."

"What the … ? You pulled a train on her?"

He lunged at Bru, who raised his hands in surrender.

"Listen, will ya? When I came back to the room, there were some others in there."

Nick spat on the floor. "Who?"

"I kicked them all out, and then I took her home."

"Who was it? Who was in the room with her?"

"Can't tell you that. As president of this house, I have to look out for the men."

"The hell you do. It was Crouse and Trellendorf. Who else? McKinney? I'll go to the cops and rat out this entire frat if I have to."

He was ready for Bru to come at him. But he sat there draining his beer. He tossed it at a stack of empty Budweisers. The can ricocheted off the cinder-block wall, toppling the pile.

"You traitor. You'd betray your fraternity over a girl?"

"Go fuck yourself." Nick turned and walked out.

"You got a short memory."

"About what?" he asked from the doorway.

"Forget how I saved your ass in Darrtown when I cold-cocked the guy with the tire iron? And that two grand I loaned you."

"I'm paying you back," he said, staring him down.

"I know. I know," Bru said, approaching. "Come on. Don't let this come between us."

Nick's arms were folded across his chest. "She didn't deserve this. You should have taken care of her."

"What can I do to help out? She need any money?"

"Let me handle it."

"OK, I'm with you," he said, bobbing his head.

Nick was at the stairs when Bru asked, "Hey, Dago, we square?"

He turned. "Yeah, we're square. That means no more IOU. Don't owe you a goddamn thing."

"A-OK." Bru flashed a thumbs up. "Roger that."

Chapter 9

On a humid Friday morning, Nick drove the freshly tarred and tacky country roads from Carlson to Medina, Ohio. He had agreed to meet not to please Megan but for all Allyson had been through. He wondered how life had treated her after the Merriman years. He also questioned whether Megan had been straight with him on what led to this meeting.

Did Allyson call "out of the blue"? Or had Megan manipulated her as part of an anti-Van Pelt strategy? Such an effort was doomed to fail. Allyson would be labeled an unstable, vindictive woman by his Republican hit squad, if they even acknowledged her allegations.

The closer Nick got to Ohio on this hazy mid-June day, the more vivid the drama from November 1972. Following his frat house face-off with Van Pelt, he met Allyson in the student union. She said she was doing better but wasn't very convincing.

"How you holding up?"

"OK. How are you?"

"Don't know if you want to hear this," Nick said, "but he denied everything. He's lying, and I'll do whatever you want. Just tell me if you want to go to the police."

"Like I told Megan, I don't want them involved. Can't have my mom and dad find out. They're still dealing with my brother getting killed in Vietnam last year. You know, I was always the 'good girl,' the one who didn't get in trouble."

She buried her face in her hands as students turned toward them. He accepted their reproach and his guilt. He told Allyson she deserved to know about his debt to Van Pelt. How it dated back to the day he received a letter from his wife, Linda. She was filing for divorce and wanted an annulment.

"I was already bummed out because of my knee injury, and that letter set me off. A bunch of us football players went looking for trouble." He said his father had cautioned him about going to places he called "buckets of blood." They went to a biker bar in Darrtown.

The jocks taunted the motorcycle gang members, who had mocked them when they walked in. The bikers threw beer bottles, and the rumble was on. Nick and his brawny mates upped the ante by chucking chairs at the motley crew. The battle raged outside. He was pummeling a bearded hulk on the ground when Van Pelt yelled, "Dago, duck!" Bru tackled the guy with a tire iron, who was going to smash Nick's head in.

When county sheriff deputies showed up, the college men were in control. It was a shallow victory as they were all arrested, charged with assault and battery and malicious destruction of property. The judge set bail at $10,000 for the five Merriman students. The incident resulted in all of them being kicked off the team.

But Delamore's athletic future had already been decided by a torn anterior cruciate ligament. He would never again play the sport he loved. Van Pelt, who had been demoted in spring practice to third string, didn't contest the punishment. He was now free to live in the Omega house, where he would soon be elected president.

Nick didn't tell his parents about the arrest. Money was tight in the Delamore household, and they had enough to deal with. He spent one night in the Delaware County Jail. Van Pelt's father bailed out his son and four others the next day. The family attorney got the charges reduced to disorderly conduct, and the bar owner was reimbursed for building repairs, damaged furniture and furnishings, plus other expenses.

"My share came to $2,000, which Bru covered because I was broke. Was going to repay him before I graduated. But now the debt is paid off as long as I don't report what happened to you. That makes me a real lowlife, doesn't it?"

"I don't blame you," Allyson said barely above a whisper.

Nick held her cold hands in that heated cafeteria. He said his "agreement" with Van Pelt was meaningless, as if written in invisible ink.

"If you change your mind, I'll go to the cops. Don't care what I told Bru. Screw him."

"Nick, I'm not feeling very good. Have to get back to my dorm."

That same week he saw Megan Bradley arm in arm with someone in a green fatigue jacket on the Merriman quadrangle. He recognized the slight bearded man as leader of Black Students United. She called him Kwame Imani.

"Had a class with you last year," Nick said. "Weren't you ... Kevin ... ?"

"Kevin Williams," the guy with suspicious dark eyes and wide Afro said. "From Cleveland." He had a resonant tone like a radio deejay, which he was in high school.

Megan said: "He became a Muslim and changed his name this year after meeting Alex Haley at a conference. Imani means faith in Swahili." Her swift speech contrasted his measured delivery.

"That's cool," Nick said. "Haley wrote *The Autobiography of Malcolm X.*"

"Co-wrote. I'm impressed," Imani said. "You read that book?"

"Yeah, that and *Soul on Ice* for an urban lit class. By the way, you kinda look like Eldridge Cleaver," Nick said, testing the guy's sense of humor.

"Better Eldridge than Beaver," Imani said with a wry smile. "Delamore, what is that—Italian?"

"Everybody thinks it is. My nickname's Dago. Have a lot of paisan friends back in my New York hometown, but I'm French-Irish."

"Dago's a derogatory term. That doesn't bother you?"

"Not really since I'm not Italian."

Imani caught Nick eyeing Megan, and she broke the silence.

"Allyson says you've been a good friend."

"Hope so."

Nick shifted his work boots in the snow dusting the sidewalk. Imani wore black high-top sneakers as did Bradley. Maybe it was a boyfriend-girlfriend thing.

"She needs all the help we can give her because of what happened in your fucking fraternity."

"What the ... ? You one of 'em?" Imani took Megan's dark pea jacket by the arm, turning away from Nick, who barked: "Whatta ya mean 'one of 'em'?"

"Why you living in that nasty-ass place?" Imani asked. "Thought you had your act together."

"If he had it together, he never would have joined," Megan said. "You know what they should do? Burn every last one of those damn frat houses to the ground."

Imani said, "She's Irish, too, and tells it like it is."

"I believe that," Nick replied.

He was yards away when Megan said just shy of a shout: "Remembah, Dela-mah. Do the right thing. Don't fah-get-it."

With back turned, he pumped a fist in the air and kept walking to the student newspaper office.

The last time Nick heard from Allyson that fall semester was finals week. She had cancelled their last student union "date," saying she was behind in her classes. He didn't buy it; she was trying too hard to act normal.

The truth would be revealed the day before he left for the Christmas holiday at his home in Elmdale, Ohio, a couple hours north of Sussex. An envelope had been delivered to the frat house mailbox but with no return address. He thought Linda had written of their pending divorce.

"Dear Nick: Sorry for not calling you before leaving campus. Hope you know how thankful I am for all you've done during this difficult time. ..."

His eyes, trained by months of copy editing at the paper, skimmed the page for the most noticeable words: "pregnant," "abortion," "adoption," "Oregon." Letter in hand, he gazed out his window at the winter scene along Stanton Street. Guys at the TKE house next door were enjoying a snowball fight on the front lawn like youngsters at play. Others were loading up their cars.

But Allyson wasn't on any vacation. She had left Merriman for Medford, Oregon, where she would live with an aunt and uncle until she had her baby, which would then be put up for adoption. "If anyone asks, please just say I dropped out."

She described how her parents had demanded an explanation. But she refused to give details or identify the father, who she said would never learn of the pregnancy. It was her responsibility to handle the situation. As a devout Catholic, Allyson knew abortion was out of the question.

"How much simpler it would be. But I couldn't live with myself if I did. I have faith that God will strengthen me. Don't know if our paths will cross, but I wish you all the very best. And I just know you'll be famous someday. Take good care. Love, Allyson."

After reading the letter, Nick walked aimlessly, ignoring his Omega brothers as he passed their rooms. They were listening to Led Zeppelin or Grand Funk Railroad, downing Budweiser or Stroh's, or getting ready for one last "spaceflight" before sailing away high as kites. *Where was Alex?* They were supposed to go uptown for a burger at Bottom Dog Tavern before the holiday break. But he couldn't wait any longer.

He would later learn Alex was with Donna on the sudden "sad, awful" trip to New York City. Nick put on his red and black Merriman letter jacket and ink-blue Yankees baseball cap. No matter how fast he walked in the swirling snow flurries, he couldn't escape Allyson's predicament or his own condemnation. *Should have protected her. Should have kept her away from him. What the fuck is wrong with you?*

The cozy Corner Café in Medina, Ohio, was from a bygone era. No laptops, tablets or phones were visible. Customers chitchatted with pink-clad waitresses, who called them by name. The air smelled of brewed coffee, cinnamon rolls and grilled cheeseburgers. The sound of rotating metal milk shake containers made it seem as if the troubles of the last half century hadn't affected this pleasant locale off I-71.

"Dela-mah, o-vah he-ah."

Although he had seen her recently, he was struck by how pretty Megan was in a multi-colored silky top and navy blue slacks. She hated skirts, believing her legs too short and wide in the ankles ("an Irish curse"). When first dating, Nick claimed he didn't notice because he was so taken with her almond-shaped eyes.

"Total BS," she said. "Men only care about women from the neck down."

He was stiff from the backroad drive from Indiana and walked slowly through the restaurant. Allyson's appearance startled him. She was very gray, bespectacled and plump in a dark skirt and a floral blouse. She sat fidgeting when Nick drew near.

"Thanks for taking time out of your busy schedule to meet us," Megan said.

"We were married for 19 years," Nick said to Allyson. "Can you tell?"

The joking relaxed her. "Both of you being here means so much to me and my family."

"And to us," Megan said. "Before we get started, I wanted to ask Nick about Lauren Deveraux's story." She handed him a folded copy of the *Plain Dealer*.

"Read it online," he said, sliding the paper under his menu.

"Thought you would be more honest with her," Megan said.

Allyson sipped her ice water and reviewed the menu for the third time. Nick ordered a Diet Coke from the matronly waitress.

"I did the interview like you wanted me to."

"And you soft-balled it."

"Figured you gave her enough on Van Pelt. But she probably knew that without verifiable facts, she was risking a libel suit if any of those assertions were published."

"Assertions? Is that why Allyson is here because of assertions?"

Nick's pulse quickened and chest tightened.

"I told Deveraux to be diligent, to do her homework," he said, leaning toward Megan. "But you're crazy if you think I would flat out call him a rapist."

"That article is published just before Father's Day," Megan said, pointing to the newspaper. "Like he's man of the year. Sickening."

"Maybe he is a good husband and father."

"Have you lost your mind?"

"All I'm saying is ... ."

"Stop it, you two," Allyson said. "What are we back in college? I wanted to see you both, and I'm happy you're here. But I don't want you hurting each other on my account."

They hung their heads, but Megan kept talking: "You said Kwame was 'very ambitious,' like he's the bad one not Van Pelt."

"Maybe you should have written me a script," he said.

"That's enough," Allyson scolded the pair. "You're like squabbling kids. It's my turn to talk, OK?"

Her son was born August 4, 1973, in Oregon. She placed him with a Catholic adoption agency, believing he would have a better life than what she could provide as an unemployed, 19-year-old single mom. That fall she enrolled at Southern Oregon University, eventually earning a special education degree and then a master's degree in education at the University of Oregon.

She worked in the Northwest as an elementary school principal in Bend, Oregon. After marrying and raising a family out west, she came home to Ohio to care for her aging folks. She was retired and living with her husband in the same farmhouse where she had grown up. The longer she spoke, the more Nick heard the innocent "country girl" he knew at Merriman.

"I haven't told you why I wanted to meet."

She said her painful past was relived this last year when her daughter Natalie was raped at Coastal State University in Portland. Megan clasped Allyson's hand as she told them how her daughter was victimized first by "cruel, evil men," then by the school, and lastly by the justice system.

As with many freshman women in those first vulnerable weeks of college, Natalie was invited to frat parties most Fridays and Saturdays. On the night she was attacked, Natalie said she drank several draft beers. What she didn't know was she also ingested the "date rape" drug, GHB (Gamma-Hydroxybutyrate).

She had made out with a couple guys during the party and found herself fully clothed in someone's bed. When he went to the bathroom, Natalie texted her roommate that she wanted to leave. But her friend was already back at the dorm.

Allyson said, "The rest is very explicit." She read photocopied pages pulled from her big black leather purse. Natalie said she reluctantly gave him oral sex, thinking she could then go home. But she was losing consciousness and had no strength to resist when he undressed her. When she awoke, someone else was having intercourse with her, and others were watching. They took turns assaulting her there and in the basement, where Natalie was gang raped on a pool table.

She was in shock and incoherent when taken to the hospital with a head wound, multiple abrasions and vaginal and rectal injuries. Allyson said as horrible as her daughter's assault and its aftermath were, the actions of university and law enforcement officials re-traumatized them.

Coastal State's judicial panel noted contradictory statements on whether there was consent from Natalie and the fraternity members. No punitive action was taken by the school. The Multnomah County District Attorney cited a lack of evidence for prosecution of "non-consensual sex." No criminal charges were filed in the case.

Allyson, who attended the campus hearing with her husband, said the university panel consisted of a vice president of human resources, the director of the campus bookstore and an assistant professor of sociology. None of the three had any training in sexual assault cases. They normally adjudicated student violations, such as plagiarism or exam cheating. Rape kit results were available, but the academic administrator didn't provide that information.

One panelist questioned what a forensic exam entailed and why it would be an unpleasant experience. Another asked Natalie whether she enjoyed oral sex. The worst part of the hearing was when she had to describe how she was carried nude to the game room and "allegedly raped by several men." Natalie said she cried out for help but couldn't be heard above the cheering.

Allyson concluded: "The final insult was when the human resources VP asked Natalie how she got back to her dormitory that night. When she said someone in the fraternity drove her, he asked whether such 'polite behavior' was consistent with men who had violently assaulted her? How could Natalie answer that?"

"I'm so sorry for all of you," Megan said.

Nick added, "I'm sorry too." *Why did such a good person have to suffer through this again?*

With the aid of her cousin, an attorney in Eugene, Oregon, Allyson contacted the U.S. Department of Education's Office of Civil Rights and filed a formal Title IX complaint against Coastal State and the fraternity. Natalie had tried to attend classes, but she was harassed online and with threatening notes on her dormitory door, "advising" her not to cause any more trouble. She left Oregon and transferred to Baldwin-Wallace College in Berea, Ohio, less than an hour from where her mom and dad now resided.

"We're grateful to have her close by, but we worry constantly," Allyson said.

"What can I do to help?" Megan asked.

"If it's OK with you," she said, "I'll give your contact info to the Education Department liaison who was assigned to our case."

"I've worked with D.O.E. officials on these type of investigations. And thanks to Obama, we finally have real federal oversight."

"Better hope he gets re-elected," Nick said.

"We all better hope."

"Have something else that may interest you," Allyson said. "Four years ago, I heard from a man named Bernard Hart. He's an ordained minister and counselor in Michigan. He's also my son."

"The one you put up for adoption?" Nick asked as Megan shook her head.

Allyson said warmly, "Yes, Nick, that one."

"Pretty dumb of me, wasn't it?"

"But you're still so gosh darn cute."

"That's what they all say."

The two of them enjoyed their inside joke while Megan looked on, and then Allyson continued: "When Bernard turned 35, he told his precocious 9-year-old daughter he had been adopted as a baby. She was the one who motivated him to find me."

"I'm a little confused," Megan said. "What does this have to do with Natalie?"

Allyson adjusted her glasses and sat upright.

"I want people to know what happened to my daughter and me and how these crimes go unpunished," she said. "I realize I'm putting those I love at risk if I go public. But they've been so supportive, especially my courageous Natalie. And now Bernard has offered his assistance. I'm very blessed."

Megan and Nick stared at her.

"Never thought I'd see either of you at a loss for words," Allyson said.

"Are you going to say Van Pelt was the one who raped you?" Nick asked.

"If that's what it takes … yes," she said.

Megan unnerved him with her enthusiastic reaction.

"Good for you. Good for you," she said to Allyson. "I know Nick is probably figuring how it will all play out in the media. But your family story is so compelling. Let's see how Van Pelt's high and mighty campaign reacts to this."

"There are better ways to get your message across," Nick said. "I've got a friend at the *PD*, Hannah Dixon. She wrote that series on the women who were abducted on the Near West Side. I'm sure she would like to talk with you and Natalie."

"Be glad to speak with her," Allyson said. "But I was thinking of something along the lines of a press conference."

"Great idea," Megan said. "If your daughter and son participate, the three of you would be very credible."

"Listen," Nick said, surprising the women at the table with his intensity. "If you pursue him for what happened in college, you'll be written off as a vengeful old girlfriend, a nut job or worse."

"Calm down," Megan said. "Let's hear from Allyson."

She displayed a photo of Bernard on her phone.

"Oh my god," Megan said. "Spitting image of Van Pelt. The media will have a field day."

Nick said, "Looks like a good guy."

"He's remarkable, and his family has been so loving and generous with all of us." Allyson paused. "And to think how close I came to losing my faith and not having my baby. My son."

"Can I ask what made you decide?" Megan asked.

"When I saw Nick on campus before Christmas."

"Me? When?"

"You didn't see me," she said. "You were walking in the snow. It sounds crazy, but I believed somehow we could be together. I was only daydreaming, but it helped me make the right decision. That's when I knew for sure I couldn't have an abortion. That wasn't who I was, and my baby deserved a chance for a good life."

"I should have been a better friend back then," he said. "Maybe I can make it up to both of you."

They were grinning until Nick began haranguing them about the risks of a high-profile approach.

"I know you want to have a significant impact, and you might. But the Republican reaction will be unmerciful."

His hand was shaking. When he drank his soda, it spilled on his new golf shirt. "Damn it."

He went to the men's room, returning with a wet stain over his heart. Megan was checking her phone, and Allyson was searching her purse. Nick knew they had been sharing ideas when he was in the bathroom.

"You're going ahead with this, aren't you?" he asked, gripping the top of his wooden chair.

"We haven't decided anything," Megan said.

"Have a hard time believing that. Anyway, I have to go."

"Thank you for coming," Allyson said with a long embrace. "It was so good to see you. God bless you, Nick."

"God bless you, too."

"Drive safe," Megan said, offering a quick wave.

When he reached the door, Nick turned and watched the two talking. *They were waiting for me to leave.* The afternoon sun was fierce. The drive back to Carlson would be miserable on this Friday as traffic on I-71 was already backed up. *Just what I need. More damn time to think.*

Chapter 10

Megan was upset with the *Plain Dealer* article on Imani and Van Pelt, but Nick thought his interview had gone well. He and Lauren Deveraux met at the Indianapolis airport on Monday, June 11. She was cordial, noting that they could be French cousins considering their surnames.

"Oh, and Larry said to give you his best."

"Nice guy," Nick replied, thinking she would bring up Rivers' column on Van Pelt.

"And he said you might try to hit on me."

"Forget what I said about Larry. He's a jerk."

Deveraux smiled as she retrieved her notebook. She and Nick were in a small TGI Friday's, sandwiched between McDonald's and Starbucks in the terminal's public area. He had an Amstel Light; she drank iced tea. They were seated among business types on their phones and tablets and casual travelers viewing the bank of flat screen TVs.

She praised Nick's journalism career, having spent time in the archives and on Lexis-Nexis. Maybe she was schmoozing him, but he enjoyed the flattery. Megan had described her as uptight and humorless, but it was easy chatting with Deveraux. She was in her late twenties with a medium build, dark brown hair and penetrating eyes. She said she was writing an in-depth profile of the gubernatorial candidates and was curious about his friendship with them at Merriman in the 1970s.

"Wouldn't say friends necessarily."

"But more than acquaintances."

"I was on the football team with Van Pelt and in the same fraternity. I knew Imani from campus activities. He led the black student organization at Merriman, and I wrote for the college newspaper."

It was easier to begin with Imani. He provided the sanitized version minus the messy affairs. Then he described meeting Van Pelt in fall 1970. First-year athletes weren't allowed to play on the varsity, and the freshmen had an abbreviated schedule of games. They spent most of their time scrimmaging with the older players. The towering Van Pelt dominated Delamore, thwarting his aggression as they dueled for hours.

"Hold me again, and I'll kick your ass," Nick threatened.

"Why wait? Let's get it on right here, buddy boy."

He said Van Pelt wouldn't shut up on the field and in the locker room. He would parade around naked, his pecker flopping like a lizard. Nick quickly apologized.

"No problem," Deveraux responded. "You're saying he was well-endowed."

"His claim to fame in the fraternity among other things."

Nick said their on-field hostility culminated in a slugfest after practice, out of view from any coaches or staff. Each man was bloodied, bruised and stained with dirt and grass. Neither would yield.

"Hey, call it a draw. Hot as hell out here," said Bob Highland, the team's fullback.

Nobody could withstand Nick's barrage of punches. But this bigmouth kept getting up. And Van Pelt didn't believe how much punishment Delamore could take. Both were winded, hands on knees.

"A draw?"

"Draw my ass," Nick said, wincing from a kidney punch.

"You are one stubborn sonufabitch."

Nick brushed off his jeans and wiped his face with the lower half of his Merriman practice jersey.

Van Pelt persisted: "We been raggin' on each other for too long. Let's call a truce. Brewskis in my mini fridge."

He turned away, only to find himself in a fireman's lift over the big man's shoulders.

"You're having a beer with me," Van Pelt said, "if I have to carry you the whole way there."

Nick's laugh broke the tension. "Lemme down, asshole."

As they sat on his dorm bed, Van Pelt spoke of a privileged upbringing in a moneyed Lexington suburb and his two great loves—sports and pussy.

"You might say I'm blessed in the ole equipment department. And I try to share my wealth with as many lovely ladies as possible. You're a good-looking *Eye-talian.* You must be laying some mean pipe yourself with these Merriman dolls."

Nick could have corrected the reference to his ethnicity, but there was currency in teammates believing he was an Italian guy from back East. What he said next astonished Van Pelt. He was engaged to Linda Pieta, his high school sweetheart. They were to wed during the Christmas holiday and then live in married student housing.

"Say it ain't so!" Van Pelt paced as in an opera. "You're breaking my heart. You can't be getting married. This is college. You're a jock. You get mucho 'tang. That's for all the hard work you put in."

The night ended with the men shaking hands.

"Call me Bru. All my friends do. Hey, that rhymes."

Nick said he would drop by his frat. Those on athletic scholarships weren't allowed to live in fraternity houses. But they could maintain "social memberships," which translated into unobtrusively attending events.

"I'll set you up with the best sorority snatch you ever tasted," Van Pelt said with a wink and a roar.

Nick chuckled as he walked through the darkened campus. His ribs ached from the afternoon brawl, but several cold beers had eased the soreness.

Fall term ended with him barely making a 2.0 GPA and limping on a badly sprained ankle. He wasn't getting any sympathy from his fiancé.

"You swore you wouldn't get hurt before the wedding," Linda said on the phone.

"I'll be fine. Don't worry."

"I do worry," she said. "Keep away from those bimbos out there. You belong to me."

"How could I forget?"

As his nuptials approached, he wondered why he wasn't more excited. When he had first dated Linda in high school, Nick couldn't believe his good fortune. She was beautiful and kind, and she had faith in him. In later years he mused over countless scotches how and why she stopped being the center of his world. Had he allowed Van Pelt to get inside his head, planting doubts and temptations?

"Too bad it didn't work out," Deveraux said. "But you were both very young."

"That we were."

"Was sorry to hear of Alex Merten's death. Must have been tough to lose a close friend."

Nick look a long sip of his Amstel Light.

"How do you know about Alex?"

"From Megan."

"Terrific guy but too sensitive for his own good sometimes."

"Reminds me of that line in *Doctor Zhivago*—the walls of Yuri's heart being as thin as paper," she said, impressing Nick with her literary knowledge.

"Alex was like a Zhivago. Back in college he read Kerouac, Kahlil Gibran or Rod McKuen and listened to Cat Stevens albums all day."

"What made him choose the priesthood?"

"Don't really know. He became very religious after a bad breakup."

"You religious, Nick?"

"Not very," he said, trying to block any more intrusions. "Don't you have a plane to catch back to Cleveland?"

"No, I'm driving to Merriman for an interview with the president and then a tour. Having both candidates as alums is a real coup for the school."

"Need anything else from me?"

"Think I'm good, thanks," she said. "Enjoyed meeting you and hearing your stories. But we didn't get to why your relationship with Imani and Van Pelt ended after Merriman. You available this week for a short phone call?"

Nick glanced up at the bank of TV screens. He had thought today's interview would suffice.

"We all went our separate ways. Nothing unusual."

"Megan sure had strong opinions about Van Pelt."

"No surprise there. She never liked him."

Toying with her glass of iced tea, Deveraux added: "Obviously from what she told me. ... His press secretary admitted he was 'sexually active' in college but dismissed it as 'youthful indiscretions.' "

"Indiscretions? You could call it that," Nick said.

"What do you think?"

"I think we all make mistakes."

After a handshake, she said: "Been a good chat. Thanks again."

Deveraux was on her phone as soon as she departed the restaurant. Who was she calling? Her editor? Her lover? Nick sat watching the *ESPN* scroll for the score between his Yankees and the hated Red Sox. *Maybe I should write a book on all his happy horseshit. You'd like that wouldn't you, Alex?*

He wanted to spend the rest of his day on rewrites. But he had to attend a 4 p.m. meeting, touting a new public-private venture to revitalize Carlson, Indiana, this tired factory town whose halcyon days were in the mid-20th century. A leading auto industry supplier used to have thousands working at a single location, running three shifts, six days a week. That facility and others were long-since shuttered.

Founded as a settlement in 1793 by Johann Carlson, a Norwegian adventurer traveling the Northwest Territory, the city was struggling to survive. One-third of its population of 50,000 was at or below the poverty line. The largest employers were Hempstead University and a nearby food processing plant, but most new jobs were in the low-paying service sector.

Nick asked perfunctory questions of officials on their proposals to diversify the local economy. An hour later, he had written his page-one piece and submitted it for copy editing and posting to the paper's website. He left the newsroom anticipating a quiet night. Then Christopher called.

"Hey, Mitya, it's Alyosha," he said, alluding to *The Brothers Karamazov*, one of their favorite novels.

Nick welcomed Christopher's cheerfulness. He and Inez had been depressed for weeks following Miranda's assault. It was unusual for his brother to be so despondent. He was the Delamore with what their mother, Eileen, described as a "sunny disposition." Christopher said Miranda was enjoying her part-time work with Aunt Meg at A Safe Place, but she was very worried about her friend Stacy.

"Understandable," Nick said.

"I know. We're so lucky she wasn't ... ."

"Keep it together, bro. You were just saying how well she's doing."

"You're right. The main reason I called was to see how plans were coming along for Mom's birthday."

Nick had assured Christopher he would help coordinate the June 30 celebration in Cleveland. But he had dropped the ball. He could list any number of distractions and sufficient reasons why he couldn't be counted on.

The older Delamore sons were self-absorbed men, consumed by the demands of their careers and a host of private desires. Nick's world revolved around work or the state of his sex life. Matt, who most resembled their dark-haired father, was a successful junior college football coach in Sacramento. He used his job in California to rationalize minimal involvement in family issues back East.

Christopher Delamore had overcome an early disability, caused by viral encephalitis, and found success as a studio photographer. He walked with a limp, and his speech was somewhat slurred. But the rotund red-haired sibling had an infectious personality and a creative spirit that endeared him to people.

The devoted son had helped his parents move back to the Cleveland area after they spent years crisscrossing the country as Charlie chased a series of hospitality industry jobs—until his luck and health ran out. In 2000, Christopher willingly assumed the caretaker role while his dad spent months being treated for lymphoma, and infirmity was a constant companion.

Even with continual requests from Eileen and Christopher to spend more time with their ill father, Matt and Nick had each visited him just once in his final months. At his funeral they were somber and reverent to their mother. But Christopher wondered if they were merely performing expected roles. He prayed their hearts would soften one day.

Had Charlie's failures caused his oldest sons to give him such fleeting regard prior to his death? Was Harry Chapin's "The Cat's in the Cradle" song playing itself out? Charlie Delamore had been preoccupied for much of their youth. He told Eileen and Christopher he understood their aloofness as if it were an inherited trait. But wasn't a father deserving of some respect and fidelity for trying to change? Couldn't Matt and Nick forgive their dad for those ancient offenses?

Eileen believed there was an emotional black hole in two of her sons. She told Christopher that his brothers were like "tin men." As in *The Wizard of Oz,* they were clinking and clanking down the yellow brick road of life.

"That makes me the scarecrow," Christopher said, tapping his head as if it were filled with straw. "Or am I the cowardly lion?" He crouched fearfully.

"You are smart and brave," she said. "And have been a loving son to your father and me."

Christopher wanted his mother's 85th birthday to be memorable. He, Inez and Miranda had moved her from the tiny basement unit in Fairview Park to a retirement center in Westlake. She visited with relatives and friends in the area, cared for a small flower garden, read her mystery novels and wrote poetry in spiral notebooks. She seemed content, but Christopher knew she longed to see Matt, Nick and their families more often.

And he hoped for reconciliation between his older siblings. Nick hailed Christopher as mediator. "If anyone can do it, you can. That's why you're our Alyosha," he said, ending the phone call and promising to assist with birthday arrangements. "Dostoyevsky should have based that character on you and not some wimpy Russian monk."

Chapter 11

Eileen Delamore's bold red waves had vanished, replaced with wispy silver hair she put up nightly with brown bobby pins that populated nooks and crannies as they had when her sons were lads. The Delamore boys would grab a handful, sharpen their edges on flinty sidewalks and launch them in rubber band slings at unsuspecting foes and friends alike. "Mrs. D.," as she had been known by neighborhood kids in Barrington, New York, looked younger than her actual age. She credited her "milk and honey" complexion from Northern Irish ancestry.

Wearing a new Kelly green and yellow print dress for Saturday's dinner at the upscale Le Chateau restaurant, Eileen prayed for peace between Matt and Nick. There had been friction since their childhood. Seldom playmates, they preferred solitary games when sharing a bedroom. As teens they fought outright. Well past middle age, their communications were limited to birthday or holiday texts and terse phone messages.

Raised Catholic, Matt had become an evangelical, using his passion for coaching as a natural springboard for rousing sermons at Fellowship of Christian Athletes (FCA) events and other faith-based activities. His fervor was an asset, as he and his wife, Janet, became loyal members of the Amway merchandising regime. He carried his Bible almost everywhere, praising "Father God" so frequently that Nick quipped Matt prayed "more times a day than a Muslim."

By contrast he was a lackluster believer, rarely attending Mass and bypassing prayer, except when trying to make a 4-foot putt or win a bet. Matt disapproved of Nick's divorces, affairs, heavy drinking and profanity. But knowing his brother's temper could be sparked by an inadvertent comment, he had promised his wife he would be agreeable at Eileen's special dinner.

In some families, honoring an elderly mother and grandmother would attract a sizeable contingent. But this clan had been decimated by deaths, disengaged relations and relocations. Tonight there would be eight for dinner at Le Chateau: Eileen, Uncle Paul Burke, Matt and Janet (Their twin sons had stayed in California with their families.), Christopher, Inez and Miranda, and a solo Nick. His 40-year-old son, Joey, had called "Nana Eileen" earlier to wish her happy birthday. He couldn't attend due to commitments in New York.

The evening began favorably with greetings, handshakes and kisses in a small private dining room. Christopher tried to keep the conversation light with remarks on the size of his waistline, the state of his photography business and his wife's latest home improvement projects. Miranda complimented "Grammy" on her "awesome" dress, and Janet noted her new butterfly brooch.

The three Delamore men swapped darting gestures as at a poker table. Christopher took photos with his iPhone, drawing good-natured derision.

"Where's your fancy camera?" Matt asked.

"That's for paying clients," Nick said.

Christopher savored the bonhomie at tonight's gathering. But he knew how easily things could change.

Who could have guessed that Eileen would start a tussle by asking Nick about his old fraternity brother? Had he forgotten that his Kennedy-Democrat mother loved politics? She was intrigued by the contest between Cleveland Mayor Kwame Imani and Cincinnati millionaire-philanthropist Bruce Van Pelt.

Janet cited the Republican's charitable good works and a popular YouTube video describing how the Holy Spirit had rescued him from his wayward life.

"Wayward?" Nick asked.

Eileen added, "My sons had some wayward times growing up."

"I sure did," Matt said. "That's why I've confessed to my Lord and Savior. And you, Nick?"

He was working on a fresh Dewar's on the rocks. "An Act of Contrition does the trick for me."

Matt was going to respond, but he was diverted by the passing bread basket. Janet couldn't resist asking Nick, "What do you think of him?"

"Typical politician," he said, swirling the ice in his glass.

"I mean as a man, a leader," Janet said, probing her prickly brother-in-law.

He drained his drink, replaying the scene of Van Pelt screwing an unconscious sorority girl in the shower.

"Really want to know?"

"Maybe we don't," Christopher said. "Hey, those Indians are playing good ball this year."

"Let him finish," Matt said. "Go ahead, bro, we're all waiting."

"OK, you asked for it," he said. "I don't care if he's reborn, retooled, rebooted, whatever. Van Pelt's NFG as Dad would say. No freakin' good."

Nick turned to Eileen. "Like how I used PG-13 language, Mom?"

Matt said to his dark-eyed niece: "Miranda, I hear you're transferring to Cleveland State and majoring in social work. Have you taken any psychology courses yet?"

"Intro psych as a freshman at Oakwood. But I'll be taking more this fall. Why?"

"Yes, why?" asked Uncle Paul after a third refill of Chablis.

"Interpersonal conflict is psychological," Matt said. "You see my brother, your Unk, has an inferiority complex, which he compensates for by denigrating everyone he can. Tonight, it's Bruce Van Pelt. Tomorrow, who knows? Thought by now he would have gotten rid of that chip on his shoulder."

Nick's New York strip steak sizzled on his plate as he threw Matt a goofy grin. Inez clinked a fork on her water glass.

"Enough Delamore fratricide for one night," she said perkily. "Let's eat."

"Let's eat," Uncle Paul seconded.

Eileen rose from her chair, reached over and patted her sons' hands, almost spilling Nick's water glass.

"I'm so glad to have all my boys here with me tonight," she said in a lilting tone more suited to a stage actress than a frail matriarch. "If only my Charlie could be with us."

"He is, Mom," Christopher said.

"You betcha he is," said Uncle Paul. The old middle-school teacher and basketball coach could have doubled for Carroll O'Connor of Archie Bunker fame. "Goodtime Charlie Delamore loved to party."

Nick toasted his "amazing" mother for all her years of sacrifice. When he sat down, Christopher patted him on the back.

Janet whispered to Matt and awaited her husband's tribute. Would he try to outdo Nick? Matt raised his water glass at Eileen and said simply, "We love you."

Christopher added, "Always and forever."

Eileen dabbed her eyes with a linen napkin and said: "You are all my greatest joy. God bless us always and forever."

The birthday observance ended without further incident. Nick was going to Christopher and Inez's house, where Matt and Janet were staying for the weekend. But Eileen was adamant he come to her Westlake apartment, where he could sleep on the hide-a-bed in her small front room. He dreaded the morning backache that awaited after being prodded by mattress coils as if on a medieval rack.

"Whatever makes you happy, Mom."

Sure enough, Nick awoke with a stiff lower back. He shuffled to the kitchenette to make coffee and saw a jar of instant Nescafe with a three-year-old expiration date. From the bedroom came a familiar utterance, "Will you put the tea kettle on?"

Eileen emerged in a rainbow-colored robe and pink slippers, lit cigarette in her left hand. Most of her adult years she smoked Winstons and Tareytons. She now relied on discount shop generics.

"That's some robe. Does it glow in the dark?" Nick asked as his mother shushed him with a wave of her hand. She added the usual heaping teaspoons of sugar and splash of milk to her hot Lipton tea and sipped from a cherry red ceramic mug. She sat at the small round wooden dining table while he stood by the electric stove.

"How did you sleep?" she asked from a veil of grayish fumes.

"Like a Jesuit in Elizabethan England."

"Stop whining. That sofa is as good as new," she said. "Sit down. I have something for you."

"Don't need anything."

Eileen kept the cigarette in her mouth as she pushed a pile of unopened bills off a deep box, sealed with old masking tape. The word "WAR" was inscribed with a black Magic Marker.

"It's not a present," she said. "This is your father's."

"Don't follow."

"These are his memoirs and memorabilia."

Late in life, Charlie would jot down all sorts of things: jokes, golf tips, even letters to celebrities. His correspondence included "a pitch" to Oliver Stone to make a movie on the Merchant Marine.

"He was in the maritime service before Vietnam," Charlie said. "So I wrote him."

But nothing came of his proposed WWII saga.

"Didn't realize you had all this," Nick said, going through his dad's journals, news clippings, photos and mementoes, including military service bars and commendations.

"Your father and I hoped you would write a book on his war years."

"Mom," he said, "I'm a newspaper guy not a biographer. Besides, there may not be that much here storywise."

He saw the disappointment on her face.

"You know very little of his military record," she said sternly. "And you owe it to yourself to learn about the Merchant Marine in World War II. It's the least you can do for his legacy."

Nick listened to her appeal, laced with Catholic guilt ("the least you can do"). *That's why she wanted me to sleep at her place. So she could work me over.*

"All right, but I can't guarantee anything will happen."

"If nothing else, it will be a good learning experience. Maybe you'll even be inspired. Been a while, Mr. Delamore."

He drank his mug of lukewarm coffee, gagging on the bitter liquid. "Geez, Mom, don't hold back."

"Never have, never will, my talented son," she said. "So where are you taking me to brunch? Applebee's has great Eggs Benedict."

As a young boy, Nick believed his dad had been a Marine in the war. He didn't understand what the word "Merchant" referred to, so he skipped the modifier. In movies like *Sands of Iwo Jima* or *Guadalcanal Diary*, he pictured his father with John Wayne, firing his machine gun and killing enemy soldiers. But Matt dispelled such notions when he said Charlie was a glorified ferryboat captain, carrying cargo, weapons and *real* Marines.

"Dad never shot a rifle," he said to his disillusioned brother. "He wasn't a hero, you idiot."

When Nick was older and his father would say how treacherous it was being in a convoy of ships in the North Atlantic, he was skeptical. Were all those German U-boats really firing torpedoes at American merchant fleets, or was Dad exaggerating? In the 1960s, Charlie watched a television series on dramatic naval battles called *Victory at Sea*. He would get sentimental at the war footage, making it more awkward for his adolescent son.

Most Americans were unaware of the extent of Merchant Marine sacrifice in the war, their high casualty rate and the thousands who were captured as POWs by the Germans and Japanese. Even more disturbing was the fact that merchant seamen weren't treated as a branch of the armed forces, including officers like Charlie Delamore, who had graduated from the Merchant Marine Academy. They weren't accorded any of the benefits given most WWII vets. There was no GI Bill of Rights for Charlie, although he had spent four years serving in the Atlantic, Pacific and Mediterranean.

Nick would lie in bed at night listening to arguments when his dad had quit his job or been fired. He often heard his anger as old frustrations and resentments ignited: "Never got to college. Never got to buy a house. Never had any VA care. Never got any breaks like all the others did. And lots of them were pushing pencils when I was in harm's way."

It wasn't until the Reagan presidency in 1988 that Merchant Marine war vets received overdue GI Bill privileges. By then, Charlie and thousands more were senior citizens.

"Been a while, Mr. Delamore," he said in the darkness, driving back to Indiana late on Sunday night, July 1. After hours on the road, Nick's head was heavy. He tried loud bursts of rock & roll and jarring heavy metal on the radio. A rush of midnight air helped. But with 100 more miles until Carlson, he needed coffee. When his cellphone rang, he flinched.

"Dago Delamore. It's me, Bru."

A prank? Was somebody imitating Van Pelt's drawl? But who would try something like that at this hour? And the caller sounded desperate.

"Don't hang up on me, please," he said, undeterred by Nick's silence. "What's it been ... 40 years since you sucker punched me in the alley?"

"No sucker punch, man. How did you get my number?"

"Easy tracking you down. My PR guy used to work at Gannett."

"What do you want?" Nick yelled at the phone. "I'm driving and got a long way to go."

"Lot's happened to us since Merriman."

"Nothin' to talk about."

"What about Garcia's suicide? Why'd he go and do something like that?"

"You tell me."

"Not my fault, buddy boy, if old Father Alex jumped in that river," he blathered on.

"Nothin' to talk about," Nick repeated, ready to end the call when Van Pelt's demeanor changed.

"Man, Jerry fucked everything up. Spent my whole life trying to clean up his messes, and now he hosed me royally."

"I could give a rat's ass."

"Don't hang up, OK? You owe me that."

"Owe you? For what? There's no IOU. Paid that off when I let you skate on Allyson Chambers and Clarice Johnson."

"Who? All I know is we were good friends. I was your big brother, for chrissake."

"Doesn't mean squat. All in the goddamn past."

"Maybe I went a little nuts in college, but I've changed. Cleaned up my act. Even got grandkids. Can you believe that? Hey, Dago, you there?"

Nick should have ended the call. But his curiosity kept him on the line. *What did Van Pelt want?*

"Make it fast," he said.

"Need some expert advice."

He said there was a "situation" with his brother and an intern. As Omegas, Nick and Alex joked about "Fairy Jerry." How the brilliant but aloof math whiz wasn't satisfied with *Playboy*, *Oui* or *Penthouse* like the rest of the mad masturbators. He read these weird sex magazines from Japan and Korea, poring over them in his room.

His favorite preoccupation was "paratrooping" on guys having sex. Nick saw him late one night on an A-frame ladder, his head in the darkened area where suspended ceiling tiles had been removed. He was peering into the adjoining room where Bru was screwing a bar pickup.

"Hey, Casper," Nick said, trying to startle the pint-sized pervert.

Even in the dim light, Jerry's Prince Valiant hair was gleaming. He held an index finger to his plump pink lips before reclimbing the ladder to resume his fraternal observation.

"Dago, you listening?" Van Pelt asked. "We had this intern from Ohio State working with our polling data. A super stud on the OSU swim team. When my brother met him, he couldn't keep away. One night he said he wanted to review the latest survey results in his hotel room, and Jerry went ape. But the kid wanted none of it and jacked him. Then he called his parents in Toledo, and they supported him 100 percent. Just like my dear old mom and dad would have done. Ha!

"Where was I? Oh, yeah. His mother contacted Sully's office. My father-in-law the senator. But they stalled her, and that pissed her off. So she called *CNN*. Why not *FOX-News* like a good Republican?

"We said it was all a misunderstanding, and I had Jerry apologize. But nothing worked. He has so many enemies, and he's been so fuckin' careless. Four months until the election, and it's all going down the crapper."

"Payback's a bitch."

"You bringing up that old frat stuff?"

"What if I am?"

"Hey, you were no angel then, and neither was I. But I got nothing to apologize for. And I don't give a damn what you or anyone else thinks."

"Hey, Bru."

"Yeah, Dago?"

"Fuck you."

Nick pulled into a rest stop to fend off a panic attack. His hands were shaking, and he inhaled slowly to ease the pressure in his chest. But he couldn't keep his mind from racing.

"What I could never figure out is the fucking control he has over you." Megan was right. He had made excuses, looked the other way and ceded "fucking control" to an evil man. *"Sooner or later, one has to take sides. If one is to remain human."*

The next morning he spoke with Larry Rivers, who asked if he had taped the phone call.

"No, I was driving."

"What difference does that make? You've got the recorder app, don't you?"

"What app?" Nick asked. "I didn't have my recorder with me."

"It's an app for your phone."

"Don't have a smartphone, man."

"Good God, Delamore. Get out of the stone age. I can't use anything you've told me."

"Treat it as deep background. I'm giving you a heads up."

"Big whup," Rivers said. "If you had a decent phone, you would know it's too late. There's video of him being hauled off by the FBI. But at least I've got a backstory."

"I'll take that as a thank you. You owe me one."

"Put it on my tab."

Loyal Republicans tried to downplay reports of Jerome Van Pelt's seamy lifestyle and alleged felonies (e.g., embezzlement and transporting minors across state lines to engage in criminal sexual activity). Bruce spoke to media outside the church he and Susie attended in suburban Cincinnati. Surrounded by a pensive pastor and other congregants, he said his "broken and remorseful" sibling would seek treatment for his addictions.

A solemn Van Pelt added: "He has guaranteed full restitution of all missing funds and is asking for our heavenly Father's forgiveness. Let us offer our petitions to God for him and for everyone affected."

Ohio GOP officials were wagering the wheels of justice would turn slowly enough for November to come and go in advance of a publicized trial. And they prayed voters wouldn't hold his brother's sins against the pious candidate.

Chapter 12

At 61, Bruce Van Pelt boasted of his rigorous fitness routines, including Ironman Triathlons, martial arts and mountaineering. His bio referenced the distinctive broken nose that resulted from a game-winning touchdown when the collegiate tight end lost his helmet while being tackled by multiple defenders: "As usual, I led with my hard head and zigged when I should have zagged." But Delamore knew the truth behind Van Pelt's altered profile. For he had knocked him out hours after Merriman's commencement on Saturday, June 9, 1973.

Earlier that evening, Nick was with Megan at a campus barbecue. Theirs was an unforeseen affair late in the spring semester of his junior year. She had "sworn off men" following her breakup with Kwame Imani, who had been sleeping with one of her counseling center colleagues. But she was impressed by Delamore's investigative journalism, including a series of articles questioning the ethics of university investments in multinational corporations and his probe into alleged misuse of student fees.

He had also penned a provocative op-ed, stating that fraternities and sororities were an idea whose time had passed: "Forget the noble creeds or quotes from anachronistic alums. The fact is the Greek system serves no valid purpose except to house privileged men and women who want to party, to get wasted and to have as much sex as possible, without regard for anyone else."

Nick admitted to being "one of those indulgent frat jerks." But he was "moving out, moving on and moving up to become a more mature adult." His column drew the ire of Omegas and many Greeks, but he defied the criticism.

He was caught off guard when Megan contacted him about his newspaper stories and suggested they meet for coffee. Casual dates ensued with long chats on college life and topical issues: the Vietnam War, Nixon and Watergate. Then came the Clarice Johnson tragedy in early May.

The university and broader community were shocked by the local woman's death. As police investigated, suspicions were heightened of a fraternity connection, based in part on Johnson's live-in boyfriend's statements. He had told her, "Stay away from those pretty college boys."

Megan's feelings for Nick were shelved, and she retreated to her vitriol toward the Omega frat and its president Van Pelt. Nick denied knowing anything of Johnson's death beyond what had been reported. How could he do otherwise? He and Alex were sworn to secrecy.

Maybe someday he could tell her what he knew and did. She might learn how he and Alex had tried to save Johnson. But for the foreseeable future he would rely on an unshakeable lie well told. Deception was required even though it would likely end a burgeoning romance with a fascinating woman.

Megan organized a candlelight vigil, and Nick covered it for the *Daily Journal*. The long procession originated in uptown Sussex and snaked through campus. Faculty advisor Kinsey and editor Zinaman praised his work. But there was no word from Bradley for weeks until she invited him to her end-of-year cookout.

When he left, Nick was stumped. Why did she kiss him and whisper, "Keep in touch"? What was she feeling? What was he?

The next day he would leave the frat house for good, closing out a bittersweet chapter in his life. That summer he would serve an internship with the *Dayton Daily News* before returning to campus to fulfill the promise of his senior year.

Bruce Van Pelt attended a graduation dinner with his mother and father at the home of Merriman's alumni relations director, who was recognizing the family for their multi-million-dollar endowment of the university's new business school. If he hadn't met his fellow Omegas for a sendoff at Bottom Dog Tavern, he would have missed his vicious rematch with Nick Delamore.

The noise from students pouring out of uptown bars was a backdrop to the riffs of "Aqualung" blaring from an open window. A single streetlight provided ample illumination as Nick walked down an alley, a shortcut to Stanton Street. He heard a rustling from the tall bushes. He tensed and slowed his breathing, expecting a dog to come bounding out. But it was no canine. Van Pelt was tugging at his zipper.

"Takes two hands to handle a whopper," he sang, unaware he had company.

Nick cleared his throat.

"Dago? That you?" he asked, tucking his white shirt into his dress pants. "Got me some dark meat tonight. This fine black chick's been eyeballing me for weeks in my marketing class. And the rest they say is history."

Bru kept talking as Nick turned away.

"Hey, hold on, pardner."

"Let it go, man."

"Let what go? No congratulations on graduating?"

"Congratulations?" Nick scoffed. "With the crap you pulled this year?"

"The hell you talking about?"

"Nothing's ever your fault, right?"

"Come on. We're Omegas. Brothers to the end."

"Could give a flying fuck about the Omegas."

Bru grabbed him by the neck with one huge hand and snarled, "Don't you ever disrespect our fraternity."

Nick pivoted, using his leverage to drive Van Pelt backward until he lost his balance and lay on the asphalt, talking to himself.

"Ripped my pants."

"Like I care."

"You sure care about that Bradley chick," Bru said. "Been messing with your head for weeks, and I bet she's still banging that Imani guy."

He was babbling when the first punch landed flush, and he fell again. When he stood, Nick put him down a third time. It had been years since he was in a street fight. He would hurt this man before he could retaliate. Van Pelt was on all fours when Nick kicked him in the ribs, and he rolled moaning toward the hedge.

"Come on. Get up," he said, circling counter-clockwise as his boxing coach, Mr. Arturo, had instructed.

Nick had won all his fights as a furious "Tasmanian Devil" teen. But Bru was tougher than anyone he ever faced. In their brutal bout after football practice, one of his punches caused a lightning strike, temporarily numbing one side of Nick's body. Since then they had only grappled in their short beer blast skirmish. Each knew the other was a worthy combatant. And neither man wanted to tempt fate until tonight. Nick didn't wait for Bru to get set before unleashing a left-right-left combination.

"Gimme a break," Van Pelt said, gasping for air.

"A break? You didn't give any of those girls a break."

"Me? What about you, Delamore? Remember those chicks we balled when we were teammates? You always ask permission before you got laid? Any of them cry when you kept going? Face it: We're one and the same. Cut from the same cloth as my daddy would say."

Van Pelt squinted from the pain and tried to clear his senses.

"Big mistake letting me up," he said. "You must be getting soft, little bro. Tough shit. Cause now I'll kill you."

Nick was ready for the bull rush. Bru charged, fists and forearms flailing. But he fooled him by throwing a cross-body block, hearing cartilage and ligament tear and bone snap. He seized the advantage, his knees pinning the brute's shoulders.

"You're a no-good scumbag."

Van Pelt spewed bloody spittle at him, but it didn't matter. He saw his target—the bridge of his wide nose. Nick's final punch was reminiscent of Rocky Marciano's devastating knockout of Jersey Joe Walcott. Gore splattered both men. But just one was conscious and standing in that darkened alley.

Chapter 13

Ray Russo waited until 8 a.m. to call Miranda about Stacy Matlin's overdose. One of his EMT contacts had texted him after they took the lifeless 19-year-old to Lakewood Hospital. She had a high blood alcohol concentration and tested positive for Oxycodone, Diazepam, Xanax, marijuana and cocaine. Someone at the house party had found her in a bathroom puddle of vomit and called 911. Most ODs were accidental, but was Stacy's a suicide attempt?

When Miranda had questioned her days earlier on her binge drinking and drug use, she was defiant.

"I take Oxy for my migraines. You know that," Stacy said. "And what do you care how much I drink or who I screw?"

"I care because I'm your friend."

"She needs more help than you can provide," Russo told Miranda later that night.

"What are you saying? You want me to give up on her?"

Before he heard from the EMT, Ray was hoping Miranda's mood had improved so they could do something fun over the weekend. Catch an Indians game, head to Cedar Point, or a trip to Put-in-Bay. Growing up on Lake Erie, Miranda enjoyed watersports. But this Saturday, she and Russo were landlocked in the hospital expecting Stacy's parents.

Dick and Debbie Matlin were salt-of-the-earth folks from Elyria, Ohio. They had moved to Lakewood to start their family.

Stacy was the youngest of four, a "change of life" baby. The deeply religious couple considered her a blessing.

The Matlins sacrificed to send Stacy to Catholic schools as they had with the rest of their children. Dick, a machinist, took on extra work as a handyman in the evening and on weekends. Debbie, a dental hygienist, was also a seasonal sales clerk in the Great Northern Mall. Their strong marriage had anchored them, but it couldn't prepare them for Stacy's trauma.

They had been anxious about her announced transfer to Cleveland State. And they were alarmed by her late nights and erratic behavior. But they trusted her.

When the call came that she was a victim of an apparent drug overdose, Dick Matlin was in disbelief. *This must be a cruel joke. How could his daughter be "on drugs"? She was a good girl. His good girl.* Debbie recited prayers on the way to the hospital.

As soon as Stacy's mom and dad walked in the lobby, Miranda teared up.

"How is she?" Debbie asked.

"They'll only discuss her condition with each of you," Russo said, trying to console them. "The attending physician will be down in a few minutes."

"She's going to be OK," Miranda said. "I know she will."

Dick hugged his wife and blubbered unashamedly.

That week, Delamore was quoted in a *Plain Dealer* article on the Van Pelt sibling scandal: "Bruce and Jerry acted entitled in college, like they could get away with whatever they wanted." Larry Rivers described Nick as an ex-fraternity brother, "emphasis on the ex." At long last, Megan was encouraged by what she saw as a critical juncture in the campaign.

"Only the beginning," she said. "Wait until Allyson tells her story."

"So you're going ahead with the press conference?"

"Have a little faith. Can you do that?"

On his mid-August vacation, Nick read his father's memoirs. ("When Charlie Delamore was green as a fairway and naive in the ways of war.") The Merchant Marine officer was popular with the rough and tumble crews, who worked 12-hour shifts on hazardous missions. Charlie wrote that it seemed foolish giving orders to men who could have flattened him. But he treated them with respect and earned theirs.

One of the best excerpts was "Hell Ship," describing a grisly murder, resulting from a racial feud between a Tennessee-born bosun and a giant Haitian galley steward. The saddest part of his father's entries was not only the friends lost on sunken vessels, but the treatment he received as a lieutenant senior grade in the United States Maritime Service. "Fuck the Merchant Marine" was the common insult from enlisted men. The ultimate rejection came when the U.S. government denied more than 200,000 merchant seamen veteran status after World War II.

Nick recalled when Charlie entertained him and his brothers with grand tales of seafaring danger, excitement and humor. He had been an aspiring actor with a gift for impersonations. He was a one-man show in the Delamore household years before his boys would learn of his faults and misdeeds. Now Nick could revive his role as an admiring son, reviewing Charlie's handwritten pages. The more he read, the more he appreciated what his dad had experienced when he had to "start from scratch" as husband and father.

Back at work, he filed his assigned stories without complaint. But his interest in the Hempstead investigation lagged. He kept dodging Henry Marx's queries. Nick would let him down easy and suggest he contact the *Indianapolis Star*. Maybe that would placate him.

With the new school year underway, he thought Marx would be busy with classes and academic duties. But there he was hurrying through the *T-U* newsroom one stifling August day when the air conditioning was on the fritz. Box-type floor fans blew hot air on an irritated bullpen. This sweltering afternoon, Nick wasn't about to be lectured by the dogmatic professor.

"Henry, been meaning to get back to you, but it's been crazy lately," he said, cutting off a breathless Marx.

"This couldn't wait. Found new information on Worthington's collusion with the campus cops."

"Collusion? Pull up a chair."

Marx had learned that Dean Worthington and the Hempstead University police chief were old college buddies.

"So they work together to keep students from filing charges," Nick said.

"Unless someone goes to the Carlson P.D., nothing is reported."

"Your president have a clue about any of this?"

"Jumping Jack Dugan? He's busy placating the board of trustees and lobbying legislators down in Indy to fund our expansion projects. That's why a lifer like the dean can do as he pleases."

He told Marx he would contact Worthington. He wasn't doing this to restore his journalistic reputation. He was going to take him down for a more primal reason. He hated bullies.

Times-Union old-timers called Worthington a true-blue "Hoosier." Nick googled the term: "A person tied to the land, a rustic. Someone who is solid and trustworthy." Others gave a bawdier interpretation, as in *"Who's yer ... daddy?"*

Dave Worthington had been an adequate high school basketball player in Winchester, Indiana. He competed as a walk-on at Hempstead, but he suffered from "WMLD" ("white man's leaping deficiency"). He used such pet phrases ad nauseum.

The homely, toupee-wearing Worthington had a potbelly from his love of pork tenderloin, Krispy Kreme donuts and beer. A bulbous nose made his small dark eyes seem more recessed. Nevertheless, he bragged about being "something of a campus Casanova."

After introductions, he studied Delamore: "You played some ball in your day, am I right? And like me probably had your fair share of the fair sex."

Nick scanned his printouts on the school's student disciplinary process, trying not to listen to the blowhard: "Let me tell you, that Viagra works like a charm. But it gives me a doozy of a headache. You know anything about low testosterone injections?"

"Can't say I do," Nick said to the pasty-faced administrator. "Dean Worthington, I'm on a tight schedule here. Would you explain how and why Hempstead adjudicates sexual assault cases?"

"Not much for small talk are you? ... OK, let's cut to the chase."

Nick anticipated the dean's evasions. He pressed him on reports of students being discouraged from pursuing rape charges and misleading university crime statistics. Worthington feigned ignorance and pledged to "investigate these insinuations."

On his way out, Nick asked if many knew that Burt Hinkle, the campus police chief, was his fraternity brother and best man in his wedding.

"Where did you hear that?"

"Got my sources."

"Sure, Burt and I go way back," Worthington said. "You meeting with him, too?"

"Should I?"

"Go ahead. He'll say the same thing I did. That we view the safety and security of our students as our primary objective here at Hempstead. And you can quote me on that."

Nick returned to campus to watch Worthington speaking at a funeral service in the Newman Center for two Hempstead students, twin brothers, who died in a tragic boating accident on Lake Michigan over the Labor Day holiday. The dean was center stage, talking with family, friends and classmates like a favorite uncle. Seeing him in action, Nick could understand why the administration was at ease with Worthington as a frontman. But when it came to researching the school's track record on sex crimes, he had to cut through all the PR hype. He wouldn't allow it to disguise the truth of how people were playing God with young lives.

With an assist from Megan, he interviewed federal education officials. They were tightlipped whether Hempstead would be fined for violating Clery Act and Title IX regulations. But he believed penalties were imminent.

When Marx told him that he would go on the record, Nick knew he had all the elements for a strong human-interest story: primary, support and expert sources, descriptive scenes and reams of reportage. He had never missed a deadline, but writing wasn't the issue. Whether he cared was the heart of the matter. And it had been a very long time since he "held fire in my hands and spread a page with shining," as the great Steinbeck testified.

Don't be a perfectionist at the outset. Get words on the page. Write by rewriting. Professor Kinsey's lessons had served him well in his career.

He used a summary lead. "The U.S. Department of Education is projected to levy a significant fine for non-compliance against Hempstead University because of its failure to ... ." He could complete the article by rote, stringing facts and stats, graphic details and analysis like sheets on a clothesline.

The *Times-Union* was printing a weekend supplement on the Hempstead investigation—the biggest local news in years. His feature was to be the centerpiece. He had read on the Poynter website that Lauren Deveraux was rumored to be on her way to the *New York Times*. And where was Nick Delamore headed?

The cursor blinked at him on page three. *It's good. Keep going. Get Hoagland off your case.* His fingers hovered above the keyboard. Then he did something very strange. He deleted every word he had written. If this *was* his swan song, he wouldn't play it safe. He was going for the long shot. The Hail Mary.

Nick remembered an anecdote involving Tom Wolfe at the outset of his freelance career. On assignment for *Esquire*, he had spent weeks researching the custom car trend in California, later published as "The Kandy-Kolored Tangerine-Flake Streamline Baby." But it nearly never was, for he had writer's block.

Byron Dobell, *Esquire's* editor, instructed him to type up his notes and deliver them to the magazine offices, and he would find a competent author. A dejected Wolfe wrote what he intended as a long letter to Dobell. Freed of the pressure to craft a story, he ignored tenets of form or function. The "letter" was published verbatim (minus the salutation), and Wolfe's innovative style came to epitomize the "New Journalism" era.

Why did Nick choose that example as the cursor blinked and threatening messages from *his* editor simmered? What did he have to lose? *Go for it, Delamore.*

He opened with a representative profile of a campus sexual assault victim:

Eighteen and away from home, on her own for the first time. Just the second weekend of fall semester. No big assignments yet. This Saturday night she and her new friends are party hopping on fraternity row. They agree to stay together no matter how hot the guys are.

She's wrecked after hitting the third frat house and doing shots of Jagermeister in the basement. Her roommate, Kelli, tries to get her to leave, but she's having too much fun with the gorgeous senior on her arm. Her head is spinning as he carries her upstairs.

The make-out session turns into a gang bang, a train, a groupshank. Crude laughter, sour breath, groping hands and unbearable pain. Walking home in the dark, disheveled and reeking, she is numb. The campus is quiet except for the comments growing louder, as if mom and dad were doling out guilt and shame.

(Shouldn't have gotten so drunk. How could I be so stupid? If only I had listened to Kelli and left with her and the others, instead of going upstairs with that guy. What did I think would happen? How could I be so stupid?)

Back at her dorm, Kelli asks: "What happened? We were looking for you? You didn't answer our texts? Are you OK?"

She replies with tears and disjointed phrases.

"Taking a shower."

"Are you OK? Should I get the RA?"

"Don't want anyone to know. Ever."

She puts on her comfy sweats and curls up, clutching her pillow. She sleeps all day into Sunday night, avoiding her parents' weekly call.

(They must never know. Never.)

She remains in bed. Kelli brings her food, but she doesn't eat. The RA stops by to talk. But there's nothing to say. She will keep pretending it didn't happen.

Nick shifted from the narrative to a conventional third-person point of view. He included a chronology of events at Hempstead and nationally, discussing federal law and local enforcement or lack thereof. He assembled a convincing case implicating Dean Worthington and the campus police. The article ended with a call for reform from students, their families, educators and activists, illustrated by a closing quote from Megan Bradley: "Colleges and universities must respond with greater urgency, transparency and responsibility regarding sexual assault and other violent crimes. Instead of focusing on branding and corporate administrative models, higher education needs more people like Henry Marx to step up, speak out and do the right thing."

Nailed it. But would the story make it past Paula Hoagland's desk without being butchered? He had to click "Submit" and hope for the best.

Chapter 14

Christopher called about their mom late on Wednesday morning when Nick was writing a follow-up to his feature story, which had been reprinted by the Associated Press. His work was well-received by readers, his newsroom peers and other journalists he had known in his career. He received many congratulations, including those from Marx, Rivers and Bradley.

Not everyone was pleased. Hempstead University was in crisis mode. Dean of Students Dave Worthington was on paid leave, pending an investigation by the U.S. Department of Education's Office for Civil Rights.

Nick's upbeat attitude ended with his brother's sad message. He stopped working and walked into Hoagland's office.

"Need some time off."

"Tell me that's a joke," she said, her face singed from the latest tanning salon visit.

"No joke. It's my mother. She's got stage-four lung cancer. I'm driving to Cleveland."

Nick stood erect, his words flat and face forlorn. Hoagland sat upright in her burgundy leather chair, tapping fingers on the desktop.

"Sorry to hear about your mother. But we need that story tomorrow. Friday at the absolute latest. I'm under pressure here, and there is major push back. Hempstead is threatening legal action. They say Marx is a disgruntled employee who violated confidentiality agreements."

"He's solid as hell. I don't give a damn what Hempstead says."

"You can't be objective. You've turned him into some kind of superhero."

"Paula, I don't know how much time my mother has left. I'll keep you posted." He walked out, hearing her tinny voice.

"I can't protect you, Delamore, if your reporting doesn't hold up."

Within the hour, Nick had his garment bag packed, including a dark suit and dress shoes. He drove north on I-69 en route to the western suburbs of Cleveland, where his mom was a patient at St. John-West Shore Hospital.

Twelve years earlier on a sunny autumn day, Charlie Delamore had been taken by ambulance to the same location. Nick was at a journalism conference in Las Vegas when a distraught Eileen called: "Your father had a turn for the worse. Don't know if he'll pull through. Please come home now. I need all my boys with me."

His brothers were already in Cleveland. Matt had driven straight through from Connecticut, where he was living in 2000. Nick caught a later flight than planned. He blamed his delay on a Vegas hangover, believing the red-eye would land early enough at Cleveland Hopkins Airport in time for him to see his father.

"Hang in there, Charlie," he muttered, hailing a cab.

He went first to the Intensive Care Unit, where his mother said they all were when she had called yesterday. After arguing with the floor nurse, he was redirected to an alternate room. He sensed something was wrong. The lights were turned down, and it was too quiet.

His mom sat bedside, holding Charlie's hand as if he were sleeping. Matt was staring out the window at I-90 in the distance. Christopher stood by Eileen, gazing lovingly at his father's body. When Nick drew closer, he greeted him.

"Dad passed in the middle of the night. Got the call at six this morning from his oncologist." Christopher spoke sluggishly, his speech impediment reappearing. As the brothers were talking, their mother turned.

"Oh, Nick, thank goodness. We only have a little time left with your father. How I wish you were here last night. He was asking for you."

"Dad rallied," Christopher said, choking back tears. "Didn't he, Matt?"

Nick's older brother was gray-haired, but the longtime coach had kept in good shape. Matt met him like a competitor at midfield before a game.

"Couldn't get an earlier flight?" he asked, watching Nick suspiciously as Charlie had often done.

"Those airlines are a mess. Got bumped. Never had that happen. Caught the red-eye."

"Well you better say goodbye to Dad. They're coming to take the body away."

He imagined at any moment Charlie would open his eyes and give him his "atta boy" wink: "Hi, ya, kiddo. How's the news biz treating you? Getting any action?"

He gripped the metal bed rail in silence. The white sheet was pulled up to his father's chin. His exposed arms showed bruises from the PICC lines and needles. Nick was shocked by the ghostly traces of his ebony mane.

But Charlie Delamore was handsome in death like an emperor lying in state. High cheekbones, a Roman nose and strong jaw line. His mouth was upturned as in pleasant reflection.

"Sorry, Dad," he whispered, stroking his cool bare arm as tears fell on the bed. "For being such a screw up. Sorry, Daddy."

An orderly arrived with the gurney, and Eileen said, "Nick, they're here for the body."

The attendant approached, mumbling a rehearsed apology. Nick shoved the pudgy man in the powder blue uniform.

"Give me another damn minute with my father."

Matt and Christopher stepped closer. Would they have to subdue their grieving sibling? Nick dropped to one knee and made the sign of the cross. He kissed Charlie on the cheek like a boy at bedtime.

"Goodbye, Dad. Love you."

Nick apologized to the orderly, who nervously accepted the handshake. "I'm an idiot. Ask my family."

Matt and Christopher nodded wearily.

"Come on, you three," Eileen said, calming her sons. "You're taking me out for breakfast."

"And Nick's buying," Christopher chimed in.

A dozen years had passed but not his regret. When Nick learned of his mother's terminal condition, he knew what he had to do. He was revisiting the same hospital where his father died, but it seemed so different.

When did medical facilities become hospitality suites with Wi-Fi hot spots and coffee bars on the main floor? Nick stopped at the information desk and then rode the elevator with chatty full-bodied women. They were visiting their bowling team captain, who had broken her ankle on the lanes.

"Only in Cleveland," he said as the noisy group left him.

Nick reached his mother's room expecting her to be asleep. But she was sitting up, her feet in pink non-slip socks, her thin legs dangling over the side of the bed. She was working at an activity on her tray, perhaps writing letters. There was no pen or paper just shiny cards. Lottery tickets. She was using a coin to reveal lotto numbers.

"Any winners?"

"Oh, sweetheart, you startled me."

He held his mom, her skeletal frame shrinking in his grip.

"No luck at all, darn it."

Eileen brightened at the arrival of her prodigal son. He was struck by how alert she was. Christopher's call had been so depressing that morning. His mother was a heavy smoker since her teenage years. A diagnosis of lung cancer wasn't surprising, but what was shocking was how rapidly the cancer had spread. Given the grim prognosis, Nick didn't think she would be very talkative.

"Where is everybody?" he asked, dragging a blue fabric chair closer.

"Went down to the cafeteria," Eileen said, scratching silver flakes from her stack of cards. "Poor souls were exhausted. They've been here since early this morning." Her voice was weak due to oxygen therapy.

"Shouldn't have left you alone," he said.

"I'm not alone. I have you with me."

"Very funny. You know what I mean."

"I may be dying, but I'm not ignorant."

"Didn't say that."

"Which part—dying or ignorant?"

"Didn't come here for a comedy routine."

"Here out of concern or obligation?"

"Mom, for chrissake."

Eileen waved an index finger at him. "No swearing in my room, mister. Asked you a simple question."

"Here because I love you."

"Good answer. Now help me get under the blankets. I'm a little chilled."

Easing her back onto the bed, he winced.

"What's wrong?"

"My sciatica."

"Sciatica? Good Lord, you can't be that old. Your father had it for years."

"Never knew that," he said, moving slowly around the room.

"I have more to say," she said, adjusting her nose tubes.

"Fire away."

"Why don't you talk to your son?"

"Joey?" Nick looked at Eileen. "I'm sure he's fine."

"I know he's fine," she said. "We had a nice long chat before you got here. Christopher told him I was in the hospital. He put his girls on the phone. My darling great-granddaughters. God love them."

"That's terrific, Mom."

"Don't be evasive."

He was limping about trying to stay calm. He didn't want to argue with his mother. *But when was the last decent conversation with his son?*

Joey Delamore was 4 years old when Phil Maraldo wed Linda. Some may have figured Nick would be outraged when his boyhood pal married his first love. But he approved of their relationship. Phil was a solid hard-working guy, who had turned his father's small-time construction business into a thriving home building enterprise. He had deep roots in the Tri-State area as did Linda. Nick believed Phil would be a good parent, and he was.

Joey had two fathers but only one "Daddy." With his dark features, he was assumed to be Phil and Linda's son. When they had kids of their own, Joey fit right in with his siblings. The Maraldos had supported Nick's participation in Joey's life, inviting him to birthdays, holidays and special occasions. But he was a remote presence.

"Mom, I don't know how everything will work out," he said. "Joey's got his own life, and he doesn't need me causing aggravation."

"Why do you say that? You're his father."

"That's what he said last time we talked. I aggravate him."

"Your pride keeps you away," Eileen said. "Like your father. You hide behind your stubborn pride."

Nick stood at the foot of the bed. "Shouldn't we be discussing other things?"

"Like what? That I'm at death's door? Maybe and maybe that's why I need to talk some sense into you."

"I'm trying to make changes. Believe it or not, I've been talking with Megan recently."

"Always liked her. Lots of Irish spunk."

"She's spunky all right," he said. "Sometimes it seems like we never split up. But it isn't like that with Linda. We were so young when we got married."

"She rushed you," Eileen said. "Now don't get me wrong; I'm very fond of her. But you didn't give yourselves a chance before Joey was born."

"Happened all so fast, I wasn't ready or mature enough to handle it."

"And like your father not so faithful a husband."

"Want a full confession here, Mom?"

"A rosary will do," she said, motioning for a motherly embrace.

The nurse in rose scrubs blushed when Eileen introduced Nick. She busied herself checking readouts and changing the sheets. The young LPN reminded him of another cute brunette— Linda Pieta on a moonlit Jones Beach in June 1969. He had proposed the night of their junior prom. The love-struck teens clung to each other as if time and gravity would pull them apart.

They were married in December 1970, and Linda joined Nick in Sussex, Ohio, living in a cramped, dreary space. He went to classes and trained for hours with the football team. As a secretary at the local high school, she felt so alone and misplaced. Her co-workers made fun of her New York dialect and gossiped about her dark skin.

"Kinda like an Arab," she overheard the principal say to a teacher one day when they thought Linda was at lunch. Most of them had never met any "real *Eye-talians.*"

She did her best to cope, fixing up their apartment and trying to make it pleasant for her husband, who was dead-tired most nights. He complained often and hardly ever thanked her. He should have been more attentive, but he was distracted by the coeds who flirted with the handsome jock. The bolder ones seemingly pursued him because he wore a wedding ring.

Nick was a gung-ho teen on a squad of horny athletes. He tried not to listen when his teammates spoke of their blowjobs and kinky partners. Making love to Linda was enjoyable, and she strived to accommodate his amorous advances. But at heart she was a good Catholic girl, unwilling to experiment. Those nuns had succeeded in brainwashing her during the formative years.

He resisted temptation for months. But when he pledged Omega Epsilon Tau in spring 1971, the allure was too enticing. He and Linda argued intensely when he became "little brother" to Van Pelt, the swaggering tight end. She couldn't stand how he leered at her whenever he was around. Her distrust of him was the main reason she didn't want her husband in the fraternity.

At the end of freshman year, Nick succumbed to easy sex, using his bloated, nauseous, cranky pregnant wife as justification. Van Pelt went out of his way to procure the most uninhibited sorority "babes" for him to party with. Linda stopped asking about his comings and goings, and his frequent lies fell on deaf ears. Two months after their son, Joey, was born at Sussex General Hospital on September 24, 1971, she and the baby were back in Barrington, New York. A long-distance separation ensued, and the Delamores were divorced in January 1973.

"You OK?" Eileen asked.

Shaken from his time travel, Nick replied: "What's wrong, Mom? What do you need?"

"Need you to listen. Promise me you'll make peace with Joey. Show him and his family how much you love them. They need that and so do you."

Just then the Delamore brood entered the room, bolstering Nick on what should have been a sad day. Inez, Miranda and Christopher were the first to greet him. The brothers had a rare bond, dating to when Christopher was an ill child, and Nick was his "buddy guard."

Feeling a hand on his right shoulder, he turned left (an old trick). Sure enough, there was Matt, Janet and their "California surfer" sons, Rick and Will. The twin 30-year-olds had their dad's height, but their fair coloring and reserved personalities mirrored their mom. Old family tensions dissolved as Nick's nephews doted on their grandmother. And the two seemed happy to be with him, which left their parents grinning.

"Since when have you two Aryans been taking steroids?" Nick asked, throwing playful punches.

Eileen was delighted seeing her children and grandchildren together in this command performance.

In a voicemail to Nick, Megan sent Eileen her best wishes and said she would make a hospital visit. She also asked if he would check on Miranda, who had been listless during shifts at the shelter. Megan had seen her crying in her car the other night.

Nick met his niece at a Starbucks. They talked of yesterday's peaceful family forum.

"Even the fighting Delamores can get along from time to time," he said.

Miranda's eyes remained downcast.

"Listen," Nick said. "I know things have been tough, and I want to help if I can."

"Thanks, but I'm fine, Unk."

"You can't BS an old BS artist like me."

When she kept drinking her coffee without reaction, he changed his tack.

"Any news on Stacy?"

"Still in a coma," Miranda said, her lower lip quivering. "And now Grammy's dying. Why is all this happening? Why is God so cruel?"

"Don't know," he said, closing the distance between them. "But I'm sure they're both getting very good medical care."

"How do you know, and how is that going to make any difference? Grammy has terminal cancer, and Stacy may never wake up."

"I was just trying to ... ."

"Make me feel better like when I was a little girl," she said.

"No, it's not like that. Aunt Meg and I are worried about you. You're dealing with a lot—school, work, Stacy and Grammy."

"I know, I know," she said. "I just wish everyone would leave me alone and stop trying to cheer me up."

In the ensuing silence, Nick was calmed by the store's familiar routines as people seemed unencumbered by any woes. When Miranda got up to use the restroom, her chair scraped the floor and started to fall. Off-balance, she bumped into the table and spilled her cup.

"Crap. ... Crap!" she said, rushing off.

He dabbed at the mess with small brown napkins as it rained on the maroon ceramic floor, until a Johnny-on-the-spot appeared with a mop. Nick reordered Miranda a new coffee.

When she returned, her eyes were puffy. But she had "freshened up a bit," as her grandmother would say.

"Hear you're working on the press conference. How are things going?"

"Aunt Meg says I'm doing a good job, but she's probably just taking pity on me."

"She doesn't cut anybody slack, and she knows how talented you are."

"Why don't you think it's a good idea?"

"Not the event itself, it's more about the response. Things can get very ugly very fast."

"Aunt Meg told me what Van Pelt did to Allyson in college, and she said you let him get away with it because he was your friend."

"What? ... Listen, I don't know all she told you. But this isn't the time or place to talk about this."

"She says you should have protected her."

"Miranda, I don't want to go into it right now."

"That's such a cop-out."

Why had Megan filled her head with all this venom?

He reached for his niece's hand, but she pulled away.

"Tell Grammy I'll see her tonight," Miranda said, striding to the door.

"OK, I sure will," he uttered moments after she left.

Before driving to the hospital, Nick sat in his car talking to Megan.

"You were right. Miranda's stressed out about Stacy and my mom."

"I'll keep an eye on her."

"Something else came up."

"What?"

"Why did you tell her about Allyson?"

"Can you be more specific?"

"That I didn't protect her from Van Pelt because he was my friend. Why would you tell Miranda that?"

"I thought she needed to know."

"Why? Because you wanted to tear me down?"

"Don't get so carried away," Megan said. "First of all, she's not your little niece anymore. She's a grown woman who's been through her own trauma. This isn't about preserving some outdated image of you."

"Outdated? She used to love and respect me. Not anymore."

"You're overreacting. She still loves you. But this has been a very rough year for her."

"I know, and it's not fair to dump this on her because you're mad at me."

"If you could stop feeling sorry for yourself and come to terms with what happened at Merriman, maybe you could finally begin healing."

"Thank you, Dr. Bradley."

"Look, I've got to go. Please give your mom my best."

"Can you do me a favor and pull the knife out of my back?"

"Relax, mister melodrama, I'll have another talk with Miranda."

Chapter 15

Eileen's hospital room was peaceful amidst the cadence of beeps, buzzes, whooshes and gongs. Nick sat near her bed as she slept. Her breathing was labored, and she wheezed with each inhale under a clear plastic oxygen mask.

He deleted a text from Hoagland. He had missed the deadline for his follow-up story. Another reporter would write it.

In her new phone message, Megan was in good spirits: "Please call me when you get a chance. Kwame's green-lighted the press conference." Delamore and Imani's one-upmanship had endured for years, and the way Megan deferred to him rankled Nick. *Let 'em both go down in flames.*

The Jerome Van Pelt fiasco had reduced Bruce's lead in the polls, but not as much as was feared by supporters. The "harassed" intern from Ohio State was awarded an out-of-court settlement. Attorneys worked to contain new accusations and delay legal action until after the election. When word leaked that Jerome was a patient at a private psychiatric hospital, spin doctors managed to create a measure of public support for his "mental illness."

But Bruce couldn't rise above the fray as more media questioned his past. One broadcast explored contemporary fraternity culture, focusing on sexual assault on campus and noting how little had changed since the 1970s when Omega president "Bru" Van Pelt attended Merriman University.

FOX-News, Limbaugh and conservative commentators came to his defense, calling him a dedicated Christian and family man. He was nothing like that White House Lothario Bill Clinton. Cincinnati businessman Mitchell Crouse compared Van Pelt in college to the irrepressible rogue Tim Matheson portrayed in the movie *Animal House*. "Just boys being boys," Crouse said, mugging for the camera.

Miranda's caustic remarks at Starbucks hadn't changed Nick's uneasiness over the risks and potential fallout from a high-profile event. But his opinion didn't matter, considering Megan's latest call on the go-ahead from Imani. And he had more important priorities. He was trying to be a dutiful son at the close of his mother's life, a man she and others could count on. He had failed his father in his dying days, and he wasn't repeating that scenario.

Eileen was tossing and turning as if trying to escape.

"Easy, Mom. You'll pull something loose."

"Get me to the bathroom."

"Wait a second. I'll call the nurse."

"No, no, no. Don't be a baby. Just help me."

Checking the myriad of tubes and cords, he noticed the catheter line.

"You don't have to get up, OK?"

"Listen, Mr. Know-It-All, I pulled it out," she said. "Want to use the toilet like a human being."

"But you're connected to oxygen and all these other things."

"I can be disconnected for a little while. Let's get a move on."

Nick supported Eileen on the perilous 11-foot journey from bed to bathroom. She leaned on her son as he guided her, one arm around her narrow shoulders, the other sliding the metal IV stand. The cords linked to her monitors were quite long. Would they stretch to the toilet? He tried to calculate how much leeway he had before an alarm rang and nurses came running.

Mother and son walked slowly, carefully. Each step was accompanied with the sound of her panting and the rattling IV stand. Nick swore softly when it slipped briefly from his grip. The cords were growing taut. But Eileen would not be deterred until the summit. Reaching the toilet, they caught their breath, inhaling the strong scent of ammonia and antiseptic.

"I'm sorry to put you through this," she said plaintively with sad blue eyes. "Funny how things turn out."

"What do you mean?"

"Me potty training you and your brothers. Now I'm the child."

"Don't worry. Whatever you need me to do."

He eased her down, and she clasped his arm for balance. He remembered Christopher saying, "Dad was so weak from chemo, I had to hold him when he went to the bathroom."

Eileen was on the verge of tears. "Not strong enough."

"That's OK, Mamma-san. Me wipee you clean."

"You're terrible," she said as he steadied her and rearranged her hospital gown.

When she was back in bed, Nick positioned her gently, trying not to squeeze too tightly or tear anything loose. She began whimpering.

"Sorry, Mom."

"Not you," she said, eyes closed. "It's the god-awful pain. Better get the doctor."

Nick told his brothers about the decision to start a morphine drip. They stood quietly in the hospital room as she slept. None of them wanted to admit she was comatose. The night nurse had reinserted the catheter and changed the sheets. Her furrowed brow and sideways glance made Nick lower his eyes. *Don't worry, Mom, I won't spill the beans on our little excursion.* This thickset black woman, with the kind visage and reassuring manner, suggested the three Delamore boys take a dinner break.

"I'll keep a good eye on your mom. Eileen and I are chums."

The men moved hesitantly.

"Grab something in the cafeteria?"

"Got a better idea: Max's Deli," Christopher said. "Not far and it's open till 11 tonight."

"Was I ever there?" Nick asked.

"Yeah, bro. You love their carrot cake."

"Of course, Max's Deli. What's wrong with me?"

"Where you want to start?"

They returned with a coconut-frosted cupcake, which was set on the small nightstand. Frank Sinatra was there also, courtesy of iTunes. Christopher placed his cell phone on the pillow by her ear and let "Frankie" serenade Eileen. Her sons listened to songs that filled their home back when their mother and father danced before an appreciative audience.

Nick called to his brothers, "Look at Mom's hand."

The three were transfixed by her right index finger rising and falling to the beat of "Fly Me to the Moon." They were smiling as tears flowed, and Sinatra's soothing baritone filled the darkened room.

Chapter 16

Eileen Burke Delamore's funeral was in the Gothic-style St. Philomena's Church on Euclid Avenue in East Cleveland, where she had been raised in a strict Irish-Catholic home. Nick met with relatives and media colleagues prior to the ceremony. He had spoken days earlier with Joey, who was going to interrupt his family camping trip in Maine to attend. Nick said Nana Eileen wouldn't have wanted him "to make a fuss" over her.

"You, Eve and your girls made her very happy when you called her in the hospital," he said, thanking his son.

The priest in full beard and glasses looked like an Orthodox rabbi. He said Eileen grew up in the Depression in the working-class neighborhood that was transformed by 1960s "white flight" into a largely black community.

"And the Burkes were devout parishioners through all the years."

The cleric wisely left longer testimonials to her sons at the end of Mass. Matt recounted how she had taken care of them through many relocations and other tough times. Christopher described her sense of humor and love of grandchildren and great-grandchildren. Nick called his mom "an unknown but gifted poet and author," who had propelled him as a writer.

She would work in the corner of the dining room when her family went to bed. With her black Underwood manual typewriter perched on a portable card table, the wife and mother became an alchemist, producing magical words and phrases in smudged ink on yellow draft pages. Eileen used to say Nick was descended from Celtic storytellers and had a duty to use his innate creativity.

"Sounds like malarkey to me. But I'll try not to let you down, Mom."

As he concluded, Megan was teary-eyed. She gazed at him in a way he hadn't seen in a long while. When he was back sitting in the front pew with his brothers and their families, Miranda gave him a thumbs up. She had apologized to her uncle after the Starbucks confrontation.

"I had it coming," Nick said, reconciling with his niece.

Mourners exchanged condolences outside. There would be no gravesite ceremony. Eileen was cremated as was her husband. Their remains would be kept in ceramic urns on a bookshelf in Christopher's home until a decision could be made on a final resting spot.

"Lovely tribute," Megan said, kissing Nick on the cheek.

"Thanks," he said. "Where's Roger?"

"We broke up."

"That a good thing?"

"Got tired of the status quo."

"Appreciate the update." He was friendly but fatigued. "You coming to Christopher's?"

"Like to, but things are crazy back at the shelter," she said with a second light kiss before walking to her forest-green Subaru.

Nick spent a couple more days with family in Cleveland handling Eileen's affairs. They sorted through a lifetime of belongings, filling countless 30-gallon bags and making multiple trips to the dumpster or local Goodwill store. He and his brothers paid outstanding bills, ordered death certificate copies and notified Social Security, Medicare and the insurance company.

The chores were tedious, but the Delamores perked up when they discovered keepsakes in a mysterious black trunk. They included a trove of love letters Charlie had sent Eileen during their courtship, when he worked the Great Lakes as a merchant seaman. The letters were bound with pink ribbons and stored in shoeboxes. Inez took pleasure in reading them aloud.

He wanted to stay longer, but, because of an angry call and ultimatum from Hoagland, Nick said he needed to leave extra early Saturday morning. The *Times-Union* was publishing another major Hempstead-related article that week. If he wasn't in the newsroom by noon, he would be fired.

Christopher bid Nick farewell in his driveway just past dawn.

"Take it easy, buddy guard," he said, his blue eyes luminous.

"All copacetic," Nick replied. "Thanks as always for being the family rock."

"You mean rock star," said his chortling brother.

"Golden oldies" on the radio made Nick think of past road trips. The best ones were with Alex when they had just enough money for gas, smokes and munchies. How Merten could talk on those getaways, describing his dreams of adventure as in one of his cherished childhood novels.

Their last reunion was in 2002 when they met in Texas. Nick had called Alex after an SPJ (Society of Professional Journalists) conference in San Antonio. He had a day to kill until his flight home. Alex was surprised to hear from him as he was the one who normally initiated communication. That June day, Nick drove his rented Ford Taurus three-plus hours due south to McAllen, stopping at a rundown 7-Eleven store to ask directions to St. Philip's Church.

"San Filippo, senor?" the stoop-shouldered man asked at the counter.

"Huh? No, St. Philip's," Nick responded. "I'm looking for Alex Merten. Father Alex Merten."

"Si," the man said. "Padre Alejandro. San Filippo."

"Let's try this again," Nick said, exaggerating his diction. "How—do—I—get—to—San—Filippo?"

"Down that street. You can't miss it. And tell Padre Alejandro 'hola' from Javier."

"I'll tell him."

Father Merten had been working in the church garden and making minor building repairs. His skin was weathered from years in the sun and south Texas winds. He wore overalls, a white tee and high-top Chuck Taylor sneakers to their tavern lunch.

"You a priest or handyman?"

"A little of both some days," Alex said. "And I see you're going for the wannabe golf pro look."

"You lost a ton of weight, amigo."

"No late-night food runs for me these days. Seems like you've put on what I lost. Hitting the booze pretty hard?"

"Hey, ease up. You know how sensitive I am."

The men ate a simple meal of rice, beans and tortillas while catching up with their lives. Alex spoke proudly of his scrappy parish. Nick griped about his love life and latest run-ins with editors. Merten let Delamore lead the conversation until a second round of beers when he unearthed their shared dark past.

"You ever think of that night?"

"What night?"

"The night Clarice Johnson died."

"We were kids for godsakes."

"That's bullshit," Alex said, shoving his plate aside.

"You allowed to curse like that?"

"Stop changing the subject."

"I think you need to cool your jets, Padre Alejandro."

"How can you act like that horrible crime never happened? How can you wipe your conscience clear?"

"Why can't you?" Nick asked. "Aren't you all for forgiveness?"

"We were cowards," Alex said. "We let them get away with it. A woman lost her life, and we dumped her and ran off."

"We did the best we could."

Alex slapped a calloused hand on the tabletop.

"Why do you keep deceiving yourself?"

"I knew coming here was a bad idea," Nick said, digging in his pocket for cash. "Thought maybe we could get together and have some laughs. But you want to condemn us over what happened in college. Well guess what? We did our best to save that woman."

"We could have done more," Alex insisted. "We should have done more."

Nick's jaw was clenched, his voice guttural: "I try to forget that night and a bunch of other lousy ones. You want to be miserable. Go ahead. Keep carrying your cross, Father Merten."

"How's that selective amnesia working out for you?" Alex asked. "Let's see: a couple divorces, an estranged son, meaningless affairs, a floundering career and a drinking problem. Yeah, you got it all together."

"Are you freakin' kidding me?" His outburst got the attention of wary locals, who were very protective of their pastor. Alex reassured them with a nod, and Nick got the hint.

"Just because you're a priest doesn't give you any moral authority to judge me," he said, tossing two $20 bills on the table.

"I'm not judging you. I want to help you reclaim your life."

"Good luck with that." Nick extended his hand like a jab.

Alex ignored the gesture and bear-hugged him, kissing his cheek. "Love you, brother," he whispered.

As Delamore drove off, he looked in the rear-view mirror at Merten, who was waving goodbye with both hands over his head. The beatific memory ended with a trucker's shrill horn when Nick's Honda Accord drifted into the passing lane on I-69 South in Indiana.

Chapter 17

Hours before Clarice Johnson's death, neither Nick nor Alex had any premonition of the tragedy to befall them. They were focused on their upcoming senior year. By fall semester, they would be deactivated from the fraternity and living together off campus. But there was one last party at Omega Epsilon Tau.

The first Saturday in May was the annual Hawaiian Luau, featuring a roasted pig, fresh pineapples, tiki torches, sappy Polynesian music, gallons of rum punch, swimsuits and leis. As this would be his final social event, Alex wanted to have a good time, though he didn't have a date. He hoped Nick would be there but doubted it. After Delamore's editorial bashing the Greek system, he became a pariah, rejected by most of the brothers as a disloyal asshole. Alex, Gunner, Spencer Dodd and Max Klein were among his few remaining friendships.

Nick was with Megan at the University of Cincinnati, where she was a panelist at a conference on campus counseling trends. They were to attend a reception in Mount Adams and then return to Sussex. He was going to stay at her duplex, but they had clashed. He drank too much complimentary wine and became "loud and obnoxious." She said he better get his act together if he wanted to see her again.

He sulked to the Omega house. The party had ended, but tropically clad men and women roamed the fraternity's grounds and its hallways until dates had been escorted home or secured behind closed doors.

Nick and Alex sat blitzed in the tube room, watching the movie *Heaven Knows, Mr. Allison,* starring Robert Mitchum and Deborah Kerr. Mitchum played a WWII Marine who washes up on a South Pacific island and meets a stranded young nun trying to escape Japanese troops.

"Deborah Kerr was beautiful," Alex gushed.

"She's a nun. What, now you got a thing for penguins?"

Both men fell asleep. Nick sprawled on the red leather sofa. Alex was curled on the carpet when he awoke to screams from a campy horror flick. Before going to bed, he had to take a leak.

Alex froze upon entering the second-floor bathroom. Four naked Omegas were in the shower, and a nude obese woman with long black hair was on her hands and knees. Van Pelt, Crouse, Trellendorf and McKinney circled the woman, thrusting themselves at her as she grabbed for their scrotums.

"Hey, what's going on?" he shouted above the din.

"What's going on?" Van Pelt echoed.

"What do you think is going on, dumbass?" Crouse groped the woman, whose back was covered with red blotches. "We're playing sucky fucky. Right, honey? Sucky fucky."

"That's right, you dildos." She laughed hysterically and drank from a bottle of Jack Daniel's that Van Pelt gave her. Liquor bottles and beer cans lined the stall.

"Garcia, either get your ass in here or get out," Bru bellowed.

Trellendorf snared one of the woman's breasts and swatted it like a tetherball. "Your tits are humongous," he squealed.

Alex didn't recognize her. She might have been a student or a townie. It wasn't unusual for Sussex women to party with frat guys. He wanted to be brave, but the scene was so overwhelming he ran out, pelted with jeers. He was retching in the hallway, each breath buffeting his shame. *Do something.*

He had to get Nick. But he was unresponsive. Alex found a half-full red plastic cup.

"Sonufabitch! What's your fucking problem?" Nick raged, rum punch soaking his face and hair.

"They're raping someone upstairs," Alex said frantically.

Nick's eyes were glassy. He fell back and began snoring. Alex would have to act alone.

He re-entered the bathroom, and the lurid scene had turned vile. Van Pelt was ramming the woman while men jangled in front of her. She was sucking one and jerking off the other two.

"If you don't stop, I'm calling the police," Alex yelled. "I mean it."

They stared at the intruder in black and yellow striped shorts, water buffalo sandals and shirt arrayed with peacocks, flowers and fruit. Van Pelt blindsided Alex, subduing him as the other three held his legs. He struggled helplessly. They were pulling his shorts and underpants down, revealing his coiled penis and clump of dark pubic hair.

Those in the shower were frenzied as he was lowered, an offering to the drunken woman, who fellated him. He felt wet lips, a warm tongue and teeth. Afraid she would bite him, he squirmed and pleaded: "No. Don't. Stop. Please stop!"

As her mouth clamped on him, he became aroused. When she took a breath, his erection enthused the men restraining him.

"That's a helluva pecker, boys," Van Pelt said. "We have a new cocksman in the house."

"Finish him off," Crouse said, slapping the woman's wide red ass.

Alex writhed and climaxed, the pleasurable release smothered by disgust. The men applauded, and he wept. They released him, and he lay in a fetal position on the putrid shower floor.

"What a basket case," McKinney said. "Got his rocks off, and he's bawling like a damn baby."

"Come on, Garcia. Get a grip," Van Pelt said, shaking an inconsolable Merten, as the sex acts proceeded with Clarice Johnson.

When Alex awoke, his underpants and shorts were at his ankles. His shirt was drenched in soapy water, beer and whiskey. The woman was slumped across from him, vomit smearing her contorted face and stringy hair.

He pulled up his soaked clothing and crawled toward her. He tried lifting her into a sitting position. But she was so heavy and wet, he couldn't get a good grip. Tears filled his eyes as he slipped twice on the slick tiles.

He raced downstairs, determined to wake Nick up. With a surge of strength, Alex pulled him onto the dingy red and black checkerboard carpet.

"What the ... ?"

"Let's go, gawdammit!" Alex cried out, running to the stairway.

When Nick saw the woman, he knew this was no prank. The dreadful scene jolted him, and he reacted instinctively.

"Get some sheets and blankets from the rack room."

Her skin was cool and clammy. Nick probed her neck but couldn't get a pulse. He knew Van Pelt was responsible—empty liquor bottles, beer cans and the same repulsive odors he had smelled on Halloween night. Alex burst into the bathroom with an armful of bedding to use as a sling. They strained to move her, setting her down often.

"Need more help."

"No time," Nick said. "Gotta get her to the hospital."

"Then we'll go to the police."

"Just give me a hand."

It was easier to slide the woman's body along the hallway. They were careful to keep her head from hitting the stairs as they took her to the abandoned main floor. Alex pulled his Chevy Camaro onto the lawn as close to the side door as possible. Then they carried her down the brick steps to the car. Alex said he was too nervous to drive and tossed the keys to Nick. In the few minutes it took to reach the hospital, he conceived a scheme so they wouldn't be identified.

"Don't think she's breathing," Alex said, studying the woman shrouded on the back seat.

"Must be an employee entrance," Nick said.

In the rear lot there were parked cars but no one coming or going. A single light shone above a double door. They positioned the woman's body on the small concrete pad. Nick was to stay with her while Alex drove to a nearby street. When the car was out of sight, he would bang on the door and then make his escape through back yards to where the Camaro would be parked, engine running, headlights off. He was counting on Alex not to panic.

"Hey, hey, emergency!" Nick pounded the metal door five times with the fleshy part of his fist. When it began to open, he sprinted toward a hedgerow, hearing a man yell ("Hey, you!") and others calling for a gurney ("Stat! Stat! Stat!").

Nick lay on the damp grass trying to slow his breathing. He counted to 100, got to his knees and peered through the bushes. The double door had closed, and the woman's body was gone. He ran to where the Camaro was idling. Alex was at the wheel saying a string of Hail Marys.

A half-hour later, they were in the rack room, listening to their sleeping frat brothers. At Sussex General Hospital, a woman was pronounced dead on arrival, due to asphyxiation from acute alcohol poisoning. There were bruises, abrasions and bite marks on her body. She had been penetrated vaginally and anally with excessive force.

A statement was issued on Tuesday, May 8, describing a criminal investigation into the death of 23-year-old Clarice Johnson. Her live-in boyfriend identified the victim. He had called police on Sunday night to file a missing person's report. Initially thought to be a suspect, he had a solid, verified alibi.

In a local newspaper story, the self-employed handyman said Johnson was "a little slow but not retarded." She had left their mobile home in the Sunny Acres trailer park on the edge of campus after an argument on Saturday evening and hadn't returned. He said she often liked "going into town on the weekend to have some fun."

For most in the Omega house, life went on as usual. Johnson's death was discussed only in passing by a select few. But Alex's agitation remained.

"You're driving me nuts," Nick said. "Chill out, get some sleep and take a shower. You stink."

"Ask Van Pelt what happened to her."

"He'll BS his way through like he usually does."

"Then I'll talk to him," Alex said. "He knows I saw all four of them with her."

"You can't threaten them. We moved the body, remember? Besides, the newspaper said she died from alcohol poisoning."

"Because they were making her drink. And what they were doing to her was sick. Can't get it out of my head."

"Calm the fuck down. I'll handle it."

Van Pelt was alone in his room when Nick knocked on the open door.

"Yeah?"

"Need to talk."

"Nothing to say. You've written us all off. So go screw yourself."

"Just shut up and listen. What did you do to Clarice Johnson?"

"Who?"

"The woman who died."

"Don't know what you're talking about. Don't know any Clarice Johnson."

"The hell you don't. Alex saw everything going on in the shower with you guys. He tried to get me to help, but I was too out of it."

Bru spoke calmly, "Don't know what you're talking about."

"That's it?"

"Yeah, that's it. Except one thing. Alex better keep his mouth shut since he was in on the action."

"What does that mean?"

"Just what I said."

Alex didn't waver. He said he was telling the "absolute truth" and denied participating in any way, other than trying to stop them from hurting the woman. *Was Alex ashamed to admit he had been tempted?* Nick couldn't picture him screwing around in front of everybody.

There had been gang bangs in the frat house with willing townies. But Nick hadn't seen Clarice Johnson there before. Maybe she had been. Did she drink herself into a final stupor, or had someone poured the fatal amount of booze down her throat? And whose bite marks were those on her back, buttocks and breasts? Too many unanswered questions. That's why Nick maintained they couldn't and wouldn't go to the police. He and Alex vowed never to speak to anyone regarding their involvement that night.

The Sussex Police Department led the investigation. Merriman University's campus police and the Delaware County Sheriff's Department provided additional resources to support the case. They shared personnel and technical assistance to collect evidence and to conduct on- and off-campus field interviews.

"We're asking for help from those in our area and at the university, in particular, who may have information related to the death of Ms. Johnson," Sussex Police Chief Jay Krupa said in a public announcement.

Continual appeals were made to contact the authorities, but there weren't enough details forthcoming to generate leads from any of the Merriman fraternities or local residences where weekend parties were regularly held. If officers had visited Omega Epsilon Tau without a search warrant, frat president Van Pelt would have stood in the doorway and politely told them that none of the brothers had anything to offer. The police investigation continued unsuccessfully for weeks. No incriminating evidence was found, no witnesses came forward, and no charges were filed in the death of Clarice Johnson.

Delamore monitored Merten's despondency to ensure he wouldn't buckle and go to the cops. He warned that there would be serious consequences if Alex broke down and confessed. He would be putting them both at risk of prosecution and subjecting their families to ongoing scrutiny.

"And nothing we can do will bring her back," Nick said like a B-movie actor.

"Should have stopped it before it got out of hand," Alex said, recycling his soliloquy.

"You've got to move on," Nick said. "Stop obsessing."

"Easy for you to say," he replied bitterly. "You didn't see what happened in that bathroom."

When Professor Kinsey met with students in the *Daily Journal* office, he wasn't his usual jovial self. He cautioned them to be thorough and responsible in their crime coverage. Nick interviewed law enforcement and university officials, dormitory directors and Greek representatives. Megan spoke on behalf of the Campus Counseling Center, which sponsored a vigil and other events to raise public awareness of violence against women.

Privately she grilled Nick: "You swear your frat wasn't involved?"

"I swear," he said without hesitation. "You and I know it could have happened anywhere. Last week you said there was a rape at one of the Vine Street houses."

"I want you to say unequivocally that no Omegas were responsible for this woman's death."

"Unequivocally? Jeezus, Megan. I knew nothing about this until I read it in the paper. And I've been working my ass off to report on it."

"What about Van Pelt?"

"I told you. No Omegas were involved. Period."

"If I ever hear that ... ."

"Keep pushing me and we're through."

"Through? Stop being so dramatic. You act like we're going steady."

"That's it. I'm outta here."

It wasn't the first time Nick had lied to Megan. It wouldn't be the last. He would justify certain fictions to shield people, as was the case with Clarice Johnson's death. He would rationalize other inventions with less noble intention.

Chapter 18

The press conference was scheduled for 11 a.m., Saturday, October 6, 2012, at the downtown Cleveland offices of Planned Parenthood of Greater Ohio (PPGOH). Allyson Chambers Ryan, her daughter Natalie and son Bernard Hart would appear as guests of Lori Bingham, president of PPGOH. Megan Bradley would join Bingham in protesting Republican candidate Van Pelt's vows to cut funding for women's health programs.

Allyson would explain how such services had supported her and Natalie, each a survivor of sexual violence. She would then introduce Bernard as her child from a rape at Merriman University and name Bruce Van Pelt as the man who assaulted her.

Megan's voicemail for Nick was direct and unapologetic: "I know you're against us doing this. But we have no real choice. Unless something drastic occurs, Van Pelt will be elected. And I'll be damned if I let that happen without a fight. Allyson and her family understand the risks, and they're fully committed."

In advance of the big event, Miranda had befriended Allyson's biracial adopted daughter.

"We're women of color," Natalie said. "It's our time for proactive change."

Miranda was struck by her inner strength and natural beauty, without need of makeup, hair styling or the latest fashion. Natalie eschewed such embellishments, dressing in worn jeans, work boots and flannel shirts.

"Loved getting glammed up," she told Miranda. "But now the last thing I want is to be seen as a sex object. To those animals who raped me, I was only a hot piece of ass."

Natalie pointed to the scar on her face from when she was slammed into the frat house pool table. Miranda looked away.

"Hey, my brown-skinned sister," she said. "We're in this together."

She described how she was adopted in Oregon 20 years after Allyson had "lost" her firstborn. "Guess you could call me a bonus baby."

"That's very cool."

"Maybe I helped heal my mother in some way."

One day as they talked over coffee, Miranda told Natalie about what happened at Oakwood College. She asked if she should tell Stacy's parents their daughter had been raped.

"Want to know what I think?"

"Yeah," she said. "I can't make up my mind."

"You should definitely tell them."

Miranda spoke of Stacy's strict Catholic upbringing and her family's sheltered ways. Was full disclosure the correct thing to do?

"Hey, I was scared to talk to my mom and dad," Natalie said. "But they were so great, it brought us all closer. And now we're speaking truth to power."

Miranda sought Megan's counsel whether to tell Mr. and Mrs. Matlin about events leading to their daughter's overdose.

"What feels right to you?"

"I don't know. Natalie says I should do it. She said talking with her mother and father turned out for the best."

"That doesn't mean it will work for the Matlins. How long have you known them?"

"Since Stacy and I were in grade school."

"You think telling them their daughter was raped will help them sort things out?"

"Maybe," Miranda said. "But it could also be too much, especially for her father."

"If he's as protective as you say he is."

"Just don't know what to do."

"You'll work it out, sweetie," Megan said. "Would love to talk more, but so much to do before Saturday."

Nick met midweek with Nate Popovich, his confidante at the *Times-Union*.

"My condolences on your mom," he said, shaking Nick's hand. "How's it going?"

"OK, thanks. Got a minute?"

Popovich was of sturdy Slavic stock from the steel mill town of Hammond, Indiana, in the northwest part of the state. They had bonded at Jake's Grille, a downtown Carlson bar popular with newspaper workers. The men had much in common, including a satirical wit and skepticism on the state of the journalism profession and world in general. Popovich was the paper's editor before Gannett bought the *T-U* and replaced him with Paula Hoagland. Since his demotion, he had served as a features writer and Sunday columnist. A husky frosty-haired man in an olive green sweater, tan corduroy pants and worn Hush Puppy desert boots, he rocked in his squeaky desk chair.

"What's happening?" he asked impishly. "You nailing that hottie in marketing? You dirty dog."

"I wish," Nick said. "No, got some intel to run by you. Went to college with both Ohio gubernatorial candidates."

"So what? This is Indiana, nimnuts," Popovich said, downing his cup of cold coffee. "Yuck. Need some fresh java and a donut. On me."

Nick previewed the Cleveland media event as they walked to the lounge.

"Disaster waiting to happen," Popovich said. "You steer clear, or Hoagland will cut your balls off."

"Strictly behind the scenes."

"Behind the scenes? You said your ex-wife is working with the Democratic candidate ... Imani? And you were all close in college?"

"No, we weren't close. Trust me. Long story."

"Yeah, well long story, short story—don't matter. You can't participate in any way. Thought you were smarter than that."

"There's more to it than the election."

Popovich polished off a second donut and a third cup of coffee as Nick discussed Allyson's rape and pregnancy, the death of Clarice Johnson and Alex's suicide. He also included Gunner's story.

"This prick Van Pelt has hurt a lot of people. He should be locked up."

"What you've described is awful, and I'm sure it's probably all true," Popovich said. "But you and I also know that without any documentation, this is all hearsay, rumor, badmouthing. That's what his campaign will claim. And the backlash from right-wing wackos will be ruthless."

Nick seemed chastened.

"Been trying to argue them out of this for months," he said, spinning his empty coffee cup in his hands. "But they're getting desperate."

Popovich stared past him as if reading a blackboard. He licked the last bit of confectionary sugar from his upper lip as Nick tore his Styrofoam cup into a small white mound.

"Desperate can work," Popovich said. "Rumors of Van Pelt being a rapist and having an illegitimate son could go ... what's that word?"

"Huh?"

"That word when things go nuts on the internet."

"Viral?"

"Yeah, viral. All I could think of was anal. Shows you where my head is at."

"Up your ... ."

"Yeah, yeah," Popovich said. "Look, we know *FOX-News* and guys like Limbaugh will defend him. What's important is that ordinary folks start asking: Could it be true? Is Van Pelt who we think he is? Could he have done these things?"

"Raise doubts."

"Hell yes raise doubts."

"Maybe more women would step up."

"Maybe," Popovich said. "Don't forget, Gennifer Flowers had her 15 minutes. Ultimately it didn't change a thing."

"But when the Monica Lewinsky scandal hit, Clinton's backstory made it believable," Nick said. "So this kind of media coverage could be worth it."

"Could be. And we could be fired if we don't get our asses back to our desks."

"Wouldn't be the first time for me." Nick nudged Popovich at the elevator. "Thanks for listening, Nate."

"Anytime. Know the best thing about this conversation? You finally giving a damn about something."

"Amazing, huh?"

"Just watch your back. These are powerful people you and your friends are messing with."

Nick left an encouraging message for Allyson, wishing her well in the days ahead. In his call to Megan, he said he was contacting Hannah Dixon about the press conference and offered some advice: "Make sure the shelter's financials are in order. Coordinate all media inquiries, and get ready for a real shitstorm."

He phoned Dixon from a bench by a public parking lot. He had said she was a friend. That was a stretch; they had never been close.

She first worked at the *Plain Dealer* in 1985 as a minority program intern from Ball State University (BSU). A slender African-American woman in oversized glasses, she was reticent as if awed by the newsroom pace. But she hung in there, constantly scribbling in her notebook with a cardinal red pen from the BSU Summer Journalism Workshop she had attended as a student at Broad Ripple H.S. in Indianapolis. Dixon was later hired at the *PD* as a general assignment reporter. Her writing was clean and concise but not engaging.

"You'll get tired of the same inverted pyramid stories," Nick said one day in the break room. "Familiar with Tom Wolfe?"

"The novelist?" Dixon asked, trying not to be intimidated by her older, brash associate.

"No, that's Thomas Wolfe. Tom Wolfe was one of the 'new journalists' who were famous in the sixties and seventies," he said. "They used literary techniques in their writing. Much freer form of journalism. You should try to be more creative when you write."

"And not so boring?"

"Didn't mean that," Nick said. "No offense?"

"No offense," she said, shaking hands with him before he left to see his friends at the sports desk.

Dixon would become an award-winning writer, praised for her reporting and unique style that made readers know the people and settings she described in evocative detail. How ironic that the conceited Nick Delamore now needed her help.

"Not comfortable with this call," she said. "And on deadline."

The shy intern had matured into a seasoned journalist. She had covered the wars in Iraq and Afghanistan, major crimes, and tragedies like the Oklahoma City bombing, Columbine and Hurricane Katrina. These credentials had earned her a fellowship with the Dart Center for Journalism and Trauma, based at

Columbia University, where she analyzed the emotional impact of such stories.

When Nick mentioned the press conference, Dixon said curtly: "Don't do politics. Talk with Stan Albrecht. He replaced Lauren Deveraux. Hold on, I'll transfer you."

"Hannah, please hear me out. This is your type of story. Allyson Chambers was raped in college by Bruce Van Pelt. She got pregnant and put the baby up for adoption. Years later the son contacted her, and they have been reunited. He's an ordained minister and has agreed to be with his mother when she goes public with her announcement. ... Hannah, you there?"

"Don't want any part of this media circus," Dixon said. "Imani's campaign is struggling, so they roll out a woman who was allegedly raped by Van Pelt and secretly had his baby. And she shows up a month before the election? This is toxic and patently ridiculous."

"I know it sounds unbelievable, but there's more."

"Don't care if this woman is Mother Teresa. Try peddling it to the *National Enquirer* or *TMZ*. Don't have any more time to talk."

"What if I said he was a serial rapist and responsible for a woman's death in college?"

"I'd say you were a biased and unreliable source."

"It all leads back to Van Pelt. I was in his fraternity, and I can verify everything."

"I'll contact you if I'm interested."

"Thanks for hearing me out."

"Better not be some trick to get me to attend this press conference."

"No trick. Thanks again, Hannah."

Nick clicked off the call and bounced a victorious fist off his chest.

Chapter 19

How could Nick ever defend his actions surrounding Clarice Johnson's death, months after the alleged rape of Allyson Chambers? How had he lived with himself, knowing he did nothing to hold the guilty accountable? Hannah Dixon asked these and other pointed questions in their subsequent phone call.

Nick answered with one of his own: "How do any of us deal with our failures and what we're ashamed of?"

Dixon didn't commiserate, staying in crime reporter mode.

"There would be records for Johnson," she said. "But did Chambers file a police report?"

Nick said there were no charges filed. He spoke of Megan's role at Merriman University in the 1970s and how she had met Allyson when an RA brought her to the Campus Counseling Center. Megan then took her to the hospital.

"Even an anonymous sexual assault victim would have a paper trail," Dixon said. "Was Megan with her during the exam?"

"Yes."

"Could she identify the ER doc or a nurse?"

"Don't know, but I'll find out."

"If they're to have any credibility, they need a third party to validate their story. Or this will all unravel. And it still won't prove Van Pelt raped the woman or is the father."

"There's a birth certificate from August '73, nine months to the day after the frat party assault," Nick said. "But you're right. No proof of paternity without a DNA test."

"Correct. You realize how weak this all sounds."

"I do, but Allyson wants her story told."

"I'll deny saying this," Dixon added. "But if what you've said is true, I hope he gets what's coming to him."

"Me too," Nick said. "And, for the record, I apologize."

"For?"

"For being such a jerk to you way back when."

"Yeah, you were a jerk. But you made me a better writer."

Minutes later, Nick phoned Megan and relayed what Dixon said on corroborating Allyson's ER visit.

"I can corroborate all of it. I was there, remember?"

"That isn't enough," he said. "The media know you're working with Imani."

"I'm not making anything up to win an election."

"The point is to find an impartial source."

"I contacted the hospital for records from that day, but they said years of old files were lost in a stock room fire."

"Do you recall anyone on duty?"

"The doctor was in and out. Nothing memorable about him. But the nurse was terrific, and she had flaming red hair."

"Like my mom."

"Yes, and she was very compassionate."

"I'll see what I can do to track her down," Nick said. "Doubt it will be before Saturday."

"Appreciate it, regardless."

Miranda and Stacy had loved Fridays in high school and freshman year at Oakwood. They would count down the hours until "party time." This afternoon there was no happy hour for Cleveland State sophomore Miranda Delamore. She was driving to a long-term care facility on Detroit Avenue to meet Dick and Debbie Matlin.

She hadn't decided whether to tell Stacy's parents about their daughter's rape. She had prayed to the Virgin Mary for wisdom and strength. Natalie offered to join her, but Miranda knew she had to handle this on her own. Ray Russo's black and white Cleveland police car was waiting in the parking lot.

"Want me to come up with you?"

"No, Ray. I'm not a child."

"Only thought that ... ."

"Thanks, but this is my responsibility."

Miranda rode the elevator, reliving a heated conversation with Stacy.

"Just talk to your mom and dad about what happened. They'll understand."

"You don't know that," Stacy argued. "And I don't want to hurt them."

"But you keep hurting yourself, blaming yourself, and it wasn't your fault."

"If I hadn't been so wasted, I could have seen it coming."

"How do you know? You did nothing wrong. They did."

"Whatever you say, Oprah."

When Miranda entered the room, Debbie Matlin was brushing Stacy's hair as Dick held his daughter's hand and wiped away tears.

"Look who's here," Debbie said cheerfully.

With her pale placid face, Stacy was more of a mannequin than a once vibrant young woman.

"The doctor said her vital signs are good, and there was new brain wave activity. Isn't that right, dear?"

"Right," Dick said glumly from his chair.

"Everyone has been so kind," Debbie added. "Arranging prayer circles and spending time with us. See all the flowers."

"They're very pretty," Miranda said. "Sorry, but I have to go."

"But you just got here."

"I'd like to stay longer, but I have to work my shift at the women's shelter downtown."

"Proud of you and all you're doing."

"Thanks," she said, kissing the Matlins goodbye and waving to her unconscious friend.

Miranda knew that if and when Stacy came out of her coma, there would likely be brain damage, requiring months of rehab and therapy to regain her speech and cognitive functions. Miranda also knew she would bear the burden and never divulge Stacy's painful past to her mother and father.

Russo was waiting in the lobby.

"How did they take it?" he asked, walking to her car.

"Couldn't do it," she said, holding his hand.

"S'okay."

"Breaks my heart seeing them with her."

"That's what good parents do," Russo said. "Love their kids no matter what."

The October 6 press conference opened with Lori Bingham and Megan Bradley deploring Van Pelt's attacks on government-sponsored women's health programs. They cited the thousands of preventive screenings, counseling interventions and other services provided annually by their respective agencies.

"And the vast majority helped by our shelter and crisis center, as with Planned Parenthood's clients, are the poor and most vulnerable," said Megan, a 5-foot dynamo in shiny black work boots.

When it was Allyson's turn to speak, she was poised. And more stylish than when she had met Nick and Megan at the Medina, Ohio, restaurant. She had toned down the gray in her hair and wore a new cranberry skirt and matching jacket over a champagne blouse. Sitting between Natalie and Bernard at a long table, draped with a blue and silver PPGOH banner, she said: "I endorse programs like Planned Parenthood and A Safe Place because they provide invaluable services to women. But I'm here today as a mother of a sexual assault survivor and as one who suffered in silence for too long."

Nick watched the Saturday morning activities from a streaming laptop video feed in Carlson. The *Times-Union* "techie" had showed him how to access the press conference. He took notes, impressed with the tenor and pacing of the event.

Natalie followed her mom. Her Afro was in retro Angela Davis mode. She said she had coped with her trauma through the love of family and friends, counseling and other social services. She was speaking out to empower college-age women.

Bernard Hart introduced himself as an ordained minister and counselor from Bloomfield Hills, Michigan, and a happily married father of three "fantastic" daughters. He wore a black turtleneck and heather gray suit jacket. In dress and demeanor he was aligned with his mentor, evangelical social justice activist Jim Wallis.

Hart said he was Allyson's biological son, nurtured by loving parents who had adopted him as a newborn. He was grateful for connecting with his birth mother and blessed to be with her and "my little sister." He smiled at Natalie and Allyson, who patted her son's hand and resumed her remarks.

"Some may believe this is purely political and that I am lying about being sexually assaulted," she said. "But the fact is Bruce Van Pelt raped me at a fraternity party on November 4, 1972, at Merriman University. I became pregnant with his child, a baby I reluctantly put up for adoption. With the grace of God and my son's love, we were reunited. I'm so thankful for Bernard and my daughter Natalie for being here with me."

The media nearly impaled Allyson and her children with their microphones, recorders and cameras.

"Are you saying that Bernard Hart is Bruce Van Pelt's son?" a *WKYC-TV* reporter asked, his eyes bulging with anticipation.

"Yes," Allyson replied. "That's what I'm saying."

"Will you file a paternity suit to try and force a DNA test?"

"Bernard and I are not interested in a lawsuit or a financial settlement," Allyson said, straining to be heard above the hubbub. "We want the truth known about a man who is running for office on the strength of his character and religious conviction. My children here today and the rest of my family pray that we may give courage to others."

Megan stepped to the podium: "Allyson Chambers Ryan is one of the bravest individuals I've ever met. And what she said is true because I was with her at Merriman in 1972."

By the time Hannah Dixon left the chaotic Cleveland conference room, many had already pounced on the story. YouTube videos, such as "Republican Rape Charges" and "Candidate's Love Child," included split-screen photos of Bruce Van Pelt and Bernard Hart. Close-ups of the men's wide brows, widow's peaks, hazel eyes and cleft chins were shared as postings grew exponentially, spurred by insatiable curiosity over the "mystery woman's" relationship with the candidate.

Politico and the *Huffington Post* were among the first to contact Allyson and Megan, with *MSNBC, CNN, NBC*'s *Today Show* and *CBS TV*'s *60 Minutes* close behind. *FOX-News* refused to do any post-event coverage, awaiting official word from Van Pelt's campaign.

Advisor and spokesperson Rachel Long, who had a J.D. degree and Ph.D. in political economy and government from Harvard, responded from what looked like a law library. She would not dignify the allegations of a "disturbed person and her Democrat conspirators," who would resort to such disgusting and defamatory remarks weeks before the election.

"Our focus is on important issues affecting Ohioans now and in the future," Long said. The elegant copper-skinned woman, daughter of Jamaican immigrants, wore an emerald green tweed jacket and a stunning Akoya pearl necklace. "We will have no further commentary on this incredibly sad spectacle."

As the Bruce Van Pelt tsunami hit the airwaves, digital media and the blogosphere, Nick Delamore relied on old-fashioned reporting. He would try to find the ER nurse who had treated Allyson. The first call he made was to the *Sussex Record*, a southern Ohio weekly newspaper, late on Saturday afternoon.

"Mike Kinsey. What can I do for you?"

Nick asked for the editor.

"Speaking," Kinsey said. "Editor and publisher. What can I do for you?"

"Did you say Kinsey? You related to Jeff Kinsey, English professor at Merriman?"

"My father."

"He was my professor and advisor at the student paper in the seventies. Made me a journalist."

"Dad passed away a few years back. Heart trouble."

"Sorry to hear that. Your father was a great man."

"He gave everything he had to this paper when he left the university."

"How are things going?"

"We're getting by. Weeklies are actually doing better than most dailies," he said. "But I'm preaching to the choir."

Nick shifted the conversation to his search for the ER nurse.

"I know the hospital's administrator," Kinsey said. "On the same Rotary bowling team."

"Appreciate if you can find anything out. Not much to go on except she was working there in 1972 and had flaming red hair. My sources say she was very compassionate."

"This have to do with what went down in Cleveland today?"

"Just trying to help out some old Merriman classmates."

"Let me see what I can do."

Nick updated Megan on his outreach to Mike Kinsey and complimented her on the press conference ("Solid effort by everyone, especially Allyson."). He later learned Hannah Dixon was writing a story on campus sex crimes. She wanted to interview Natalie but not her mother.

"Don't want to go near that sideshow," Dixon said.

She had briefly discussed Clarice Johnson's cold case files with the Sussex Police Department: "Jane Doe (later identified as Johnson) D.O.A. at 2:57 a.m., May 6, 1973. Asphyxiation from acute alcohol poisoning. Evidence of sexual battery. No leads or suspects after boyfriend's alibi confirmed." Dixon told Nick she had gone as far as she could.

FOX-News derided Allyson Chambers Ryan as a "crackpot and opportunist," dreaming of fame from her delusional affair with the candidate. The network also disclosed how Kwame Imani and Megan Bradley had been romantically linked in college. The married Imani and divorcée Bradley were shown in a recent phone video, dining by candlelight at a Cleveland night club. Rush Limbaugh dismissed Allyson's and Megan's accusations as "the mindless ramblings of frustrated old sluts who can't accept the fact that a man they supposedly knew in college could one day be on his way to the White House, while their lives had gone to hell."

On Thursday, October 11, Mike Kinsey called Nick with good news. He had a lead on the ER nurse. Kendra Jenkins was legendary at Sussex General. She was the county's first certified S.A.N.E. (sexual assault nurse examiner) health professional and an early advocate for use of rape kits. The tip on "flaming red hair" was key as longtime staff noted her "fiery personality and hair to match."

Kinsey said he had heard Jenkins resided in a local assisted living community. Nick thanked him and was ending the call when Kinsey asked, "You caught up in all this Van Pelt controversy?"

"Could say that," he said. "Off the record."

"You know what Dad thought about OTR."

"He hated it and so do I," Nick said. "And I also know he was a mensch and so are you, Mike."

Delamore then left a message for Hoagland, saying he needed a "mental health" day off, knowing full well she wouldn't authorize it and would dock him vacation time. Finding Kendra Jenkins was more important than warming his seat in the newsroom on Friday.

When the investigative series on Hempstead was published, a national organization called Safety on Campus (SOC) credited the *Times-Union,* citing how the university had consistently misrepresented the reporting of violent crimes, in violation of federal law. Misrepresented was an understatement. For the last decade, the school had recorded no rapes or sexual assaults. According to "official" statistics, bicycle theft and dorm marijuana busts were the most serious crimes at the school known as "Hemp U."

SOC's executive director further stated the university and Worthington, in particular, had consistently dissuaded female students from pursuing felony charges in "an environment of intimidation and collusion" that existed between his office and the campus police. Dave Worthington resigned midterm due to "health issues." The university feted him with a hastily scheduled sendoff dinner. That same night, Henry Marx toasted Nick with cocktails at his house. Delamore was appreciative and cautiously optimistic. He knew chronicling Bruce Van Pelt's crimes would be more difficult than exposing a duplicitous dean of students.

Nick assumed Kendra Jenkins would be living in a drab institutional setting. But the Millville Retirement Village featured new brick condominiums encircling a modern main building. The lobby had polished wood treatments, comfortable furniture and painted landscapes. It smelled of floral fragrances, and the personnel were dressed more like corporate types than health-care workers.

Jenkins didn't seem impaired at all, opening the door and ushering Nick in. She had smudged her ruby lipstick, and the rouge on her cheeks was theatrical. Her bright red hair had to be a dye job. In another age she might have been a Gaelic priestess. The mythological allusion was warranted, for she was combative from the outset.

"First of all, Mr. Delamore, stop acting like I'm a doddering old lady," she said, sitting in an aqua-colored micro-fiber armchair and directing him to the similarly upholstered loveseat. He set his digital recorder on the wooden coffee table.

"Glad to see how well you're doing. Mike Kinsey at the *Sussex Record* said he thought you were in assisted living."

"Who?" she asked. "I don't know any Mike—whatever you said his name was. And, yes, I was in assisted living after a nasty fall. But I'm back and very independent as you can see. Better get your facts straight."

"Understood," he said, glancing about and trying to warm the icy reception. "Are those your grandchildren?" Nick asked, noticing a framed photograph on her bookshelf.

"Yes, my son and his family," she said, a slight grin creasing her stern face.

"Handsome group. And I want to thank you for giving me time to chat. As I said on the phone, I went to Merriman years ago."

"That's what you said." Jenkins eyed Nick. "But you're not here to talk about your college days are you?"

"Not exactly."

Her hand tapped the armrest. "How I miss smoking."

"You remind me of my mother," he said. "Always with a cigarette in her hand. She also had red hair. Irish Catholic through and through."

"I'm Scots-Irish Protestant," Jenkins said. "But that's neither here nor there. What can I do for you, Mr. Delamore?"

"You can call me Nick, and I'm trying to find information on a student you may have treated in the 1970s."

"Are you writing about all that commotion in the governor's race?"

He knew he couldn't underestimate this woman as she kept talking.

"This part of Ohio is royal red Republican, and nothing you or anyone else says or does is going to change that."

"I understand, Miss Jenkins."

"Mrs. Jenkins, if you please. My late husband would raise Cain if he knew I was talking to a reporter."

"Some of us are nice guys," Nick said, attempting to establish minimal rapport. When she didn't react, he added, "If you've been following the news, you probably heard that Allyson Chambers was an emergency room patient at Sussex General in November 1972."

"She was examined and released but no police report."

"Do you remember her?"

"Didn't say that. Only repeating what's been on the news and in the paper. This woman appears after 40 years, saying she was raped in college by Bruce Van Pelt, who seems like a solid individual if you ask me."

"Mrs. Jenkins, were you on duty when Allyson Chambers was treated? She would have been with a university counselor named Megan Bradley."

Jenkins watched Nick fumble with his recorder, which he had forgotten to turn on.

"We hardly ever had any Merriman students in the ER. They usually went to the campus infirmary. That day was different. We had two come in—a young lady in shock, who cried the whole time, and another who kept trying to answer for her. The mouthy one was a short firecracker, who sounded like she was from New York or thereabouts."

"Actually Boston," Nick said. "So you do remember? Did you examine Allyson?"

"I'm getting to that," she snapped. "Don't you want background information? What kind of journalist are you?"

"Not a very good one, obviously," he said. "Go on."

"I knew right off there was trauma."

"How could you tell?"

"How could I tell? Good Lord," Jenkins said. "She had abrasions, bruises and was hemorrhaging from the rectum. Her vagina was torn, requiring several stitches. That's how I knew."

Nick tried not to succumb to the imagery, but she was so precise in recreating the ER scene.

"A doctor did the sutures?"

"Correct, and I had to have little Miss Firecracker help me hold her down," she said, again tapping her armrest.

"Is it true hospital files from that time period were lost in a fire?"

"If you wanted to find a record of that exam, you're probably out of luck. And you should also know that none of what I've told you can be used in any kind of criminal investigation."

"How do you know that?"

"My son is a deputy sheriff."

"No offense, but I doubt your statements would be relevant without any other supporting evidence."

"Except my recollection matches up with what those women have been saying."

"Do you know what going on the record means?"

"That you can publish what I've told you. This isn't my first newspaper interview, Mr. Delamore."

"Mrs. Jenkins, I came here to do research and verify facts not write a story. But if you give me permission to share this information, there will be media interest. However, some may question you and your motives."

"My motives? What motives would I have?" she asked, looking at the wall clock. "Tell whoever you want. Now leave me be. It's time for my soap opera."

Nick called Megan after his productive meeting with the saucy old ER nurse. He didn't say he was going to visit Merriman because he wasn't sure until he was on campus that Friday. This was no mere nostalgia trip. For it would prove to be more about penance than reminiscence.

Chapter 20

First stop: The stadium where Nick was a fearless linebacker until the end of his sophomore season. Replaying the knee injury on that muddy field had him limping to his car. He drove to where married student housing had been located south of campus, today site of an expansive recreational complex. In another lifetime, he carried Linda over the threshold into their tiny apartment. As dusk fell, Nick could have ended his flashbacks, left the confessional and departed for Indiana. But there was still plenty to account for on this mild autumn eve.

Arriving at the Omega house, he thought men would be sitting on the wall fronting the limestone and brick structure, downing beers and flirting with passing women students. But Nick was alone surveying the scene. Lost in retrospection, he was startled by a lanky fellow in dark blue and gold Greek T-shirt, torn jeans and flip-flops.

"Can I help you?"

"Didn't see you there," Nick said.

"You an alum? Welcome back," the Omega said, giving him the secret handshake.

"Was here in the seventies."

"That's awesome. Come in if you want, but it's fall break. Most of the brothers went home."

"Holding down the fort?"

"Yeah, holding down the fort. That's what my grandpa says."

"I'm a grandpa myself."

"Awesome. Want to come in?"

"Thanks, but I'll hang out here."

"Sounds good," he said. "Hey, what's your name? I'll look you up. We've digitized the old composites."

"Delamore. Nick Delamore."

The amiable young man entered the wooden front door as he remained outside. Darkness descended and upper-floor windows were illuminated. Gunner's Kenwood stereo began playing "Stairway to Heaven" for the thousandth time as Nick and Alex shared a joint before dinner. Bru was down the hall cheating at euchre, his band of merry men none the wiser. Nick might have expected such visions. But he was unprepared for another stowed away—the tumultuous shack up with Jessica Stewart, wisecracking bartender from Bottom Dog Tavern, St. Patrick's Day 1973.

She was a former basketball star with long limbs, cinnamon curls and a toothy smile. Stewart wasn't Nick's type, but he liked hanging out with her bar side. And that was that until he trashed the script.

The night had started with Nick and Alex knocking back cans of Busch beer from their Daytona Beach trip. When sold to hordes of college students, the promotional price was 99 cents a six-pack. They had stockpiled cases in the trunk of Alex's Camaro for the ride north.

Neither of them had dates for the Boone's Farm Apple Wine party, a St. Patrick's Day hoedown, popularized by Omegas from southern Ohio, Indiana and Kentucky. The basement was converted into a "redneck palace," complete with bales of hay and country music, straight-leg jeans, cowboy boots and flannel shirts on the men and women. Nick and Alex were going uptown, where green beer flowed from dawn 'till midnight.

Everything was on schedule until Spencer Dodd glided into their room with an unlit joint in one hand and a white envelope in the other. Son of a cardiologist from Upper Arlington, Ohio, Dodd and his roommate, Max Klein (Omega's "toking token Jew"), also dispensed medications as the biggest pot and hash dealers on Merriman's campus.

Dodd had cruised through his college years. Tonight he entertained his frat brothers as a court jester, jumping about with his disposable lighter. "Presto!" He handed a lit joint to Alex as the familiar herbal aroma filled the small room. Dodd bowed and gave the envelope to Nick. It was from the Archdiocese of White Plains, N.Y.

"This was in your mailbox," he said. "You becoming a priest, Dago?"

Alex took a hit and offered one to Nick, but he was busy reading the letter.

"Fuck it," he said, crumpling the paper and tossing it aside.

"What's up?" Alex asked, handing the joint back to Dodd.

"Gracias, mi amigo, Garcia," he serenaded. "Dago, take the edge off. Primo pot. No Indiana ditch weed."

Nick forced the dope into his lungs.

"Marriage annulled," he said with a long exhale.

"Thought you were divorced."

"He was in January," Alex interjected. "But this is important in the Catholic Church."

"No it isn't," Nick groused. "Who cares what some bishop says? Does this mean my son's suddenly illegitimate? It's all a crock. Got any more weed?"

"Come to the pharmacy, boys. Hundred percent customer satisfaction," Dodd said, reeling in his more than willing friends.

Nick left Alex sleeping on their tartan pattern Goodwill couch. The party was underway in the basement rec room. He heard Johnny Cash blaring and Van Pelt's wolfman cry: "Cut loose the wagons, boys!"

Someone called to him as he went out the door: "Where the hell you going, Dago?" Though he was high, the walk in the brisk air didn't ease the funk that had descended on him when he read the annulment letter. *Who are they to decide if I was married or not? So now Linda can walk down the aisle in another white dress? Too bad, babe, but you can't get your virginity back. Don't care what the holy pooh-bahs say.*

Student revelers surrounded the Bottom Dog Tavern. Many had been drinking for hours. Some were puking in bushes and alleyways before hurrying back inside for more green 3.2 beer. Nick went to the far end of the bar near the jukebox, Jessica Stewart's crowded serving side. She refilled several pitchers before recognizing him among the patrons.

"Hey, Delamore, what's biting your ass tonight? Why the sad face?"

"You keep turning me down, Jess. You broke my heart."

She stretched out her arm, handing him a bottle of Budweiser.

"Suck on that and quit complaining."

Nick heard Stewart's hearty laugh as he sat in his Accord, adjacent to what had been a bike shop but today was an organic grocery. Antique street lamps lined the charming college town. But there was nothing quaint about his remembrance.

He had fallen asleep in one of the bar's wooden booths and was snoring away when she shook him from a dream.

"Huh?"

"Closing time, sweetie," she said. "Heading home."

"Want some company?"

Stewart's studio was smartly decorated with colorful furnishings, dried flowers and knickknacks. Nick walked through the spic and span kitchen area into the main room. A pale blue dollhouse sat on a wooden bench near a wide waterbed. He performed a backflip off an imaginary high board and giggled as the waves sloshed him to and fro.

"This is a blast."

"Need it for my back," Stewart said. "Had surgery at the end of last season."

"That's why you had to quit the team."

"You're quick, Delamore. Some wine in the fridge. You like white?"

"Anything with alcohol is fine with me," he said, stretching out.

"Sit up," she ordered, carrying juice glasses of Chardonnay. "Don't want you getting wine on my comforter. That was a gift from my mamaw."

"Your who?"

"Mamaw. My grandmother, you dope."

"Never heard that word."

They sat drinking on the wooden waterbed frame. Nick looked at the dollhouse and a rocking chair filled with stuffed animals.

"From when you were a little kid?"

"Wow, it's like you have ESP or something."

"Hey, be nice."

"Okey-dokey."

Vanilla-scented candles highlighted a glimmering lacquered wine bottle on a small side table.

"Cool. That's macramé, right?" he asked.

"Decoupage not macramé, dumbo."

"At least I knew it was French."

"Speaking of which."

When they had finished their wine, he tossed his jacket onto the rocking chair menagerie of puppies, kittens, rabbits and teddy bears. As he stood, so did Stewart. She kicked off her size 11 tennis shoes and reclined barefoot. Nick undid his boots and playfully unloosened his belt.

"In your dreams, Delamore."

"What? Why not?"

"Keep the pants on and get over here," she said. "It's chilly, and I want to snuggle."

"Okey-dokey."

And for a second time, Nick performed his backflip onto the waterbed. He and Stewart made out, maneuvering on the undulating surface. He slipped his hand underneath her red and white Merriman sweatshirt. Her breasts were small and firm. But the exploration was blocked when Stewart yanked his fingers away, her large hands resisting his advances.

"Why aren't you guys ever satisfied?"

"Don't know, Jess. Don't get me wrong; I like kissing."

"But you don't want to stop there."

"No way. Too many hormones."

"Here are your options: You and your hormones go to sleep or go home. What'll it be?"

The Delamore charm sure wasn't working with Stewart. But he didn't want to leave on this cold night. "OK, promise I'll be a good boy."

They blew out the candles, took off their jeans and got into bed. When he rolled toward Stewart, she elbowed him in the ribs.

"Keep away or else."

He whined, "No goodnight kiss?"

"Love hurts," she said. "Go to sleep."

How easy it could have been for this "date" to end innocently with them awakening in each other's arms and maybe enjoying some breakfast. That should have been enough for Nick. They were friends. Why jeopardize that?

The rationale was quite logical, but his body had different notions. He had fallen into a deep sleep, waking abruptly with an erection. In the darkened room he tried to get oriented. *Who was he with? How had he gotten here?* Stewart was on her left side, her long frame adjoining Nick. *Time for Act Two. Why not screw?*

He carefully slid off her panties and mounted Stewart, using his thick thighs to open hers. She awoke with an expression racing from peaceful to alarmed.

"Get off me!" she screeched, her hands slamming into his sternum.

He fell off the bed and lay dazed as she delivered a string of epithets. Nick checked the back of his head for any swelling or blood. His mouth was sandpaper dry. The throbbing in his temples was nonstop. This was one of those Thor, god of thunder, hangovers.

"What you do that for?"

"Said no screwing, and I meant it." Stewart pulled the thick quilted blanket over her and lay back down.

His arousal was *going, going, gone* as he sat bare-assed on the wood floor. He wasn't thinking of the furious woman across from him. He was recalling excerpts from the annulment letter: *"Serial infidelity. ... Emotional instability. ... In the eyes of God, this marriage is null and void."*

He scrambled to his feet and flung the comforter, toppling the dollhouse. Stewart heaved upright cursing Delamore, who pinned her on the waterbed. She slapped at him, gouging his cheeks with her fingernails. Despite her size and years of competitive athletics, she was no match for a man of his strength.

But he had exerted so much energy trying to subdue Stewart, he couldn't perform. When he reached between his legs, she grabbed the decoupage bottle. Nick recoiled onto the floor, clutching the gash above his right ear.

"Get out before I hit you again." She stood over him, weapon raised as he begged for mercy.

"I'm going," he said. "Don't hit me, OK? I'm going."

She swung at him when he got to his knees. He ducked.

"Not fucking around, Delamore."

"Hey, you got a towel? I'm bleeding," he said, crawling toward his scattered clothes.

Stewart had slipped on gray sweatpants and still held the bottle. In her other hand was the yellow kitchen telephone. A flickering fluorescent light displayed a pink stove and avocado green refrigerator.

"Calling the police unless you get out of here—now!"

She shrieked like a banshee. He had his boots on but didn't tie them when he saw her dialing the phone. He snatched his letter jacket, tipping the chair and releasing a herd of toy animals. He made it out the door, thumping his way down the stairs.

He had no idea what time it was, only that it was dark and freezing. His head wound was oozing, and his face stung from where Stewart had raked him. *Would she follow through on her threat? Would there be cops waiting at the frat house?* He would know soon enough. He ran in his untied boots, the March wind slicing his lungs as he gasped for air.

Sitting in his Accord, Nick could feel the burning in his chest from that distant mad dash. He clicked on the interior light and gazed in the mirror. The deep scratches had blended in over the years. But above his right ear, the old lesion was more visible without his dense brown curls. The decoupage scar, he called it this October night in 2012. The drive west to Indiana was marked not by music or cellphone calls but with more Merriman scenes, jumpstarted from his campus visit.

In those wee hours after St. Patrick's Day, he thought all would be bedded down in the fraternity. It had to be 3 or 4 a.m. when he made it to College Avenue and Stanton Street. He had walked the rest of the way, being too tired to run. No police cars. Maybe Stewart had reconsidered. Or maybe she was waiting until daylight to have him arrested.

Furniture was askew in the Omega house living room. Red and blue plastic cups were scattered everywhere, and strawberry puddles dotted the foyer and first-floor hallway. He heard conversations from around the corner. The tube room was filled with men, lit by a low-wattage lamp.

"Dago, what the hell happened to you?"

"Face plant on the sidewalk coming out of Bottom Dog."

"Ouch."

"Missed an incredible fight tonight."

"Bru took on a gang all by his lonesome."

"Looked like Jim fuckin' Bowie when he stabbed that guy."

Van Pelt's lackeys weren't lying about his exploits. He had saved his brethren, including Alex, when "crazy-ass townies" invaded the party. Merten later told Delamore how he had come out of his stupor to find him gone. He was nursing a beer and listening to the new "Catch Bull at Four" Cat Stevens album. He never intended to go down to the party. He was barefoot in blue sweatpants and scarlet and gray Princeton High football jersey. Hadn't shaved since spring break. Hadn't showered in days.

He kept berating himself over Donna's December abortion in New York City, for which he would certainly spend an eternity in purgatory if not hell itself. Though he didn't feel ready to be a husband or father, things might have been different if she had wanted to keep him and his baby. But her words doomed them: "We were never good for each other and never will be."

He ended up at the basement bar, where Boone's Farm bottles stood like sentries. He gulped rotgut apple- and strawberry-flavored wine as his brothers mocked him. Performing for an amused audience, he danced in place, unaware how closely Van Pelt had been studying him. Bru announced, "Garcia, our very own queer hermit, has joined us." They serenaded him with "The Sweetheart of Omega" song, raising their cups as he thrust his arms in triumph.

Then the first Huns broke through the French doors. Were these Sigma Chis or TKEs crashing their party? Turnabout was fair play. Fraternities raided each other's houses, trying to steal booze and hustle sorority girls. But these were no frat boys.

A shaggy guy in a red bandana tackled Alex, and someone screamed, "Townies!" Thugs in dirty jeans and steel-toed boots were beating the crap out of Omegas, sending their dates clucking from the mayhem. Tom McKinney dangled upside down before two goons threw him aside. Mitchell Crouse cowered as more men came at them, overturning tables and hurling metal folding chairs.

A few tried to fight back, throwing pathetic fists in the air. But they were no match for these badasses. Alex was down, mouth bloody and face misshapen from the punches. His head thudded against the wall like a Raggedy Andy. Losing consciousness, he heard Van Pelt yell: "Hey, asshole, get off him!"

Bru was stripped to the waist, his shoulders, chest and arms imposing in the harsh basement light. He stood without fear, his tight jeans tucked inside polished cowboy boots as he shouted again at the bandana-wearing cretin.

"Let's get it on, motherfucker."

The guy lunged at Van Pelt, who hit him so hard he smashed into the flimsy wall paneling and crumpled. Two more came from behind, ramming Bru into the biggest, grossest man in the room. The giant wrapped him in his massive arms. Van Pelt's face was ablaze in pain.

"Squeeze the ever-living shit out of him, Darrell," someone hollered as his buddies whooped it up.

Omegas far outnumbered the intruders, but no one budged to rescue their president. Chip Trellendorf ran for the stairs to call the police. But he tripped and fell onto a hay bale, where he dared not move.

When it seemed he would be another casualty, Bru arched his back and headbutted the ogre three times, turning his nose into red pulp. Suddenly free, he kicked Darrell in the crotch with his custom-made boots. Three more rushed Van Pelt, who unveiled a hunting knife. They roared to a stop, eyes riveted on the blade. He slashed one across his chin.

"He cut me! He fuckin' cut me!" the guy wailed, grasping his wound.

"We're outta here," another yelled, helping his crimson comrade.

Others dragged the goliath Darrell. They barreled into the patio doors, shattering glass and splintering wood. The bitter night air couldn't chill the enthusiastic Omegas, who celebrated their hero, slapping him on the back as Crouse raised the champion's brawny right arm.

"Bru's our man. If Bru can't do it, nobody can!"

Deafening cheers of "Bru, Bru, Bru" resounded in the topsy-turvy rec room.

"Need a towel and ice," Van Pelt commanded as he tended to a battered Alex Merten. "Garcia's in bad shape. Get your asses in gear!"

Men in jeans and flannel shirts scurried. They ran for bath towels and to the kitchen ice machine. After taking Alex to his room, Bru bid his adoring frat brothers farewell and retired to his suite, where his raven-haired Pi Phi pinmate awaited.

When Nick heard of the battle with the townies, he knew Van Pelt would become a fraternity legend, and many more would be indebted to him as he had been.

Chapter 21

With Election Day three weeks away, polls showed Imani down by 5 to 8 percentage points. Months earlier, it was anticipated Van Pelt would win in a landslide. But his setbacks and inroads made by his opponent, with a strict stance on crime, moderate tax policies and progressive economic proposals, had closed the gap. Imani received endorsements from traditional Democratic blocs, such as the American Federation of Teachers and the AFL-CIO, and he added testimonials from current and former presidents Barack Obama, Bill Clinton and Jimmy Carter, as well as sports icons LeBron James and Jim Brown.

Nick credited Allyson and Megan for challenging Van Pelt while facing a fierce reaction from right-wingers. The women pursued the defiant candidate and raised awareness of sexual assault and domestic violence issues.

As the race tightened, more media called for DNA testing to resolve the paternity of Bernard Hart. *Plain Dealer* columnist Rivers wrote: "If Van Pelt has nothing to hide, why not submit a swab of saliva and be done with it? He can silence the critics with wit, grit and spit."

Adding to his woes were Jerome's legal problems: multiple counts, including possessing and distributing child pornography, statutory rape and sex trafficking. His lawyers had won an extension, postponing the trial until January 2013. However, based on the latest polls, the timing seemed secondary to more imminent obstacles.

Nick's visit with Kendra Jenkins had paid dividends as the feisty woman became a popular guest on numerous talk shows, including a *60 Minutes* episode with Lesley Stahl. The retired ER nurse discussed when she had treated a rape victim, later identified as Allyson Chambers Ryan. Jenkins' memory was aided by records located when newspaper editor Mike Kinsey filed requests for documents from Sussex General Hospital. Many files hadn't perished in a fire but were misplaced during an expansion project.

After Rachel Long's initial reply to the now-infamous Planned Parenthood event ("this incredibly sad spectacle"), the Van Pelt campaign didn't comment for nearly two weeks, choosing instead to hold raucous rallies with only "friendly" press invited. Critics called it a failed bunker mentality.

Then the Republicans announced a limited media briefing on Friday, October 19 at the Cincinnati Marriott RiverCenter Hotel, where the GOP gubernatorial candidate was headlining a national evangelical conference. The news release read in part: "Bruce Van Pelt offers comprehensive strategies for Ohio's future and rejects the slurs that have defiled his good name and derailed discussion of vital issues."

When Nick heard about the event from Megan, he knew he was going to attend. *"Sooner or later, one has to take sides. If one is to remain human."* He called Larry Rivers, who arranged for his press credentials as a *Plain Dealer* "special correspondent." For the first time since their alley brawl, he and Bru would be face to face.

U.S. and State of Ohio flags bookended the dais in the hotel ballroom. Beyond the staging area was a broad gray banner with red script lettering: "Onward Ohio! Vote Van Pelt!" Grand chandeliers sparkled above. The walls were cream with golden swirls. Tall rectangular mirrors were hung at 12-foot intervals. The carpeting was navy blue with mustard fleur-de-lis. Rows of cushioned folding chairs were divided by a wide center aisle.

Journalists were interspersed among the conference attendees. While media lined the room with cameras, boom mics and a sea of mobile technology, Nick carried a blue and white "Professional Reporter's Notebook" and his trusty Radio Shack digital recorder.

"Delamore, that you? What are you doing here?"

Rollo Standish was Midwest bureau chief for *TIME* before becoming a senior editor at *Politico*. They had been rookies together at the *Plain Dealer*. The dapper black journalist would have Nick review his copy prior to submitting stories in the "Tom Vail" days.

Vail was editor and publisher of the *PD* from the late sixties through early nineties. A reserved, respected man, he continually sought the elusive Pulitzer Prize. But the newspaper never received one on his watch. The closest Vail came was when Delamore was a Pulitzer finalist for reporting on organized crime's rise and fall in Northeast Ohio. He also garnered a number of prestigious awards—Sigma Delta Chi, IRE (Investigative Reporters and Editors) and APME (Associated Press Managing Editors).

When he was covering the Murray Hill gang, Standish would warn him: "Don't get blown up like Danny Greene, man. No story's worth getting killed over."

And Nick would lecture him on ending a sentence with a preposition: "Didn't they teach you grammar in the ghetto, Rollo?"

"Ghetto? I grew up in Grosse Pointe, brother."

Then he would erupt in one of his Carl Weathers-Apollo Creed guffaws, the Hollywood reference appropriate given his looks.

"Seriously, man, how'd you get in here?" he asked Nick. "Thought you were in Iowa."

"Indiana, but I'm on assignment for the *PD*," he said, flashing his badge. "Ya dig?"

"Ya dig?" Standish's voice resonated, attracting attention. "Damn, Delamore, you talk like it's 1969. You're in a time warp. Why you care about this guy anyway?"

"We were frat brothers in college."

"That true what he did to that woman?"

"And much more that will never come out." Nick checked his watch. "They're late. Not a good sign."

Standish straightened his pink silk tie, eyeing a striking *CNN* reporter.

"You haven't changed, Rollo. Could be her grandfather. What are you on ... wife number four?"

"Three and she's crazy for me."

"How you think this election will play out?" Nick asked as more attendees filed in.

"Van Pelt's unbeatable. Tea Party. Big-time Christian. Sully Kirby's son-in-law. Slam dunk. He'll keep dodging those rumors."

"Never say never."

"Whatever," Standish said, drawing closer. "When they look twice, you're on the ice. Time to meet that sweet young thing."

Nick was enjoying his antics when he saw the entourage. In addition to the usual political team members were a pair of behemoths as big as NFL linemen. *Why did he need bodyguards?*

Van Pelt made an impressive entrance: lean and broad-shouldered with pewter hair. He wore a charcoal suit with a starched white shirt and blood-red tie. His smirk was unmistakable as were his piercing eyes. He scanned the room between handshakes for the most desirable women.

Nick thought Rachel Long, who had been an effective spokesperson, would handle the introduction. But it was press secretary Barry Devonshire at the podium, a heavy man in an ill-fitting sport coat, his forehead lathered in sweat.

"Ladies and gentlemen," Devonshire said timidly. "After Mr. Van Pelt's opening remarks, we will have a limited time for Q and A."

But that didn't satisfy this impatient gathering. Hands shot up, and the bombardment began. Devonshire recoiled like a clumsy ballerina. He turned toward the candidate and then back to the clustered media, stammering as the ginger-bearded campaign manager in the corner issued a death stare. Van Pelt stepped forward, put a hand on Devonshire's shoulder and pushed by him, baring his teeth like a Doberman.

"You're all champing at the bit. Can't wait to get to me, can you? Well you heard what Barry said before you all mugged him. I've got a prepared statement, and then we'll open up the floor."

The noise died down.

"That's better," he said. "At the very least, let's agree to be civil. I want to begin by introducing my beautiful wife and daughters."

On cue, four slim, radiant women with flowing blonde hair entered the room in pastel dresses and high heels. The daughters were in their twenties and thirties, and their mother could pass for an older sister. A model family portrait. For a moment, Nick questioned if Bru had evolved. *Did marriage and fatherhood drive the demons away?*

Not a chance. There was that cocksure pose: left foot ahead of the right, hands on hips. Van Pelt's eyes shifted to where the fair-haired reporter was standing too close to "Romeo" Rollo Standish. Then his wife coughed, and he refocused.

"Let me start by saying how blessed I am to be here with Susie and my girls, Sarah, Sheryl and Susannah. So proud of them and my record of empowering women as an elected official, businessman and philanthropist. When I was in Congress, most of my senior staff were female. In our charity, Gather My Sheep, women worldwide are in executive positions. And in our household, I assure you ladies run the operation."

He heard some light chuckling and proceeded: "What I'm truly excited to announce today is the establishment of the Christian Adoption Network—C.A.N. This organization will address the crushing problem of unwanted pregnancies and the tragedy of more than a million abortions annually nationwide. It is a 'CAN-Do' solution to one of our nation's gravest social, moral and spiritual problems.

"We're giving women positive alternatives like prenatal counseling and other essential services. And I ask my liberal Democrat challenger, Mayor Imani, to promote this resource rather than Planned Parenthood, which incentivizes women to find an easy way out. Our Christian Adoption Network, CAN and will save and restore lives."

Those who had predicted a defensive posture were out-maneuvered. Van Pelt was diverting the media's focus by initiating a faith-based program for women. *Some things never change.* Nick cued the line from a Bob Seger tune: *"You always won every time you placed a bet."*

Concluding, the candidate acknowledged applause from the handpicked business, civic and religious leaders. But the respite was temporary. The *CNN* reporter stepped away from Standish and closer to Van Pelt, where he was beaming at his wife and daughters.

Her voice unnerved him: "Allyson Chambers Ryan has said she chose adoption over abortion as an unwed mother and college student. But she also states you sexually assaulted her and is the father of her first-born son."

News crews captured the candidate's intensity. They rushed microphones and recorders to the podium as he set his shoulders.

"Let me be very, very clear," he said, his words rising like a Pentecostal preacher. "I have never, EVER sexually assaulted anyone in my life. These attacks are salacious and insulting. This is the lowest form of character assassination, and it's happening at a critical time for Ohioans."

Someone asked: "But you're campaigning as a man of Christian values. Isn't this level of scrutiny appropriate for candidates?"

Van Pelt: "Scrutiny is appropriate. Witch hunts and slander are not. Next question."

Nick was reading a text from Megan ("Can U believe this?") when he heard, "Do you deny having sex with Allyson Chambers when you were a student at Merriman University?"

His response: "I've admitted I was with many women before marriage. And I've repented for my past. Can all of you in the media say the same about your lives?"

The *CNN* reporter sharpened her pursuit: "Did you rape Allyson Chambers in November 1972 at a fraternity party?"

Van Pelt glared at her for several awkward seconds before answering: "Have you no shame? Have you no shame? We have just introduced a new program to help women in need, and I refuse to let you drag me and my family through the mud. We have a prayer service to attend."

He and his attendants left in a flurry of activity as Barry Devonshire blabbered, pointing to a stack of glossy folders: "The Christian Adoption Network's 'CAN-Do Program' is detailed in these press kits. Please take one."

Nick hurried to a rear exit. He had worked enough scandals and investigations to know that whether you were a candidate or a crime boss, you sent your flunkies out the front to distract while you used an escape route. When he reached the back parking lot, Van Pelt was getting into a black Escalade, joining his wife. Men in dark pants, windbreakers and sunglasses blocked any access. But Nick was well within shouting distance for a native New Yorker.

"Hey, Bru. Bru!"

Hearing his college nickname, he took the bait, his eyes settling on Nick.

"Dago Delamore. What are you doing in Ohio? You work for an Indiana paper," he said confidently.

They were a study in contrasts. Van Pelt wore an expensive tailored suit. He was trim, well-coiffed and polished down to his supple black Italian loafers. Delamore was paunchy and rumpled in khakis, an open-necked blue shirt and off-the-rack blazer from

J.C. Penney. He wore brown Nunn Bush Comfort Gel shoes. His windblown hair completed the guise of an adjunct instructor caught between classes.

"Here as a special correspondent," he said, fingering his ID.

"Well good for you."

"How about a question for old times' sake? Unless you're gonna chicken out."

A bodyguard approached, but Nick stood his ground. More media appeared on the scene. Word had spread of a skirmish between the candidate and an unidentified man. Cameras were rolling. Wary of any surprises, he removed his wire-rim glasses and put them in his coat pocket.

Van Pelt spoke to his wife and then came at him. They were at arm's length, sizing each other up as if punches would be thrown. Instead they tried to wound with words.

"Give it your best shot, Delamore," he said aloud on this blustery day. "The way your career has tanked, this is your last stand."

Nick was unfazed. "Bruce, why weren't you charged in the death of Clarice Johnson at Merriman University in May 1973? Did your father's lawyers make a plea deal with the local prosecutor?" He added the second query to confuse him. It felt as good as slamming a sudden left hook to the body.

Van Pelt waved him off as one would a heckler at a ball game. He retreated to his Escalade while breezes rustled the trees. The press trailed the candidate's car, then turned and shouted at Delamore: "Who are you?"; "How do you know Van Pelt?"; "Who is Clarice Johnson?"

He motioned, and Standish nodded.

"Guys, *Politico* has an exclusive on this," Nick said.

"A joint *CNN-Politico* exclusive."

Hearing his new female colleague's proclamation, Standish shrugged his shoulders. Nick walked among the media politely declining questions. He shook hands with Standish.

"Ready to go?"

"Right on. Whose car?"

"Hers."

He pointed to a white CR-V with the engine running. Nick recognized the cameraman with the Reds cap from the hotel ballroom.

"My folks live near here, and they're out of town," the freelance videographer said, driving through Covington,

Kentucky, minutes from downtown Cincinnati. "We can do the taping at their house."

"If we're being followed, it'll be a goddamn disaster," Ms. *CNN* sniped from the front seat as the men rode like obedient children in the rear.

Standish whispered: "Eye of the storm, brother. Balls to the wall."

The CR-V whipped into the driveway of a stately brick home with a wide attached rear garage, below street level and out of view from passing traffic.

"Breaking News" alerts dominated afternoon media coverage: "Ohio Republican candidate named in 1970s campus death." Video footage showed the one-time fraternity brothers squaring off in a hotel parking lot.

Nick knew the reaction from Van Pelt's team would be savage. *"Delamore is a disgraced and deeply troubled man, recruited by the Democrats to sabotage our candidate."* He also knew his fate at the *Times-Union*. He would be dismissed for ethical violations.

In his interview, Nick fully supported Allyson's account of her rape in November 1972. He said he should have gone to the police, though she asked him not to. He then reconstructed the tragic night six months later when a Sussex, Ohio, woman, later identified as Clarice Johnson, died of acute alcohol poisoning. He said she had been sexually assaulted by Omega frat brothers led by Bruce Van Pelt.

"My roommate, Alex Merten, had confronted the men in our fraternity bathroom after a Hawaiian luau party. But he was unsuccessful in stopping them." Nick described how he and Merten tried to save Johnson, taking her to the hospital. Looking into the camera, he added: "But it was too late. We should have reported what happened. Alex wanted to, but I stopped him because I was afraid we could be implicated."

The *CNN* reporter asked: "Where is Alex Merten now? We would like to speak with him."

"He passed away earlier this year."

"Are there any other witnesses, including former fraternity members, who can confirm your version of events?" she asked.

"No. Those who took part will deny it and call me a liar or worse."

"Nick," Standish asked with a dramatic pause. "How do you respond that you could be part of a ... ploy by Kwame Imani?"

"Why would I do that?"

"Maybe it's a vendetta between you and Van Pelt. Or because of your ex-wife's involvement with Imani. I mean with his campaign."

"Listen," Nick said. "This isn't a vendetta. And Megan Bradley can speak for herself. She has done remarkable work for years running Ohio's oldest women's shelter and crisis center. I don't care what others say about me. All I know is I'm telling the truth."

When the taping ended, Nick clasped Standish's arm. "Cheap shot bringing Megan into this."

"Have to uphold my journalistic integrity."

"Among other things," Ms. *CNN* said, trying to lighten the mood as Nick imagined what lay ahead.

"Eye of the storm, brother. Balls to the wall."

Chapter 22

On I-70 West, Nick called Megan, who answered on the second ring. "I sure as hell didn't expect this," she said, confusing him. It seemed she was speaking to someone else, and he had accidentally joined the conversation.

"What did you say?"

"Clarice Johnson. All this time lying about her death. That's pathological. How do you live with yourself?"

The day had taken its toll. Nick was light-headed. All he could muster was: "I don't know, Megan. I'm sorry for hurting you. But I was trying to look out for Alex."

"You were covering your own ass," she said, dismantling his meager defense. "Hope to God you weren't involved in her death."

"How can you say that?" he asked. "How can you think I hurt that woman? Alex and I wanted to help her."

"Maybe now I understand his suicide," she said. "He felt guilty all this time. But you were his best friend, the one who convinced him not to go to the police."

"Thought it was the right call."

"You could have brought charges against Van Pelt and the others even years later."

"What difference does it make? In your mind, I let them get away with it. Like with Allyson, no matter what I do to make good, it will never be enough," he said, awaiting her final censure.

Megan's anger eased: "Hold on. I don't believe it. They've already lined up a Swift Boat group of old frat guys to denounce you—CEOs, a Christian college president, even an Air Force colonel. They're all saying you're a lying, jealous drunk."

"Can they say I'm a drunk on the air?"

"Not funny," she said. "Your reputation is shot."

"Couldn't get much worse."

"You shouldn't make light of this."

"Not many options."

"By the way, Kwame wants to talk with you."

"Why?"

"To thank you for what you did."

"Whatever. He can call me. If nothing else, we can discuss you."

"You're unbelievable."

"My consistency should count for something."

"I'm still pissed," she said. "But you handled yourself well today."

"Can I get that in writing?"

"Don't push your luck, Delamore," she said, ending the call.

Again the phone rang. *What else did Megan have to say?* It wasn't her but Miranda. When they last spoke, she was very subdued. This call was different; she sounded happy.

"Hey, Unk, you're a big-time celebrity."

"Yeah, right."

"For real," she said. "You're rocking the internet."

"Things just sort of happened."

"You were very brave."

"Finally, huh?"

"Didn't mean it that way. Hope you know that."

"I do, hon. Thanks. So how's everything going?"

"Awesome news on Stacy," Miranda said. "She's out of her coma. Her mom said the doctor is only allowing family to visit until she can adjust to all the stimuli. But she's finally awake. Isn't that great?"

"That's wonderful. You've been such a good friend to her and her parents."

"Maybe we're both on a roll."

"Make mine a sweet roll."

"That's so lame," she said. "But I love you, Unk, even when you say the dumbest things."

"Love you too," Nick said.

"See you soon?"

"Absolutely. Take care, punkin."

"You haven't called me that since I was a little girl."

"Must be feeling nostalgic."

After Miranda's call, Nick cruised the last 50 miles, even welcoming the highway sign for Carlson. That night he reviewed his messages, which included praise from both brothers. Christopher: "Mom and Dad are bursting with pride for what you did. Bless you, bro." Matt: "Maybe you're not a washed-up journalist. Stay strong. Keep punching."

The good vibes lasted only a couple days following the "Van Pelt Ambush," as *MSNBC* called it. Most *Times-Union* personnel avoided eye contact when Nick crossed the newsroom. On Mondays in the fall, sports editor Sam Miller would usually drop by to settle lost football bets. But there was no friendly chatter this morning. One person who had greeted him was Thalia Smart, the lanky security guard and former captain of Carlson High School's 1998 state championship girls volleyball team.

"Mr. Delamore, you're all over YouTube," she said. "What's next—*The Daily Show*?"

He deflected her compliment. *Lot of good it did.* Van Pelt had retained his lead in the polls despite the Clarice Johnson revelation.

Nate Popovich stood by Nick's desk, handed him a glazed donut and unloaded.

"Jesus H. Christ, Delamore," he said. "Did you have a nervous breakdown on Friday?"

"Just sort of happened."

"Most train wrecks just sort of happen."

"Good metaphor."

"Ms. Paula will have your head on a plate for this."

"You laying odds?"

"Can I have your laptop?" he asked when Nick received a call to meet with Hoagland. He flipped off Popovich and sauntered to the editor's office.

Paula Hoagland was an attractive fortysomething with a prominent bust, tempting eyes and naughty laugh. But her Nordic skin had been disfigured by years of artificial tanning. It had the color and texture of a basketball. She dressed boldly chic, boosted by tight blouses and mid-thigh skirts. Her adornments included a small red rose at the tip of her spine.

Nick knew many of Hoagland's intimacies, becoming her lover within weeks of his joining the newspaper in 2011. They had taken precautions to allay suspicions. Their "rendezvous" were arranged at a motel by the Indianapolis airport, an hour from Carlson.

In bed she was a notch above satisfactory by Nick's late-life standards, more nimble than predicted and within a reasonable age range. His flings with much younger women had ended due to incompatibility. That was his official explanation. The reality was he couldn't perform as in his glory days, and he wouldn't rely on a little blue pill.

He hadn't developed any romantic feelings for Hoagland, but the sex was preferable to cyberporn or bar pickups. He rejected online dating services. They were as feeble as classified ads in alternative newsweeklies.

The more they saw each other, the kinkier Hoagland's carnal preferences. She knew there wasn't a chance for love with this dour loner. To keep him energized, she intensified their conjugal visits. But her risqué methods had backfired on Memorial Day weekend.

Nick said he needed a break. Translation: *Leave me alone.* But Hoagland misinterpreted him and booked a weekend for them at a pricey downtown Indianapolis B&B. He agreed to go on the condition he would get an extra day off the next week. He was irritable upon arriving, and things only got worse when she gave him a box containing handcuffs, a miniature whip, a studded neck collar and black vibrator.

"What is this crap?" he asked, tossing aside the paraphernalia.

"You big prude," she chided him, adjusting her collar and rolling on the bed in various nude poses. "Come on, loosen up. Even Ben Franklin liked a little S&M."

"Then go screw Franklin," Nick said, removing her fingers from his crotch. He zipped up his jeans and marched to the door as she unleashed a vulgar hailstorm. Unrepentant, he said they had been using each other.

"No harm, no foul."

"Get out, you bastard!" She hurled her vibrator, narrowly missing him.

"Does this mean no extra day off?"

Since their "breakup," Hoagland had treated him with indifference. He was merely an employee and an unreliable one at that. There would be no mercy for Delamore in the wake of the Van Pelt episode.

Entering the executive office, he saw her Valencia facial. *Just in time for Halloween.*

"Please sit down," she said stiffly.

Another demerit in a checkered journalistic career.

"Paula, want to apologize for ... ."

"For what, Nick? For being an arrogant prick?"

"I know you're still mad at me for Memorial Day weekend. But is this a personal or professional reprimand?"

"Don't kid yourself. This has nothing to do with us and everything to do with your reckless, unethical behavior."

She stood with her back to him, watching the street scene below. Ashen skies cast a dull sheen on the potholed roads and sidewalks littered with hamburger wrappers, plastic slushy cups and cigarette butts. A nondescript Puerta del Sol Mexican restaurant, a pawnshop and a bail bonds storefront flanked the *Times-Union* building.

"What were you thinking?" she asked, turning around. "Do you realize how many rules you violated by attending an Ohio media event without permission, posing as a *Plain Dealer* correspondent and accosting a candidate?"

"It's complicated."

"No, it isn't," she replied. "Last night a Gannett VP asked who hired this lunatic?"

Nick almost said, "You did, Paula," when she threw her pen, hitting him in the forehead.

"Hey, that hurt."

"This is how you repay me for giving you a chance when no one else would? By pulling this stunt?"

"I am sorry, Paula," he said standing. But she thrust out her palm to stiff-arm him.

"You need to go to HR," she said, facing the tinted glass windows. "They'll discuss the severance package and health insurance."

He put the red and gold *T-U* pen on her desk and slowly closed the office door. This wasn't the first time he had to vacate a newsroom. Didn't take long to load one Bankers Box. No trinkets or photographs. A coffee mug, flash drives, a digital recorder, notebooks, Webster's dictionary, Roget's Thesaurus, Bartlett's Book of Quotations and a dog-eared AP Stylebook. Earlier he had turned in his Dell laptop to the HR Nazis.

People were muted but observant as he packed up. They weren't mourning his departure. Other than Nate Popovich, Sam Miller and copy editor Jeanne Thompson, he didn't know most of his co-workers. It made leaving that much easier.

Nick had moved often as a kid. He knew what it was like to be in one school, one classroom, one lunchroom, one playground one day and at a new locale the next. Compared with those situations, this farewell was easy.

Termination pay was for 90 days instead of the usual 30. He was receiving the added compensation, having negotiated that bump in benefits in lieu of a higher starting salary. A lesson learned from prior dismissals.

Next step? Take advantage of his month-to-month lease, leave Carlson and relocate to a better climate. He didn't want to be in Indiana any longer than necessary. The holidays were coming and so was the bad weather.

He could call in some favors for freelance writing jobs. His journalism career may have ended, but he could produce clean copy. *Words, words, words. Words that work.* Maybe he would print up business cards.

After three scotches and a bland sirloin steak dinner at the local Applebee's, Nick watched the latest NFL news on *SportsCenter*. He had two calls. One was from a columnist with *The Cincinnati Enquirer*, who had also attended Merriman in the early 1970s. The other call was from Megan.

"I know you had your reasons for not telling me about Clarice Johnson," she said. "Like trying to protect Alex."

"Should have told you sooner. No excuses."

She was sympathetic about his firing and he whimsical.

"Maybe I could be Imani's press secretary if he gets elected."

"Wouldn't that be ironic," she said. "I'll let you know if I hear of anything."

Their relationship had endured despite the disagreements and deceptions. Why hadn't she written him off? Why the second chances? Maybe it was pity, certainly not obligation. All the credit belonged to her. Quite simply, she was a better person than ... him. *Yes, him not he.*

Nick regretted how inconsiderate he had been as her husband. Before Megan became shelter director, she was a case manager and on call as a member of the SART (Sexual Assault Response Team) protocol. She spent long hours in emergency rooms as a client advocate. Compared to her, he was a shallow scribe courting fame, who grew to resent her zeal.

His typical complaint: "Why do you have to be the one to go? Can't someone else do it?" When she described how the ER shifts rotated, he could only think how it affected him. He said her work schedule was sabotaging their marriage. And that rationalization made him hunt for romance when he was a hotshot Cleveland reporter.

Larry Rivers said it was a good thing Nick didn't care about social media. He was getting hammered for assailing "a good Christian family man who was destined to be Ohio's next governor." Such reaction could have hurt a more sensitive soul, but he cavalierly rejected the criticism: "Fuck 'em if they can't take a joke."

Gunner Gunderson wrote a letter, praising his long overdue reckoning with Van Pelt. It was the exception as much of Nick's "fan mail" was full of disgust and condemnation. Jim Merten called to say he knew Alex would be grateful. Allyson sent a sweet card, thanking him for standing by her when it mattered.

"You're a good man, Nick Delamore."

Chapter 23

Van Pelt and his team were smug in the campaign's last days. On Tuesday evening, October 30, there was an executive meeting in a downtown Cincinnati boardroom high in the Carew Tower. Built in 1930, the 49-story, 574-foot Art Deco structure was a historic edifice in the Queen City, providing a panoramic view of the Ohio River, the Great American Baseball Park, where the Reds played, and northern Kentucky, where Bruce was a child of privilege.

Tonight, emboldened by trappings of success, he felt invincible. The election was a week away, and he was ahead in most polls. An ad barrage challenging Imani's smear tactics was airing hourly in all major Ohio markets. Cronies Mitchell Crouse, Chip Trellendorf and Tom McKinney were featured in interviews and commercials. The 80-year-old pastor of the family church in Lexington was enlisted as part of the media effort. He was filmed leafing through a scrapbook of boyhood photos of an angelic Van Pelt. The video was a hit.

But Senator Sully Kirby wasn't taking anything for granted. He had flown in from Washington to run the meeting. In attendance were Bruce and Susie, along with consultants, statisticians, scribes and party loyalists. Conspicuously absent was advisor Rachel Long.

Men and women in business attire lined the dark cherry wood conference table. Legal pads and sharpened pencils were at the ready in gleaming silver trays. Ice water pitchers and crystal glass tumblers sat on imported brass coasters.

"Let's get moving," Kirby said. "Meter's running."

"Lot of firepower here. Right, Susie?" Bruce asked.

His wife was feverishly working her phone. She blurted out: "Where's Rachel? Why isn't she here?"

Bruce replied: "I told her to take the night off to be with Lara. Some school function."

"You told her? Never mind. Keep going," Susie directed.

"My sentiments exactly," Kirby said. "Let's see the latest Imani ad."

The 10- by 15-foot screen dropped with a barely audible hum. A consultant with gelled hair clicked away on his MacBook Pro, playing the 60-second spot. The life and times of Kwame Imani were presented in a rapid collage of photos and clips, portraying his visionary passage from social worker to city councilman to years as Cleveland's mayor, guiding the city through crisis and conflict. The video emphasized the stark contrast between the wealthy Republican with a questionable past and this inspirational Democrat, who overcame hardship to enhance people's lives in his native Ohio. It ended with the tag line: "A man and leader you can trust."

"I'm all weepy inside," said one of the suits, sparking snide comments in the room.

"Could swing undecideds," said Howard Sykes, the goateed pollster, scrolling his tablet. "They're stressing the reliability angle."

"It's no angle," Kirby said. "They're discrediting our candidate's legitimacy."

"Come on, Sully, a silly slogan won't change anything at this stage. Howard said we had a solid lead."

"Listen, plenty of votes can turn in the final week," Kirby said, aiming his Cross ballpoint pen like a derringer at his son-in-law. "This is no time to be complacent. Who else has something to say? Stop staring at your damn phones, or I'll throw your fancy asses out of here."

At Imani headquarters in Cleveland's landmark Terminal Tower, the candidate was in his spartan office on a call with Nick Delamore, while a skeleton crew monitored TV and other media.

"Wanted to thank you for what you did," Imani said flatly, viewing poll results on his laptop.

"You're welcome, Kevin. I mean Kwame," Nick said from his recliner.

"You love doing that don't you—messing with my name?"

"Maybe I like ruffling your feathers."

"Heard you were let go at your paper. What's next?"

"You know as well as I do. I'm damaged goods. Although I did get a call from some third-rate publisher to write a book on our Merriman years. You, me, Van Pelt ... ."

"And Megan?"

"Knew you would bring her into this," Nick said, feigning anger. "You always had the hots for her."

"The hots? Who uses language like that anymore?"

"How's obfuscation? That better?"

"If you only knew how much she cares, you'd get your ass back to Cleveland and ... ."

"And what? You offering me a job if you get elected?"

"Very funny. You couldn't stand working for me. But you should hang out your shingle."

"Appreciate the advice and your thanks. Though you give me too much credit. I didn't have any plan to go after Van Pelt. Just couldn't let that self-righteous sonufabitch get away with it."

"How do you think it was being on stage debating him, knowing what he did in college? And word is he's just as bad today, but he's got his own Gestapo and fixers."

"That's why I'm rooting for the good guys. So keep hope alive, *Kwame*."

Imani was cackling as the call ended.

On Thursday, November 1, many Ohio residents awoke to snowfall dusting yards and slickening streets. The winter weather led morning newscasts. But by midday, meteorological updates were replaced with shocking headlines: Ohio Republican gubernatorial candidate Bruce Van Pelt was accused of statutory rape by a senior advisor, who claimed he had been molesting her 15-year-old daughter.

Wearing a black cashmere Burberry coat, a composed Rachel Long spoke with the assembled press outside the Indian Hill Police Department. Her beauty and erudite persona captivated viewers. She said she had met with law enforcement officials, including the district attorney. Her genteel words were laced with outrage.

"I discovered within the last 24 hours that Bruce Van Pelt has had illicit sexual relations with my underage daughter since early this summer. We are pursuing rape charges."

What Long didn't include in her statement was Lara's pregnancy and that Van Pelt had urged her to have an abortion without Rachel's knowledge. Lara overcame her fear, confided in her mother, and the sordid tale was exposed. The vivacious teenager had been a straight-A student at the elite Miami Valley Christian Academy, the preparatory school the Van Pelt daughters had attended. The families also went to the same church. Rachel had known Bruce and Susie since her divorce and relocation to hometown Cincinnati in 2004. The senior campaign aide had also been legal counsel to and a board member of the Gather My Sheep charity.

Because of her history with the Van Pelts, Rachel was pleased that Lara enjoyed working as a babysitter for their daughter Susannah. Summer duties included supervising the children in their spacious swimming pool. Bruce had been respectful toward Rachel and protective of Lara when she was a chubby kid, giving her access to his personal driver and indulging her with the latest iPhones and iPads. But he turned predatory as she blossomed in pubescence, and her mother's taxing schedule kept her away from their luxury condominium on Hickory Lane in Indian Hill, the affluent Cincinnati hamlet where the Van Pelts lived.

In a recent puff piece, Bruce discussed how close he had grown to Lara: "I feel like a father figure, or maybe a grandfather figure would be more fitting." Now, in light of the tawdry allegations, that narrative was utter fiction, a facade for repeated encounters involving alcohol, marijuana, Quaaludes and Ecstasy to manipulate Lara into compliance. She became withdrawn, and Rachel said her academics and extra-curricular activities had suffered.

"I should have been more aware of what was happening to my own daughter," Long told *CNN*'s Anderson Cooper. "But I was betrayed by a man I believed was a close friend."

When asked by Cooper when she had last spoken with Van Pelt, Long stated that early on the morning of November 1, hours before she went public with the rape charges, he offered a $5 million bribe for her silence. He said if Lara didn't want an abortion, he could assist with his newly formed Christian Adoption Network.

"And what did you say?" Cooper asked, his azure eyes exuding empathy.

"Told him I was recording the call. Then I hung up and contacted the police."

Van Pelt defined Long's assertions as a "premeditated, slanderous performance by an ambitious woman with a promiscuous daughter, who tried to entice him." He said he had retained Rachel Long as an advisor because of her excellent qualifications and work history with his wife's charity. But she had exploited him. He vigorously denied acting inappropriately with Lara, whom he had known "since she was a little girl."

He implored supporters to consider his years of public service. With the sincerity of a televangelist, he spoke on *FOX-News*: "I hope and pray you will trust in what I have said. Thank you so very much. God bless you all." The segment ended with him looking weary and dejected.

On Sunday, November 4, Van Pelt launched his last resort to salvage the election, which some analysts called "Nixonian" and others "Clintonian." He bought prime-time spots in Cincinnati, Dayton and Columbus. With his stone-faced wife sitting by him on the dark leather sofa and a blazing fireplace in the background, he issued a long-winded confession. Denying he had engaged in sexual intercourse, he admitted to "ill-advised and immoral relations." Out of vanity and weakness, he had succumbed to a beguiling temptress and compromised his Christian values. He apologized to "all those he had hurt," concluding with a final plea to voters: "If you will forgive me, I vow to learn from this terrible mistake and to be a faithful steward for the citizens of this great state."

He could have saved his empty appeals and fortune spent in desperation. His staunchest allies abandoned him. Cleveland Mayor Kwame Imani was elected governor of Ohio by a margin of 72 percent to 23 percent (a majority early absentee votes). Five percent of the ballots went to the Libertarian candidate. With Van Pelt's life upended and political career in ashes, it would be up to his legal team to manage his defense. Meanwhile, news junkies fed on scurrilous details.

Nick fielded media inquiries on the prurient nature of Van Pelt's downfall. He reminded interviewers of the 2005 Pulitzer Prize for investigative reporting won by Nigel Jaquiss of Oregon's *Willamette Week*. The 2004 newspaper series revealed an extensive cover-up in the administration of popular Democratic governor Neil Goldschmidt, who at 49 surprised many by announcing in February 1990 he would not seek reelection.

Jaquiss detailed how years earlier as mayor of Portland, Goldschmidt had conducted a three-year liaison with his family's babysitter. He was in his mid-thirties and she a young teen. The abused victim, a parochial school honor student, subsequently had psychological problems and drug dependency issues, several arrests, a rape in Seattle and a federal prison term. In 1994, she received a $350,000 out-of-court settlement from Goldschmidt in exchange for her silence.

"As evil as Bruce Van Pelt's actions are, the Neil Goldschmidt story shows the extent to which people will shield those in power, even if they are corrupt and criminal. That's a valuable lesson to glean from all of this," Nick told *Politico*'s Rollo Standish.

Megan should have been elated by the election result, but she said a better word was relieved. Nick agreed with her assessment.

"Glad the way things turned out?" she asked.

"Do you mean am I glad Kwame won?"

"Not exactly what I meant, but are you?"

"Sure, even though he still has a thing for you."

"And you're still wacked," she said warmly. "Can we please move on? ... Any final thoughts on Van Pelt?"

"Never really understood him," Nick said. "All I had were memories masquerading as insight."

"Very profound. Any regrets?"

"Sorry that Alex couldn't be here."

"For sure," she said. "Last thing before I go. You want to come to my house for Thanksgiving? Getting some old friends together, including a few who would like to see you after all these years."

"Can't be many left."

"Some people can be very forgiving."

"Thanks for the invite, but I'm going East. Been in contact pretty regularly with Joey since Mom died. Many mea culpas on my part. He invited me to spend Turkey Day with the Maraldo clan in New York."

"That's great. Please give him and the family my best. Good to hear you're trying to make things right."

"We'll see," he said. "Let's not get ahead of ourselves. This is me we're talking about."

"This is I," she corrected.

"I'm impressed."

"You should be."

"Have been for a long time. ... What's this? ... Megan Bradley speechless? I don't believe it."

"Maybe we're both impressed."

Now it was his turn to pause.

"Any more thoughts on Cleveland?" she asked.

"Christopher said I could stay with him and Inez for a while."

"Nice of them to offer, but do they have room?"

"If not I can put things in storage."

"Listen," she said. "May be crazy for suggesting this. Getting all sentimental with Christmas coming."

"You sentimental?"

"Watch it or you'll blow a good opportunity."

"Fire away."

"Have all kinds of space in my basement. Should have downsized, but I love this drafty old house."

"You always did. This invitation for me or my stuff?"

"You ... maybe," she said. "Your stuff definitely."

"Appreciate it. OK if I let you know in a week or so?"

"No problem. Just keep me posted."

"Will do," he said. "And thanks for not giving up on me."

"Call me a soft touch. Safe travels to New York."

Clicking off his phone, Nick poured a nightcap and lifted his glass.

"Onward, Father Alex. Adelante, Padre Alejandro!"

Muy bueno, mi amigo.

"Haunting my ass? Well, I deserve it."

Chapter 24

Nick told Christopher that rebuilding his life at 60 was like training for a bout in a *Rocky* movie. The holiday season kicked off with his "apology tour." He drove to Carmel, New York, for Linda Maraldo's Thanksgiving feast.

Joey, his wife, Eve, and their teen daughters, Jennifer and Emily, were the first to meet him. Phil and Linda's daughters, Claire and Becky, their husbands and Claire's three rambunctious boys came later. One of the black-haired lads strutted up to him and asked, "Who the heck are you?"

"I'm Papa Nick."

"Yeah, he's Saint Nick's cousin," Phil howled from the kitchen.

"Good one, Maraldo. Forgot how witty you are."

After dinner, Joey brought his daughters to where Nick sat with a mug of coffee watching the snowfall. Father and son were similar in size and shape. Joey had also been a linebacker on his high school football team. Slowed by an arthritic hip, he too lumbered like his dad. Apart from that resemblance, they differed. Joey had an easygoing disposition like his mother's side of the family. The darkly handsome son had a light Bronx accent, rounding off consonants and "tawking" as Nick did growing up in Barrington, New York.

"My girls are aspiring writers," Joey said. "Jennifer works on her high school newspaper and yearbook, and Emily enjoys poetry and short stories."

He and his daughters sat on the flowered print couch next to the matching loveseat. Nick had a short interview with each grandchild, asking about their favorite books and authors and other literary topics.

"I have trouble getting started sometimes," Emily said.

"They call that writer's block," said her big sister.

"Had that disease my entire life," Nick said, amusing the girls and their dad. "Worse than the flu."

"Never liked writing," Joey said. "I'm a numbers guy."

"And it's served you well," Nick said, tapping his son's knee. "Corporate reinsurance, correct? Don't know much about the business, but kudos to you on your success."

Joey looked kindly at his father. He had spent many years viewing photos of a youthful, barrel-chested, curly-haired Nick Delamore. Now this man wore bifocals, had a well-creased face and a sagging midsection.

He was glad his girls had the chance to be with their grandfather, if only briefly. Joey was a pragmatist. His mom had prepared him as a child not to get his hopes up when it came to relying on Nick.

"Take it as it comes," Linda would tell her son when he asked when he would hear from his "real" father. For all intents and purposes, Phil was his dad. Nick was an enigmatic man who would occasionally drop in.

Maybe this Thanksgiving would lead to more get-togethers. That would be great, but we'll take it as it comes, Joey decided. As the daylight dimmed, making Linda and Phil's house seem that much cozier, he left his daughters with Papa Nick. He regaled them with stories of tracking down "bad guys" in Cleveland when he was an intrepid crime reporter for a newspaper called the *Plain Dealer*.

"That's a funny name," Emily said, pronouncing it "newspaypah." She was blonde-haired and blue-eyed like her mother. And much shyer than her very assured older sister.

"I've heard stranger ones," Jennifer said. "The *Times-Picayune* in New Orleans."

"Good job," he told his outspoken granddaughter. "That sure is one strange name."

When Nick found Linda, she was cleaning up the kitchen and putting dishes away in leaded-glass cabinets. He and Phil had been toasting with Amaretto. Maybe it was the liqueur that elicited his apology. But he believed his desire to make amends came from good intentions.

"I forgave you long ago," she said, her face still lovely.

"I was immature and stupid. Not to mention selfish."

"And very frisky," she said, smiling and shaking her head.

"Yeah, that too," Nick said. "But I'm sorry for hurting you and Joey. I'm thankful Phil stepped in and was the father I wasn't. He's a great guy."

"The best," Linda said. "No offense."

"None taken. You both have done well."

"I wish you never went to Ohio," she said. "You changed when you went out there. And then you met that horrible Van Pelt. Like he was the devil himself."

"Maybe he was," Nick said. "You follow all that political hoopla?"

"And the filth from his disgusting life," Linda said. "But that was something seeing you on TV."

"Things happen for a reason."

"They do," she said, stroking his cheek. "Thanks for coming. It meant a great deal to Joey, Eve and the girls. And to me."

"Not me, you no good bum," Phil said, entering the kitchen. For a hefty man, he had quick feet, dodging Nick and throwing a light jab at his chin. "Don't you owe me dough from the old days?"

"Dream on," he said, patting Phil's bulging stomach. "Sure you're not pregnant? Marone, that's a big labanz!"

The three embraced, and it was the happiest Nick had felt ... in forever.

He spent an extra night in Carmel after Linda and Phil lured him with a homemade "macaroni and gravy" dinner. Phil translated: "It's pasta and sauce, spazzdick. That's what you get for eating at the freakin' Olive Garden out in those cornfields."

When Eve asked Nick about his retirement plans, the room grew quiet. He sipped from his glass of Lambrusco. He could have taken offense, but there was no tension in his reply.

"Guess it's one step at a time, as my dad used to say."

"That means he's S.O.L."

Linda scolded her husband: "Phil, your mouth. The girls."

"What's S.O.L. mean, Daddy?" Emily asked Joey.

"It's dirty," Jennifer said.

"No it isn't," Joey said, trying to keep a straight face. "Papa Phil is only kidding with Papa Nick."

"But what's it mean, S.O.L.?" Emily asked, swiveling her head between her father and laughing grandfathers.

"It means *sure ... outta ... luck* ... S.O.L.," Nick said with a wink. "Sometimes I'm sure outta luck."

"Can say that again," Phil said, trying to mess with his old buddy's hair.

"You're just jealous cuz you're bald as a cue ball."

The men kept joking while Linda shared stories from when their kinship was in full bloom. Joey listened intently, holding hands with Eve.

Nick left Saturday morning, pledging to revisit in the new year. He drove south toward New York City, stopping in Valhalla to visit the Gates of Heaven Cemetery. He had made calls to Westchester County listings, trying to track down his boxing coach. An aged cousin said that Ken Arturo had died months earlier from Parkinson's.

He would pay his last respects to the man who transformed him when he was an insecure boy in a roughneck town. Mr. Arturo trained Nick as a fighter and was a no-nonsense mentor, who called him out when he screwed up in the gym or elsewhere in his teen years. With his swarthy chiseled face and muscular physique, Mr. Arturo resembled many hard men from gritty New York neighborhoods. But he didn't need to prove his toughness. His years in the ring had mellowed him. He was like a warrior home from an epic quest. There was no more enmity left in his bones.

As an up-and-coming journalist, Nick dreamed of getting rich by writing a screenplay about Mr. Arturo (dogged detective and ex-champion boxer from Hell's Kitchen). He envisioned Robert De Niro portraying him in an acclaimed movie. But as with most of his ambitions, this one never came to fruition. Nick was too undisciplined as a man and author.

An icy wind swept the hilly cemetery as he knelt on the ground and hugged the headstone.

"Thanks for everything, Mr. Arturo," he said, his voice breaking. "If it weren't for you ... ."

He rose and pulled a plastic bag from his parka. He laid a child's red boxing glove at the gravesite and made the sign of the cross. He took his stance and threw punches in the frigid air, seeking his coach's final approval.

Back in Carlson, Nick began packing in advance of his return to Ohio. Sure there was harsh weather and a host of socio-economic problems in Greater Cleveland. But this was more than a blue-collar region of loveable losers, and Megan Bradley was one of its best ambassadors. He told Christopher he would live *temporarily* in the basement of her Dutch Colonial in Lakewood.

"I'll be like Alyosha leading a monk's existence."

"Nice of Megan to put you up. But you can stay with us if and when she throws you out."

His offer wasn't the only item on the agenda. He had asked Nick to go into business with him. Christopher's photo studio work had grown steadily, and his Warehouse District lease was coming up for renewal. A freelance graphic artist had proposed renting a larger location on the same block of West 3rd Street and Lakeside Avenue. With Nick as a consulting writer, Christopher could compete for Cleveland-area marketing communication clients.

"I don't have any money to put in the game, and I don't want charity."

"No charity, bro. But we could sure use you on a part-time basis."

He had to hand it to his persuasive kid brother. Nick might have adjunct teaching opportunities at Cleveland State or Cuyahoga Community College. But that wouldn't be until summer at the earliest. Megan was glad to learn of their potential working arrangement. However, Nick would be "on probation" in her house.

"No drunken tirades," she said in their phone call the day before he was leaving Indiana.

"And no funny business," he added. "Got it."

"Absolutely no funny business. I'm putting a lock on the basement door in case you get any midnight urges."

"The only urges I get are to go to the bathroom two or three times a night. You locking me in like a mutt?"

"Want to be very clear so there are no misunderstandings."

"Know you're nervous about my moving in. So am I. But it's only until I find a place. Any more rules?"

"No rules but a request. Would you be one of our public speakers? I'm creating a new program with area high schools on dating violence, targeting jocks."

"Will this count toward my rent?"

"Drive safe."

One thing was certain. Nick would tread carefully in his "new-old" abode. He and Megan kept their distance in the first days of cohabitation. They barely spoke or so it seemed with her long hours on the job and him getting squared away.

She had said he could come upstairs to eat his meals, watch TV or listen to music. ("You don't have to be a subterranean.") But he was fine in the heated partially completed basement. When the marriage ended, he had scrapped his master plan for a combination home office, workout area and game room (poker, pool and ping pong). His living space was lined with remnants of gray Berber carpet and items jettisoned from upstairs: a brown velour sleeper sofa and faux leather easy chair, a black floor lamp and slightly warped bookshelf. Nick was comforted by the furnace clicking on, creaking floor joists and Megan's light footsteps overhead.

He spent most of his free time on his Gateway laptop, napping or reading. Christopher had loaned him a copy of Thomas Merton's *The Seven Storey Mountain*.

"Appropriate for your new monastic lifestyle," his brother said.

Nick had previously read the autobiography. But today the book had more relevance. As with Merton, he had also separated from the world, so to speak. *They say it's never too late to reinvent yourself.*

On his second Sunday as a "tenant," he was invited "above ground" for a home-cooked meal. He wore faded jeans and a slate turtleneck. He climbed the wooden basement stairs in his old Florsheim Imperial loafers. Megan was dressed in jeans, a Cleveland Browns sweatshirt (jarring orange letters on a bland chocolate background) and Irish wool socks. She had used a little mascara and blush but no perfume. He enjoyed the scent of her cocoanut-lime shampoo as she brushed past him to set the table. She had the same ("Dorothy Hamill") hairstyle as in college, and it flattered her.

"You smell like a walking pina colada."

"On that note," she said, "there'll be no alcohol at dinner not even wine. What you drink on your own time is your business. But we're flying sober when we're together. And if you can't handle it ... ."

"Whoa! I didn't say anything. I'm fine with that. It's not like I'm a ... ."

"A what?"

"You know."

"An alcoholic? You sure?"

"Positive," he said, not wanting to sound antagonistic. "Actually drinking less lately."

"Actions speak louder than words."

"Geez, never heard that one before."

Megan accepted his compliments on the meatloaf dinner, steering the discussion back to his drinking.

"You're in denial over the booze and have been for years."

"I like my scotch and a good bottle of wine. But am I out of control? Don't think so."

"Geez, never heard that one before."

"Touché. You'll just have to ... ."

"Trust you? So said the man with a shaky track record."

"As noted by his probation officer," Nick said, raising his glass of water.

Megan's no-alcohol policy was in effect when dining out. She made a point of meeting at casual restaurants like Bearden's for hamburgers and shakes and Max's Deli, where he astonished her one night buying a three-tier carrot cake. Such indulgences took their toll. He had to get into better shape or else, the doctor had warned him in his last exam.

Nick drew on his post-Thanksgiving visit to Mr. Arturo's grave for motivation. He would honor his late boxing coach by hitting the gym. He saw an online listing for Richie G's in the Flats.

Clevelander Richie Giachetti had trained heavyweight champ Larry Holmes and other contenders for decades. One son had been operating the gym since 2006. When Delamore showed up on a mid-December day, the scowling, tattooed black and Latino young guns studied the chunky old white dude in his maroon gym shorts, crew neck T-shirt, calf-length gray socks and black Nike sneakers. Giachetti was dumbfounded.

"You ever boxed?"

"A while ago."

"This is a real friggin' gym. No time to teach you fundamentals," he said.

Each man was stout, though Giachetti was heavier with darker features. His thick beard, sunken eyes and gruff tone made him look more pirate captain than pugilist.

"Don't need no babysitting," Nick said, carrying his vintage Everlast gloves. "If you want, I'll sign a release form in case I croak. Only want to hit the bags and go a few rounds with the hand pads. No sparring unless you get some more geezers in here. How's twenty bucks an hour?"

"Twenty-five," Giachetti said. "Knock yourself out."

He picked a jump rope from those hanging on the wall near the boxing ring. Years since he had regularly exercised, there were a few missteps until he found his pace and even added some crisscross moves.

"Not bad, old man," Giachetti shouted from inside the ring.

Being here was like a second home. It wasn't a pristine carpeted health club with rows of ellipticals, stair steppers and cardio bikes, high-def screens and the smell of Lysol from everybody cleaning off their equipment or exercise mats. In Giachetti's gym the air smelled funky from sweaty, sleekly muscled guys who didn't care if they stunk up the joint. Nick was immersed in a timeless cacophony—the thudding of padded gloves against bloated black heavy bags wrapped in duct tape, the rat-tat-tat-tat of the pear-shaped speed bags in hypnotic rhythm, and the jarring "DING-DING-DING" of the oversized red clock timer above the main entrance.

Trainers growled instructions: "One-two, one-two. Upper cut. Body shot. Hook. Don't slough off. One-two, one-two. Hands up, gawdammit!" Boxers grunted, groaned and taunted each other. Nick roamed the gym, working the bags and talking with the "kids."

"You wuz goin' Golden Gloves?" asked a wide-eyed teen.

"True that," Nick said. "Liked to bang heads in and out of the ring."

"*You* ... a gang banger? *That* I have a hard time believin'."

"You and me both."

After declining Christopher's invitations to join him at Sunday Mass, Nick relented and went to an Advent service at a small church on the Near West Side in Inez's old neighborhood. Miranda attended with Ray Russo. She sat happily between her boyfriend and Unk.

The chapel was decorated with evergreen wreaths by each of the Stations of the Cross. It smelled of incense and was adorned with numerous candles. A choir filled the sacred space with stirring music and hymns.

"You doing all this to prove something to me?" Megan asked. "Or are you really trying to get your act together?"

"Remember when I was into Yukio Mishima, the Japanese poet who followed the Samurai Code?"

"He the one who committed hara-kiri?"

"When he was at his physical and intellectual peak."

"You trying to reach yours?"

"My peak has come and gone. But I can keep trying."

"As long as there's no hara-kiri in my house, Mr. Samurai."

On Christmas Eve, Nick rode with Megan to find a decent tree. But the lots were either sold out or had a slim selection. They went west on Lorain Avenue as the night grew colder with snow in the forecast.

"My folks would hold off until the last minute," he said. "Supposedly a Delamore tradition. But they were actually hunting for cheap Charlie Brown trees. One year Dad had to tie two scraggly ones together."

"Been too busy," she said. "You know how crazy things get at the shelter during the holidays."

"Sure do," he said, spying a small lot by a Quonset hut-type VFW hall at the Cuyahoga-Lorain County border. "Hey, I see some trees."

"It's a mirage," she said. "You're hallucinating."

"Could be, but I think we're in luck."

They decorated the squat Scotch pine in Megan's living room. She asked him to build a fire, and he moved contentedly through the house in preparation. When the yellow and orange flames grew higher, he wiped his hands on his old corduroys.

"Now that's a yuletide blaze," he said as she sat in a wingback chair gazing at him. "What's wrong?"

"Nothing. Was thinking of having a glass of wine."

"You mean I'm off probation?"

"Didn't say that. It's just ... ."

Nick didn't wait for her to finish.

"Red or white?" he asked, examining the wooden kitchen wine rack.

"Surprise me."

"Got that right," he said, selecting a bottle of Merlot. "At our ages, there will definitely be surprises."

Epilogue

Nick's interest in editing his father's WWII Merchant Marine stories had waned. His prose was flat, driven more by a son's devotion than true inspiration. On a crisp late December night, he stopped working and strolled through Lakewood, Ohio, savoring his Macanudo. The Christmas gift from Christopher was quite the stogie. Nick cocked his head back and swaggered with gusto, a la Tony Soprano.

The longer he walked in the festive setting, the more his mind drifted. What triggered tonight's contemplation? Maybe it was the aroma of his cigar or the stocky man with dark moustache herding his children from a yellow Dodge Caravan into their brick home on Detroit Avenue. He was chuckling as he chased the little ones inside. Nick stomped his feet and blew on his fingers. A recollection granted him relief from frosty Ohio as he journeyed to sunny Daytona Beach, March 1973.

He and Alex were cruising the busy main drag, beat from their 900-mile drive but psyched for the week ahead. Most Omegas were on a Caribbean cruise. Delamore and Merten didn't have the money or desire to go. After midterms in gloomy Sussex, they had headed to Florida in Alex's 1968 Camaro, the car Nick dubbed the Banana-Rama. Fueled by coffee, junk food, weed and Moody Blues 8-track tapes, they drove straight through, rapping for hours on their "days of future passed." They spotted an economical motel near the ocean and settled in.

The amigos sat on a patch of beach, getting high as the sun set. It may have been the violet-streaked sky, the sultry southern breezes or the Acapulco Gold, but their aspirations seemed within reach. Alex would graduate from a prestigious law school and find fame in jurisprudence. Nick would win a slew of journalism awards and write bestselling books. They would marry fantastic women and stay close friends for the long haul.

In the short term, the two agreed to refrain from any "downers." Nothing better to soothe heartache and loss than a week in the sun, fortified by strong dope and cheap beer, surrounded by glistening beauties. *Man, that was a great spring break.*

Nick returned home and started writing in earnest on a modified basement workbench. The standing desk eased the toll on his ailing back as he conjured away.

"What the hell is this, the Elliott Gould look-alike contest?"

A wiry ponytailed bouncer at the Tit-for-Tat strip club turned carnival barker when the Merriman duo appeared, $5 bills in hand.

"Want an autograph?" Nick asked.

"Just your money," said the guy in jeans, black and orange Harley-Davidson shirt and sandals. A pack of Marlboros rested on a stool by the darkened doorway.

Nick was in red gym shorts, a gray Merriman Football XXL shirt and flip-flops. Alex wore a tie-dyed rainbow tee, white painter's pants and tan moccasins.

"Really worth five bucks in there?"

"Guaranteed hard-on," the bouncer said, taking their cash.

"You're on, slim jim," Nick said. "Money-back guarantee?"

"My ass," he replied.

"No thanks," Alex said. "We'll stick with women. Can I bum a smoke?"

The three men roared as Nick and Alex entered the funhouse. They exited with wallets lightened by garter belt outlays and pricey drafts. But neither of them complained.

They left a Piggly Wiggly supermarket with their cart piled high with cheap six-packs of Busch beer, jumbo bags of potato chips and rolls of paper towels to distract the checkout girl from sirloin steaks wedged on the bottom rack.

"Nothing to it," Nick said as they hauled the groceries up to their motel kitchenette. "We'll eat like kings tonight."

His words drifted as smoke in a stiff breeze because Alex was mesmerized by bikinis three doors down.

"Invite 'em to dinner. We got steak, beer and pot. They'll be down in a flash."

"Seriously?"

"Positively, Waldo. Don't be such a wimp. Ask 'em."

Toni and Jamie were freshman roommates at Ohio State. They brought munchies and a bottle of Chianti. Each wore fringed jean shorts. Toni's bright green halter displayed her cleavage. The thinner Jamie wore a blue and white striped tube top. Alex predictably went for the buxom blonde.

The four emerged hysterical from the small bathroom as cannabis clouds swirled around them. Alex gazed into Toni's bloodshot eyes and was smitten. She cradled his numb noggin, and they tumbled onto a double bed, where Alex was reborn. She tasted of beer and menthol cigarettes. He was in the undertow and didn't care if he drowned. Nick called from the shore, "Hey, come up for air."

Alex and Toni kissed throughout dinner. Nick and Jamie were more laid back. At this point, it was logistics—who got the room and when?

Those schemes detoured when three loud stooges in surfer swimsuits poked their heads in the doorway. The shortest of the trio with cascading ringlets and dancing eyes yodeled: "Listen up, lovebirds. Party at the Marina Lodge, room 503. Be there, aloha!"

Toni and Jamie began singing: "Par-tee. Par-tee. Par-tee."

Nick pointed the empty wine bottle at Alex. "We're going to a party."

They joined the serpentine line of college students ambling to the Marina, which dwarfed other beachfront motels. Music blared from the fifth floor to an eager overflow crowd. After an endless wait, the quartet was turned away with dozens more. Fire hazard.

"That sucks," Toni whined.

"Guess you're stuck with us," Nick said.

"That's not so bad," Jamie added, interlocking arms with him.

"Yeah, not so bad, right?" Alex asked the elusive Toni.

Nick whispered, "Let her come to you."

They shared another joint in the motel room and then separated with their dates. Nick chose a secluded grassy area near the sand dunes. The scene evoked the 1969 post-junior prom at New York's Jones Beach, when he was infatuated with Linda Pieta. Four years later, he lay on a Florida shore with a sexy stranger.

Jamie smelled of arousal and Intimate perfume. Nick tasted the musky fragrance behind her ears, down her neck and around her nipples, while probing the dampness between her legs.

"You ready?"

"Did you bring a rubber?"

He thought a little more foreplay could persuade her to bypass the dreaded condom. But when she asked again, he simply stopped trying. Calmed by hours of pot smoking, he lay staring at the stars.

"I'm sorry," she said. "I really want to, ya know. You turn me on, but … ."

"Me too, you," he said like a total dork.

"Should have told you. I have a boyfriend. But I can still get you off. Don't want you thinking I'm just a tease."

"That's OK. Don't worry about it. … He's a helluva lucky guy."

"Who? Oh yeah, my boyfriend. Thanks again for being so nice," Jamie said, kissing him on the cheek as she slid into her clothes.

"That's what they all say."

Nick sighed pulling up his gym shorts. Back in the room, he smoked a solitary joint and masturbated.

When he awoke, the other bed was empty. *At least one of us scored.* The morning was overcast. Delamore put on a sweatshirt and grabbed a beer. Maybe Merten was walking the beach with his new sweetheart. Someone was perched like a sad pelican on a faraway dune, watching the roiling ocean as pounding surf drowned out the seagulls. When Nick approached, Alex wiped his eyes.

"What's the matter, lover boy? Couldn't get it up, or did Toni turn you down?" he asked, tousling his mop of hair.

Alex smacked his hand away.

"Not her. It's Donna, Donna, Donna. Like I'm cursed."

Nick couldn't find anything uplifting to say in the raw wind.

"You're cursed. We're all cursed."

"Not you. Not love 'em and leave 'em Delamore. Dumped your wife and kid so you could go screw sorority girls."

"Crossing the line, man," he said, kicking Alex with the edge of his flip-flop.

"Like I give a crap."

Nick walked off before the argument escalated. By noon the skies had cleared. They were out by the pool reviewing the new arrivals. One babe was oiled up in a tan mesh bikini. She swiveled and wiggled before enchanted spectators. Men tugged at their swim trunks, but there was no whistling. This wasn't *Beach Blanket Bingo*.

Alex kept glancing at Toni and Jamie's motel room door.

"Go on up and check," Nick said. "They're probably just hung over."

When there was no answer, Alex went to the front desk, learning they had already left.

"Toni and I were supposed to have another date tonight," he said, sulking as Nick dozed in the hazy sunshine. "We were getting along good, talking about cool things ... movies, music ... ."

"This before or after the hand job?"

"Hey," Alex said. Then he giggled.

"Way to go, Mighty Manfred."

"Actually, she was dumb as a rock. Said Cat Stevens was weird. Can you believe it? How could I fall for a slutbag like that?"

"Happens to the best of us. Let's hit the beach and get some bodysurfing in. Waves are huge."

On their last night in Florida, they pooled their money and went to Joe's Crab Shack. They were eating dinner when Alex asked what it was like being married.

"I'm no expert, considering how I screwed mine up," Nick said. "But I can tell you that it isn't non-stop sex. Your wife won't always be in the mood. And you can't be a caveman and haul her off to the bedroom whenever you want."

"But it's nice, isn't it? I mean living together."

"It's nice if you find the right woman."

"Was Linda the right woman?"

"She probably was," Nick said, eyeing the Asian hostess by the door. "But I wasn't the right guy at the time. Wasn't ready."

"Wonder if I'll ever be ready."

"You were born ready. Hell, you would have proposed if Toni went all the way with you."

Alex sprayed his mouthful of Coke at Nick, who barely dodged the soda shower.

The drive back to Ohio was uneventful except for a stop at a mom and pop eatery outside Nashville, where the tanned, wild-haired, mustachioed men were ignored. When Nick complained, the grizzled waitress said, "Don't want no beaners in here." The cockeyed grill cook added, "Taco Bell's down the road." Alex had to pull his enraged friend out of there. They arrived on campus with drifting snow and freezing temperatures.

"Great way to end the break," Alex said, lighting up a fresh joint.

"Can you believe we were on a beach yesterday?" Nick asked as the blizzard continued.

"Think Toni and Jamie are back at OSU?"

"Think those were their real names?"

"Don't you?"

"I looked in Jamie's ... I mean Carol's purse. Turns out she's from Daytona Beach. She and Toni, or whatever her name is, are in high school."

"No way."

"Saw her driver's license. She turned 18 in February."

Alex exhaled a long "Wowww!"

"Yeah, wow. You got it on with a hot teeny bopper."

Nick cracked up as his often melancholy pal shimmied on their crummy couch. Their smiles remained, though both knew the good times and good feelings wouldn't last. The goal was to end the term with no major hassles. In June they would leave the Omega house and have one last year of school together until the real world beckoned beyond Merriman's hallowed halls.

For the first time as college students, they wouldn't have to worry about the Vietnam War. The Paris peace treaty had been signed in January. U.S. troops were coming home. No more sweating out grades and low draft numbers or losing deferments like sad sack Omega Ben Tarpley, who blew off his classes, flunked out and was reclassified 1-A.

During the war years, some might have been tempted to talk with Vietnam veterans on campus regarding their experiences. But no one dared disturb Merriman's vets, who congregated most mornings over bottomless cups of coffee and full ashtrays in the same corner of the cafeteria. Nick watched these bearded men huddled in intense conversations. *How can the rest of us possibly measure up?*

These days, Delamore had other concerns. Would he make it to his seventies, eighties or beyond? Or drop dead from a heart attack, the big "C" or a gruesome disease such as ALS? Maybe a stroke. Parkinson's. Or the latest 21st-century rage, Alzheimer's.

But he could stick it to Father Time by rekindling tales like the last hurrah with Alex before everything changed. Another New Year's Eve had arrived, and his reflections were accompanied by treasured lyrics: *"Now I've been happy lately. Thinking about the good things to come. And I believe it could be. Something good has begun."*

Megan called down: "Got a fire going. You coming up, or will I be drinking this champagne alone?"

Nick brightened at the sound of her voice.

"Don't you dare! Almost done. Be right there."

Climbing the stairs this wintry night, he paused. *"And I believe it could be. Something good has begun."*

The End.

About the Author

Mark H. Massé's novels include *HONOR HOUSE, WHATEVER COMES* and *DELAMORE'S DREAMS*. He has also written three books of narrative nonfiction (*VIETNAM WARRIOR VOICES, TRAUMA JOURNALISM* and *INSPIRED TO SERVE*). The retired educator and award-winning author is completing a new dark comedy and short story collection. ***www.markmasse.com***

CPSIA information can be obtained
at www.ICGtesting.com
Printed in the USA
BVHW032205180621
609955BV00007B/175

9 781090 977427